# MY DAUGHTER'S KEEPER

SHEILA NORTON

Boldwood

First published in Great Britain in 2025 by Boldwood Books Ltd.

Cover Design by Colin Thomas

Cover Images: Colin Thomas

A CIP catalogue record for this book is available from the British Library.

Paperback ISBN 978-1-78513-689-4

Large Print ISBN 978-1-78513-690-0

Hardback ISBN 978-1-78513-688-7

Ebook ISBN 978-1-78513-691-7

Kindle ISBN 978-1-78513-692-4

Audio CD ISBN 978-1-78513-683-2

MP3 CD ISBN 978-1-78513-684-9

Digital audio download ISBN 978-1-78513-686-3

This book is printed on certified sustainable paper. Boldwood Books is dedicated to putting sustainability at the heart of our business. For more information please visit https://www.boldwoodbooks.com/about-us/sustainability/

Boldwood Books Ltd, 23 Bowerdean Street, London, SW6 3TN

www.boldwoodbooks.com

# 1

On the day after my fortieth birthday, my husband told me he was leaving me.

'I didn't want to spoil your special day,' he said, bringing me a cup of tea in bed, sitting back down beside me and looking at me with those deep brown, puppy-dog beautiful eyes of his that had made me fall for him in the first place, his voice oozing with sincerity and care. 'But I need to get this off my chest. You deserve to know the truth.'

And he proceeded to break my heart, while I stared into my teacup, feeling too sick to drink.

Afterwards, I reflected that he didn't even have the decency to let me deride him for being the predictable stereotype of a middle-aged man, finding himself a new, younger model. No, he'd not only fallen for somebody wealthier, more successful, more elegant and beautiful (yes, I'd met her, unfortunately, and at the time I thought she seemed nice) but she was *older* than me. Just turned forty-six, apparently. And she was his boss. Not even just the managing director but the actual owner of his company.

Until that moment, I'd had no idea he'd been seeing someone. The shock of it actually made me vomit. When I jumped out of bed to rush to the bathroom, he settled back against the pillows, waiting for me, so that he could continue with his story of how he and Kirsty had fallen in love. How they'd tried so hard to fight it, poor things, but eventually realised they'd have to suffer the guilt of hurting me, in order to *live the lives they were destined for.*

By now I felt like being sick again, from disgust at the verbal bilge he was spouting. I couldn't believe it. This was the man who'd sworn to love me forever. It had never even occurred to me that he wouldn't keep his promise. We'd never actually married – we'd decided there was no need – but we called each other husband and wife. Now I wished we'd made it official, if only to make his escape more difficult for him. Why shouldn't it be difficult? We had a child; he couldn't just walk away from us.

'What about Daisy?' I interrupted his rhetoric of anguished love, impatiently. I wasn't even crying yet. I don't think it had sunk in – my stomach might have reacted, but my brain was still struggling to catch up.

'Don't worry,' he soothed me at once. 'We've worked that out.'

*Worked that out* – as if our little girl were just a problem to be solved. Just a minor irritation, a little hiccup on the road to the fulfilment of their love's desire.

'How? What exactly have you worked out?' I demanded.

'Well.' He sat up, looking almost excited about it. 'Here's the plan—'

'No!' Anger was overtaking the nausea. Perhaps the tears would come later – I was quite puzzled myself by the lack of them. 'No, I'm sorry, but you – you and her, *she* – don't get to make a plan, and expect me, and our daughter, to fit in with it. What if I want to make a plan for myself?'

'Well,' he said, looking surprised, 'of course, if you've got a plan...?'

'Of course I haven't!' I spat back at him – literally spat, which couldn't have been very pleasant, given that I'd just been throwing up. 'I haven't exactly had time to think of a plan, have I, as you've only just announced your *plan* to leave me.'

'No, I don't suppose you have.'

He looked at me sadly, almost sympathetically, and my anger slowly deflated like a wrinkled old balloon. I was never going to have a plan for my future with Daisy, was I? How could I possibly come up with one, however long I waited, however hard I tried? How was I ever going to have enough money, as a hairdresser, to support myself, to look after Daisy, to give her the sort of life I wanted for her? How was I going to manage? What exactly was I going to do and where were we going to live? Because I sure as hell wouldn't be able to afford the mortgage on this place on my own.

'So what's your plan, then?' I muttered crossly, feeling defeated already.

'Well, obviously I'll be moving in with Kirsty.' He wasn't even making any attempt not to sound excited about it. 'So—'

'You won't be taking Daisy with you!' I interrupted, sitting up straight, raising my voice. 'No way.'

'No. Of course not.' He looked hurt. 'I'm not a monster, Tash. I wouldn't take her away from you, but I'd like to still see as much of her as possible.'

I just nodded. Daisy loved her daddy, even if I was moving from love to hate at a rate of knots I'd never have imagined possible.

'So what we thought was—'

His use of the word *we,* about himself and Kirsty, made me flinch. The implication, that they were already a couple, with me on the outside, felt like a cold flannel slapping me across the face. I put my head in my hands.

'Are you all right?' he asked, with just a hint of irritation. 'Not going to be sick again, are you?'

'Not yet,' I muttered crossly. 'Carry on.'

'We thought, if you and Daisy move nearer to us—'

'No way!' I was still just as annoyed by the 'we' and the 'us' as I was by 'their' sheer cheek in suggesting that Daisy and I should be the ones to uproot. 'Why should we move away from the area, as if *we've* done something wrong? I'm not moving Daisy from her school, I'm not leaving my job, just to make your life more convenient. And that's the end of it.'

Except that it wasn't. It wasn't the end of it – well, it was temporarily, because at that point I walked out of the bedroom, slamming the door, and after trying to compose myself had to get breakfast ready for my daughter and take her to school, pretending to act normally, like a cheerful, happy, in-control mummy rather than a screaming, vomiting madwoman. The screaming, vomiting madwoman reappeared later, in the empty house on my own, after I'd returned from the school run to find Craig gone – off to work, off to his new high-flying executive girlfriend – to no doubt tell her his confession had gone as well as could be expected, that I hadn't made too much fuss and he'd soon be free to move in with her. And he'd left me a note on the kitchen table, saying:

*Sorry if it was upsetting for you to hear my news. I thought you might have guessed already. Have a good day.*

'Have a good day?' A good fucking day? I screwed up the

note and threw it as hard as I could in the general direction of the bin, before sitting down at the table and finally crying my eyes out. He 'thought I might have guessed already'? Did he really think I'd have gone on so blithely, so happily, going out the previous day with him and Daisy and our friends to celebrate my birthday with lunch at our village pub? Smiling as they all sang 'Happy Birthday', kissing him in front of everyone to thank him for my present – the jacket I'd been eyeing up on my favourite website for months, dropping hints but thinking it was too expensive? Could he really have believed I'd be that good an actress, or prepared to pretend, for the sake of a birthday party, for my friends' sake, even for Daisy's sake, that I didn't know? No! No, I wouldn't have; I'd have had to have it out with him as soon as I suspected anything. But like a fool, I'd still been so in love with him I'd assumed he felt the same.

I called my work that morning and pretended I had a bad cold.

'It might be flu, or Covid or something, so I'd better not come in,' I said.

'You do sound a bit rough,' my colleague Jackie said. 'Not the after-effects of yesterday, is it?' she added with a little laugh.

She was only teasing. Jackie had been at my birthday party, but she knew I hadn't had much to drink; I wouldn't have done that while I had Daisy with me. However, the thought of getting completely wiped out on white wine right now suddenly held a strong appeal. *I can't*, I reminded myself sternly as I ended the call. *I've got to be OK for Daisy again later.*

Daisy had to be my priority now. And I had to come up with a plan. I couldn't just roll over and give in to whatever Craig wanted us to do.

* * *

A couple of days later, after talking to Daisy, making her cry too, Craig moved out. And six months after that, I rolled over and gave in to what Craig and Kirsty wanted. Because – however much I hated to admit it – it had actually turned out to be the only sensible plan. We sold the home we'd bought together, and, with my share of the little equity we had in it, I took out a new mortgage on a little house in a run-down area of Radcombe, the nearest town, twenty miles from our village. It was actually where I worked: the salon was in the town centre, so it was going to make my life easier in that respect, at least. And on the other side of Radcombe, on *The Hill*, the most upmarket part of town, of course, was Whitegate House, where Craig now lived with Kirsty. I hadn't wanted to give in to him, but there was something in it for me. The deal included free childcare.

## 2

'I want to go home,' Daisy said as she toyed with her breakfast, picking up spoonfuls of cereal and milk and letting them dribble back into her bowl without eating.

'Sweetie, we *are* home,' I reminded her with a smile. I'd already told her this at least ten times that morning. 'This is our home now, our new little house, and we're going to be living here together, and, well, I know it's not looking very nice at the moment but we're going to make it nice, OK?'

'But I want to go back to our other home.'

She looked so forlorn and sad, her big blue eyes starting to fill up with tears, her shoulders slumped in misery, that my heart gave a lurch of sympathy. I wanted nothing more than to take her in my arms and tell her it was OK, we didn't have to stay there, we'd go back, she could have her pink rabbit-themed bedroom back again and we'd forget all about moving house. But I couldn't, of course. We'd moved; it was done, and we both had to get used to it.

'I know it's hard,' I said. 'It feels strange at the moment, for me too, but I promise you, we'll both soon get used to living here. The important thing is that we're together – you and me. Together forever, yeah?'

I held out my fist to bump with hers, the way we'd been doing ever since we'd been on our own together. I considered by now that we'd moved on, Daisy and I. We were a little team, we told each other we were OK and that everything was still fine, because break-up etiquette dictated that I mustn't blame her daddy for anything, I mustn't say anything to spoil her relationship with him – and of course, I loved her far too much to do that to her.

And to be fair, it was partly for the sake of Daisy's relationship with her daddy that we'd agreed to the move here, closer to Craig's new home. Correction: *Kirsty's* home. Kirsty's beautiful five-bedroom, three-bathroom home with an acre of garden and a swimming pool – all hers, mortgage paid off, hers alone since her late husband, John, who was CEO of her company, died suddenly four years previously while mowing the lawn. She joked – actually joked – that he didn't quite manage to finish the job before he collapsed. Craig told me that was how she'd coped afterwards – by joking. Personally I couldn't quite comprehend it. I wondered if she'd make a joke about it when, eventually, she tired of Craig. Because, while it was quite obvious to me why Craig had become infatuated with a wealthy, beautiful woman who was in a position of power over him, I still couldn't quite understand what she'd seen in him. Of course, he was a good-looking man, hard-working, reasonably intelligent and – until recently – I'd always thought of him as a decent, caring man, too. But there were plenty of those around, surely, who would have been willing, if not eager, to move in with her. Why mine?

I'd tried my best to explain the situation to Daisy. She was six now, and she'd been settled at her school and doing well;

she was happy, she had friends, friends I promised her she could still see during the school holidays.

'If we move into town, near where Daddy lives now, you'll be able to see him much more often.'

Up until the day we moved, the visits had mostly been at weekends. Usually Craig came to pick her up and took her out somewhere, but after a while he started taking her back to Whitegate House – Kirsty's place. He told me she'd been very shy around Kirsty and her two daughters, completely silent in fact, but we'd both hoped that she'd soon feel more at ease with them if she started going there more often. Because that was the plan: Daisy would gradually go there more often, and Craig was going to look after her every day after school. For this to work, she was moving from the village school where she'd been settled for her first two years, to the larger primary school in town, a short walk from Whitegate House. I didn't like it; I still referred to it as Craig and Kirsty's plan – not mine – but the bottom line was I had to make it work. It was the only way I could continue in my job, and work longer hours, which I was going to need to do if Daisy and I were going to survive on our own. Craig worked from home and, quite honestly, never seemed to be particularly busy these days, either. I was beginning to wonder whether Kirsty had always treated him favourably, keeping his workload light. Or perhaps she liked keeping him in his place, as her junior, and didn't want him having any more responsibility. But whatever the intricacies of their relationship, all I knew was that:

(1) he'd apparently be available from three-fifteen every afternoon to collect Daisy from school and look after her until I finished working my new full-time hours;

(2) my work was only a five-minute drive from Whitegate House, massively cutting my commute, which would have

been a lot busier in the rush-hour than previously when I'd finished at three o'clock. And,

(3) he was apparently also going to be able to cover the school holidays. This was so extraordinary an offer that I began to wonder if Kirsty was actually bribing Craig to move in with her by giving him thirteen weeks' paid leave per year. But no, apparently Kirsty herself didn't even really need to work – she just had to chair various online meetings occasionally and read important documents from time to time.

'So, she can supervise all three girls during the holidays,' Craig had said, sounding thrilled with himself for having landed such a fantastic specimen of a woman.

The problem was I didn't want the woman who stole my man anywhere near my little girl, let alone left in charge of her. But free childcare, as opposed to paying for a school holiday club for two weeks and trying to manage all the other holidays by begging, stealing or borrowing favours from other mums, repaying them by having four or five of their kids back to my house during my own annual leave – which gave the word *holiday* a whole new and contrary meaning – held an undeniable appeal which somehow overcame my reluctance.

And so it had been decided. Our nice three-bed semi in a desirable village had sold quickly, leaving me to buy my two-up, two-down end-of-terrace ex-council house on, let's face it, the wrong side of town. It was fine. I'd never been acquisitive; I'd been happy in our previous house and I was sure I'd be happy here, too, once we were settled. But I couldn't deny I felt resentful about Whitegate House. Not jealous, just resentful – because Craig didn't seem to care that he'd just upped and moved in there, to a life of comparative luxury. After nearly ten years together, I felt cast off. It was hardly fair. But worse than that, it hurt. Because I was sorry to admit it –

and I felt an idiot for admitting it – but I still would have taken him back. I loved him even while I was hating him for what he'd done to us, and I didn't need a psychiatrist to tell me I was taking out the hatred on the woman who'd stolen him away from me, the very woman who was going to be enabling me to survive the school holidays by caring for my daughter. I had to justify it to myself by reminding myself that she was doing it for nothing. Not that she'd have needed the money anyway.

I'd deliberately timed our move into our new house for the beginning of the school summer break, so Daisy and I could get used to living here before she had to start at the new school, and so she could also get used to going to Whitegate House more often. I had two weeks' leave from work to help us both settle in, but the reality of the move had hit home now. It was a Saturday, and Craig was coming to pick Daisy up that morning so I could try to finish the unpacking, get the house straight and everything put away. And Daisy didn't want to go.

'I want to stay with you, Mummy,' she said sadly, letting another spoonful of milk drip back into her bowl.

'I know, sweetheart, but it's only for a little while, so that I can get everything tidied up, and make your new bedroom all nice for you.'

'I don't like my new bedroom. I want my old one.'

'You'll like it better soon. When we've had time to settle in, I'll take you out to choose some lovely new wallpaper.'

'I want my old wallpaper.'

'We'll see if we can get the same one, if you like. Or something very similar. OK?' I gave her a smile. 'Come on, eat up your breakfast. Daddy will be here soon.'

In fact Craig arrived just as she was finally, reluctantly, shovelling some cereal into her mouth. He breezed into the kitchen, all smiles, pulling Daisy towards him for a hug and exclaiming at the expression of misery on her face.

'What's the matter with my little princess?' he teased. 'No smiles for Daddy today?'

'I want to stay with Mummy. I want to go home – to our *other* home.' She glared at him. 'I want us *all* to go back there.'

'But this is a nice house, Daise!' he said cheerfully, looking around at the little kitchen with forced enthusiasm. 'You and Mummy will be as snug as two bugs in a rug here when everything's unpacked and tidied up.'

I had to turn away, taking our dishes to the sink, to avoid looking at him. How condescending of him to call our new little house *nice* and *snug*, before taking his daughter back to his new woman's mansion.

'I don't want to be a bug in a rug,' Daisy said mournfully. But she hugged him back, and allowed herself to be encouraged into putting on her shoes, finding a couple of favourite toys to take with her, and eventually she returned to me, the mournful look still on her face, to be kissed goodbye.

'You'll have a lovely time with Daddy,' I said, stroking her hair, marvelling as always at the way the blonde curls framed her beautiful little face – beautiful despite the downward turn of her mouth at that moment. 'And when you come back, your bedroom will be looking much nicer, I promise.'

'Will there be rabbit wallpaper?'

'No, not yet!' I laughed. 'But it'll be all tidied up, and the cardboard boxes will be gone.'

Craig shepherded her to the door. His car was on the road outside – there was only room for mine on the drive. Well, it wasn't a drive, really, just a *frontage*, as the estate agent called it. Enough room for one small car, so that it was only just off the pavement.

That first day passed quickly. By four o'clock I'd unpacked the final box, hung the curtains in the lounge – they were from the other house and far too long, but I wasn't going worry about that – and I'd worked out how to connect the washing machine. I'd taken readings from the gas and electric meters and had even called the last few people and businesses on my change-of-address list. I was shattered, frankly, but I'd told Craig that I'd like to pick Daisy up from his place, rather than letting him bring her back. I needed to speak to Kirsty.

She answered the door to me; I could hear her coming, clip-clopping across the hall floor. Who wears high heels indoors? She was wearing a plain green dress that fitted her slim figure beautifully – it hung like velvet and shone like silk – and she was in full make-up, at home, on a Saturday. Despite her being more than six years my senior, she made me suddenly feel old and scruffy and boring. Although I'd met her at a company function once, it was only in passing, so shortly after he moved in with her Craig had brought me here, to *introduce us*. I thought it was an odd idea, and to say I didn't want to come would have been an understatement, but he insisted it would be good manners. No mention of the appallingly *bad* manners involved in her stealing my husband, of course. But in the end, I agreed out of curiosity. I wanted to know what she was like, this older woman, this pathetic, past-it, menopausal crone who seemed to have an unhealthy interest in younger men. And of course, the reality wiped the sneer from my face. Not only was she beautiful, she was charming, and she managed, somehow, much as I hated to admit it, to convey an air of... not quite apology, more like actual sympathy towards me, for the loss of my husband. As if it was something that had happened accidentally, nobody's fault and certainly not hers. As if I'd just mislaid him while out shopping: *never mind, these*

*things happen, don't they, let's have a nice bone-china cup of Earl*
*Grey and a chat, woman to woman; we've all been there, can't count*
*on men – my last one actually died, can you believe it?* I wouldn't
say I fell for the charm offensive, but it did disarm me. I felt,
unequivocally, the message that there was no point in me
trying to fight her for Craig: she'd won, and would keep on
winning.

She gave me her gracious smile again now, all sympathy
and concern, ushering me into her huge hallway.

'How are you getting on, Tasha? It's such hard work, isn't it,
moving house? I do feel for you, you poor thing, you must be
exhausted. I told Craig he should have been there with you
today, helping you – I would have been more than happy to
look after poor little Daisy on my own. But he insisted he
should be here with her himself, as she's probably feeling a bit
unsettled.'

I felt a shiver of irritation at 'poor little Daisy'.

'She's fine,' I said. I didn't want Kirsty feeling sorry for my
daughter, pitying her for being the child Craig left behind.

'Well, she's been no trouble at all, quiet as a mouse, in fact.
I think Freya's probably scared the life out of her.'

Freya was Kirsty's younger daughter; she was nearly eight,
more than a year older than Daisy, and Craig had already told
me she was a bit of an extrovert – by which I guessed he probably meant she was a pain in the neck. As I was remembering
this, Freya herself came hurtling down the stairs, yelling, at the
top of her voice, 'Your mum's here, Daisy!' And Daisy followed
her, slowly, the look of relief on her face when she caught sight
of me both gratifying and worrying at the same time.

'Can we go home now, Mummy?' she asked very quietly,
looking at her feet.

'Yes, of course. Have you had a good time?' I judged from

her face that it was best not to wait for a reply. 'Go and say goodbye to Daddy – ah, here he is. And say thank you to Kirsty for letting you come and play with Freya.'

'Bye, Daddy.' She hugged him, and he gave me a nod and a smile and asked the same questions about how I'd got on in the house. 'Thank you,' Daisy added obediently in a whisper to Kirsty. She looked almost as if she didn't really want to say it.

'So are we having her again during the week?' Kirsty asked. 'Whenever you like.'

'Well, I've got two weeks' holiday from work,' I said. 'So it won't really be necessary until after that.'

'But we want Daisy to get used to coming here – don't we, Freya? You'd like Daisy to come again during the week, wouldn't you?'

'Yes!' Freya shouted. 'Come again tomorrow, Daisy.'

Daisy was shaking her head, looking at me with wide, anxious eyes.

'Not tomorrow,' I said. 'But maybe one day in the week, then, if you're sure – just for a little while, though. As long as it doesn't interrupt your work, having an extra one here?'

How she managed to concentrate on her apparently-very-important Teams meetings at all, with Freya yelling around the house, was difficult to imagine, but she smiled and shook her head.

'Oh, not at all. As long as I'm available in case anyone needs my input, I only have to be actually there – online – for the occasional meeting. So it's fine.'

'Unbelievable!' I muttered to myself, after settling Daisy in the car and starting the engine for the short drive back. Presumably paid a fortune, for doing next to nothing.

'What's unbelievable, Mummy?' Daisy asked.

'Um, unbelievable how lucky you are.' I smiled at her in

the mirror. 'You'll be going to Daddy's new house quite a lot now. It'll be just like having another home. Like having another family.'

'I don't want another family,' she said sadly. 'I want *our* one. When Daddy still lived with us.'

And of course, the sad fact was, there was nothing whatsoever I could do to provide her with that.

## 3

Our first week in the new house passed quickly. I liked having time to take Daisy out, exploring our new neighbourhood, the local parks and shops, but I also still had things to do – shelves to put up, things to put away – and besides, I knew Craig and Kirsty were right, unfortunately, to say that Daisy needed to get used to being at their house before I went back to work and actually needed to send her there.

'Perhaps it'll be nice for you to go to Daddy's house tomorrow while I get on with some of these jobs,' I suggested on the Thursday afternoon. 'You can play with Freya instead of being bored.'

'I don't want to play with Freya,' she said immediately. 'She shouts, and she's bossy.'

'Well, it's her house, and she's a little bit older than you so perhaps she just likes to be in charge. You've only met her a couple of times; now you're going there more often I'm sure she'll settle down a bit.'

'I don't want to go there more often.'

'I know, sweetie, but I've got to go back to work soon, and

you know we moved here so that Daddy and Kirsty could look after you at their house when I'm working – in the holidays, and after school. You know Daddy works from home, and Kirsty—' I just managed to stop myself from saying that she hardly worked at all. 'Kirsty doesn't have to work many hours. So they can keep an eye on you, and you and Freya can be company for each other.'

Daisy was silent for a couple of minutes, looking down at her feet, before ducking her head even lower and saying, so quietly that I had to lean closer to hear her, 'Freya kept asking me why I was being quiet.'

I smiled. 'Well, perhaps she's used to people being as noisy as she is! You probably feel a bit shy with her at the moment, don't you.'

She shrugged, looking uncomfortable. 'Kirsty keeps asking why I'm quiet, too.'

'Ah, I expect they're just not used to shy people. I'll tell her you're—'

'No! Don't say anything, Mummy,' she said, looking worried.

I felt a shiver of concern. 'You're not scared of Kirsty, are you, sweetie? *She* doesn't shout, does she?'

Another shake of her head. 'No. She was nice. She gave me and Freya cakes and told Freya to calm down.'

'Well, that's good, isn't it? I'm glad Kirsty's nice to you.' I held out my arms to her. 'Don't worry, Daisy. The more you go to Kirsty's house, the more you'll get used to them and you'll soon stop feeling so shy.'

'But don't talk to her, don't tell her I'm shy, will you, Mummy? She'll think I'm a baby.'

'Of course she won't, she just wants you to be happy at her house. OK, don't cry, don't cry! I won't tell her, then, but you must promise to always tell me if anything's upsetting you, or I won't be able to do anything to help you.'

'You can't help me, anyway,' she said miserably. 'You won't, cos you'll just say I have to go there, and I don't want to, I want to stay with you.'

'I know you'd rather stay at home but honestly, I think you'll love going to Whitegate House after a little while, playing with Freya. It doesn't sound like anything happened that you really didn't like. Everyone seems nice, and—'

'Not everyone,' she whispered into my ear, before covering her face as if she was ashamed of saying anything.

'What? Who wasn't nice? You said Kirsty was, and Freya was—'

'Amelia,' she said from behind her hands.

'Amelia?' I repeated, surprised. 'But... she's...'

I wanted to say that Amelia, Kirsty's older daughter, probably wasn't even interested in Daisy. I'd only met her once, and I got the impression she struggled to even speak to me, only wanting to go back upstairs to her bedroom ('her lair', as Kirsty referred to it when she told me, eyes raised, that she was 'twelve, going on fifteen'). Craig had told me she'd been a bit difficult – not so much rude as uncommunicative, responding to anything he said with monosyllables, sloping around the house disconsolately, wearing a lot of black and spending a long time scowling at herself in mirrors. It had sounded like fairly normal pre-teen hormonal moodiness to me, so I didn't take too much notice. But if she was being mean to my baby girl, that was different.

'Has she been horrible to you?' I asked Daisy. 'You must tell me, if she has.'

'No.' She was avoiding my eyes again. 'But she's scary.'

'Because of the way she dresses? Wearing all black clothes?'

She shrugged. 'I just don't like her. She's scary.'

I racked my brain, trying to think of what Amelia might be doing to frighten Daisy. Perhaps she was playing loud music; perhaps she argued with her mum; perhaps she argued with Freya in front of Daisy. Being an only child, Daisy wasn't used to the bickering that goes on between siblings – and there were four, nearly five years between Amelia and Freya so, at this stage, they probably didn't have a lot in common. Perhaps the atmosphere between them was really combative. Daisy wouldn't have liked that, she wouldn't have understood it.

And she wouldn't like what I was going to do either, but I'd already decided: I was going to have to have a word with Kirsty about it. After she was asleep that evening, I called Craig and asked if I could take Daisy to Whitegate House again the next morning.

'Of course,' he agreed immediately. 'As Kirsty said, it's a good idea for her to get more used to being here, before you go back to work. I'm not too busy at the moment and Kirsty hasn't got a meeting tomorrow, so that'll be perfect.'

'Do you think Kirsty's girls mind, though?'

'Mind?' he said, sounding puzzled. 'Why would they mind?'

Why was I even bothering to ask him? Men never picked up on this kind of thing.

'Well, because she's coming into their home, invading their space. Perhaps they don't like it.'

'Don't be silly. Freya loved having Daisy here. She says it's like having a new friend. One who's almost kind of related.'

'Kind of related?' I muttered to myself, instantly disliking the phrase. 'What about Amelia? Daisy seems a bit nervous of her. I think perhaps I should speak to Kirsty about it.'

He laughed. 'Oh, Amelia's just at that age. We're all nervous of her!'

'Yes, well, Daisy's not used to older girls.'

'I'm surprised Daisy even saw her. Amelia spends most of her time in her bedroom. Don't mention it to Kirsty, she's worried enough about Amelia as it is. Tell Daisy to ignore her. I'll tell you what I *have* noticed, though: Daisy doesn't really speak when she's here.'

'Not at all? I know she's feeling shy, Craig, but she must be speaking a little bit, surely.'

'No. Well, only to me.'

'Not even to Freya?'

'No. Freya probably doesn't let her get a word in!' He laughed again.

I fumed to myself after I hung up. Daisy seemed really worried by Amelia, and Craig was just being dismissive about it. OK, I knew this was probably nothing, she was only little and she'd probably get used to being there. But – I wasn't supposed to tell Kirsty about it, in case it made her even more worried about her daughter? Wasn't that just typical of a man? All right, perhaps not any man, but from my recent experience, it was certainly typical of one who'd shacked up with his new woman, and who was so besotted with her that even his own little daughter now came further down his list of priorities. I mustn't upset Kirsty by mentioning the possibility that her daughter was scaring the life out of my six-year-old? Craig didn't want her *any more worried*? Well, I was sorry, Craig – but I found it hard to care about that.

When we arrived at their place in the morning, Kirsty was outside in their massive garden, wearing what looked like designer cropped jeans and a pure white T-shirt – a strange ensemble, I thought, for anyone to wear for gardening. She was pulling out weeds and complaining that the gardener wasn't doing what he was paid for. Freya was playing on the swing set further down the garden, so I sent Daisy off with her while I asked Kirsty if we could have a quick word.

'Of course, come and sit down,' she said, pointing to a pristine wooden bench on the patio. I put the same questions to her, about her daughters, that I'd asked Craig the previous night – and got more or less the same responses.

'Freya can be a bit overpowering. I'll talk to her, try to get her to tone it down. But as for Amelia, well, she hardly ever comes out of her bedroom. She's at a difficult age – you know, moody. I've had to pick her up on things recently – things like slamming doors and stomping up the stairs in a temper. She does snarl at her sister sometimes – I think Freya's exuberance gets on her nerves. But she hasn't really seemed to take any notice of Daisy when she's been here. Daisy's so... FREYA!' she yelled suddenly, startling me as she jumped up from the bench and took a few steps down the garden towards the girls. 'What have I told you about playing down the end of the garden? There are a lot of prickly bushes down there – STAY AWAY from there.'

She came to sit back down, shaking her head. 'I'd hate Daisy to get scratched – some of the rose bushes down there are lethal. But my roses are my pride and joy. I won't even let the gardener touch them.'

'OK,' I said, slightly bemused, wondering if perhaps she entered her roses for competitions or something.

'But as I was saying: Daisy's so very quiet, hardly says a word, only if I ask her a direct question, and then she only whispers.'

'Yes. Craig said he didn't think she spoke at all while she was here last time. Didn't she even speak to Freya?'

'Mostly just nodded or shook her head.' She laughed. 'Freya doesn't seem to mind, she talks enough for both of them! But I'll keep an eye on things, though. I wouldn't want poor little Daisy to be nervous of coming here.'

And although I bristled, again, at the 'poor little Daisy' bit, I had to admit I was grateful to her. She didn't take offence, as she might have done, by the implication that her older daughter was scary. And she'd promised to watch out for any signs of trouble. I even wondered, after hearing Kirsty holler down the garden to Freya about the rose bushes, if that in itself was the kind of thing that was making Daisy feel shy and a bit nervous. It might not be all about Amelia but Daisy was still a bit young to put all of her anxieties into words.

I went back to my tidying up feeling a little less worried. Kirsty might have been a bitch for stealing my husband, but, well, she was a mum, like me. So I guessed she understood a little of how I felt – probably more than Craig did.

\* \* \*

Gradually, over the next two or three visits, Daisy seemed a little less worried about going to 'the big house', as she'd started calling it. She was getting used to Freya's boisterous-ness, and when I, carefully, asked about Amelia, she just shrugged and said she'd hadn't seen her much. So, by the time I went back to work, I'd stopped feeling quite so nervous about leaving Daisy. Still, it was a big change for her that I had to work full time, to say nothing of the fact she'd soon be going to a new school. But I had no choice; things were already bound to be difficult, with nothing coming from Craig's salary now apart from what we'd agreed on, to support Daisy. I was trying not to be resentful about this, but it was difficult, in the circumstances. Craig didn't even need his salary for himself any more – Kirsty could surely have supported him. It irked me that it hardly even seemed to occur to him that I might be struggling, but that was my own fault. When we'd first discussed finances, I'd said I'd be OK. I'd even said I understood that he wouldn't want to be financially dependent on Kirsty, especially as they were in such a new relationship. Why was I trying to be so noble? Well, I didn't want us to be one of those couples who fight and spout hatred at each other after breaking up. I didn't want Daisy to see us turning into that. We would be reasonable, I'd decided, after the first few weeks of constant crying and recrimination had passed. We would treat each other civilly and make this work – even if at times I thought the pain in my heart would kill me. But since then, I'd made some stupid financial errors – starting with just one mistake and, since then, escalating the situation to the point where I was now really struggling. And I couldn't tell him that. I couldn't tell anyone. I knew what I'd done was stupid; I wanted to keep it to myself.

* * *

The salon where I worked was in the town centre, halfway between our new home and Whitegate House. So after a quick trip to drop Daisy off, I was able to go straight into work. She wasn't in a good frame of mind about it on my first day back, though.

'I thought you liked going to play with Freya now?' I tried to encourage her.

'I like it a little bit. But I'd rather stay at home with you.'

'I'm sorry, sweetie, but I can't stay at home now – my holiday's over and you know I have to go to work, don't you?'

'But I don't want to go to the big house every single day, Mummy. I'll miss you.'

I gave her a hug. 'And I'll miss you, too. But you'll be having fun, and I'll be with you all over the weekend, so we can both look forward to that, can't we? Now, come on.' I decided it was best to adopt a business-like tone rather than delaying the inevitable. 'Put your shoes on, we need to get in the car and get going.'

She was quiet on the way there, but I reasoned that she'd soon get used to the routine, that things seemed to be settling down and I just needed to keep reassuring her that everything was going to be fine.

'Come in, Daisy. Freya's so looking forward to you being here all day today,' Kirsty said in what sounded like almost genuine excitement. 'Go on, get yourself off to work,' she added to me as Daisy reluctantly stepped over the threshold. 'You don't want to be late. We'll be fine, won't we, Daisy? We're all going to have fun together. That's right, kiss Mummy good-bye. See you later, Mummy, have a nice day.'

The door was closed on me, my baby girl had been swallowed up into her other family, as I was trying not to keep thinking of them, and I was dismissed to hurry off to work. I understood Kirsty was trying to help by being so cheerfully matter-of-fact, and despite myself I was grateful to her. But still, I imagined my little Daisy feeling overwhelmed by the abruptness of our goodbye. And I knew I'd be worried about her all day at work. I supposed it went with the territory.

## 4

'I'll be glad when we're finished today.'

Jackie, my colleague, was winding down to retirement and often felt exhausted towards the end of a busy day.

'Me too.' We were passing each other at the appointment desk where I'd just said goodbye to a client while Jackie had been taking a phone call.

'Only one more lady for me – ah, here she is,' she said, as the doorbell pinged and a cheerful-looking lady with a grey perm came in. 'Hello, Mrs Dryden. Come in, take a seat.' Jackie turned to me and added, quietly, while Mrs Dryden was getting herself settled, 'Why don't you go now if you haven't got any more clients? The phone's quiet, there's nothing else for you to do at the moment – Paige can sweep up.'

Paige was our trainee, but Jackie and I both wondered for how long. She was young, but seemed so unenthusiastic about the job that I couldn't understand why she'd chosen it. She preferred the days she was at college with her friends, of course, but I'd have thought she'd also be grateful for the opportunity to have some actual paid work.

'I don't know,' I said doubtfully. 'I'd better wait in case someone comes in to make a booking. It's my first day back.'

She gave me a sympathetic smile. 'I know how worried you've been about Daisy.'

'Well, not exactly worried, just a bit anxious. Anyway, I'd better stay, I don't want you-know-who to think I'm going to start sneaking off early, now I'm working full time.'

'I can't understand why she's still here.'

'Me neither. It's so annoying.'

Camilla, the salon owner, usually referred to by the rest of us as Camel (because she always had the hump), had a habit of staying right up until we closed, even though she spent most of her time sitting in the office at the back, where she could be heard, occasionally, complaining loudly to friends on the phone. She lived in the flat above the salon and did hardly any hairdressing herself any more, but seemed determined to hang around downstairs to check up on us all. It was all right for Jackie to talk about sneaking off ten minutes early – she'd already qualified for her pension and was, in her own words, only working part-time now because she didn't want to be at home with her husband every day. But my job was absolutely essential to me, especially now.

I was tired when I finally got away, after helping Jackie and Paige sweep up, tidy everything away and put all the towels and gowns in the washing machine.

'Stay for a cup of tea before you drive home,' Kirsty offered while I waited in her hallway for Daisy to come downstairs.

I found it frankly amazing that she was talking as if we were friends – friends who'd sit and chat over a cup of tea, as if the only thing we had in common wasn't just that we'd both slept with Craig. But I supposed she was trying to give the impression she was a decent person. And of course, I was in her debt: she was having my daughter here in her house every day. I had to be polite, at least.

'Thanks,' I said. 'But I'd like to get home, if you don't mind. It's been a long day.'

'Of course, you poor thing. It must be awful, dealing with people all day.'

*'People'!* I thought to myself, wondering at the scathing way she'd said it, as if 'people' were beneath her. I supposed she only ever had to deal with them in online meetings, and – given how powerful she was – I guessed they'd all be scared of her. Not for her the strain of having to smile and make polite conversation about people's holidays and health conditions day in and day out. Not, to be honest, that I didn't enjoy my job and get on well with the majority of our clients. It was a friendly little salon and most of our customers were local people who we'd got to know over the years, many of them retirees, who seemed grateful no matter what we did to their hair, and often just liked the chat. I was pretty sure it wouldn't be the sort of salon Kirsty ever set foot in.

'Come on, Daisy,' I said now. 'Let's go home. Thanks so much for having her,' I added to Kirsty.

'No problem, it helps me too – keeps Freya happy and occupied.'

'Bye bye, Daddy,' Daisy said, as Kirsty opened the front door for us, and there was an answering call of *Bye, Daise!* from the study, where I presumed Craig was too involved with his work to come out and see her off, let alone say hello, or even goodbye, to me. I was only his ex-wife now, after all, even if I was never properly his wife.

'Did you have a nice time?' I asked Daisy as I drove her home.

'It was all right,' she said. 'Apart from the swimming pool.'

'Oh, did you go in the pool? You didn't have a swimsuit.'

'Kirsty got me an old one of Freya's.'

'Was Kirsty in the pool with you?' I asked, seized by a sudden fear that she and Freya might have been allowed in the pool without any adult supervision.

'Yes.'

'But you didn't like it?'

'No. Because I can't swim.'

'Well, you nearly can.' I'd been taking her sometimes to the public pool near our old house, and had even booked her a course of after-school swimming lessons, which had to be cancelled when our lives suddenly unravelled. 'I'll look into getting some new lessons booked in September. And meanwhile, remind me to find your armbands. Then you'll be able to swim, won't you?'

'No! I don't want armbands. I'll look like a baby. Like she said.'

'Who said?'

'Amelia. She laughed at me because I just sat on the side. I didn't want to get in the water and I didn't want to say it was cos I didn't have my armbands. And Kirsty said that's all right, just sit on the edge with your feet in. But Amelia laughed, and said I was a baby.'

This all came out in a rush of shame, and I felt an instant pang of sympathy for her – and annoyance at Amelia. OK, so it might have just been a bit of light-hearted teasing, but it had obviously upset Daisy, and surely a twelve-year-old should have known better than to tease a younger child for being nervous about getting in the water?

'Amelia and Freya can swim all the way up and down the pool with no armbands,' Daisy added sadly.

'Well, that's because they've got their own pool; they can go in it as often as they want and get better and better at swimming. If I book some lessons for you, you'll soon be able to join them, swimming up and down.'

'I don't want to.'

Was she going to be put off swimming for life by a silly, mean remark from Miss Moody-Sulker? Not if I had anything to do with it! I'd pack Daisy's swimming costume and armbands the next day, without telling her, and I'd have another quiet word with Kirsty. Perhaps – as she seemed to have all the time in the world to laze around her swimming pool doing nothing – she might be kind enough to help Daisy become more confident in the water. While also telling her elder daughter to keep her thoughts to herself.

As it happened, Amelia was apparently out the next day, at a friend's house, and when I picked Daisy up in the afternoon, she told me Kirsty had found another pair of armbands and suggested Freya wore a pair too 'so that you're both the same'.

'And Freya didn't mind?'

'No, she thought it was fun! She said they made it easier to float on her back, and I floated on my back too and we made ourselves into star-shapes on the water. And guess what, Mummy, Kirsty said she'd give me some lessons and she said she's sure I'll soon be able to swim with only one armband, and then none, because she says I'm a good floater.'

'That's brilliant, Daise,' I said. 'I'm sure she's right; you'll soon be swimming like a little fish.'

'Not a fish, a girl!' Daisy giggled. And it was so nice to hear that giggle, and to see that smile of happiness again, that I could almost have hugged Kirsty for her kindness. Much as I hated having to admit it.

'But I don't want to wear my armbands if Amelia's there,' Daisy went on in a quieter voice, her smile dropping. 'It was much nicer today at the big house, Mummy, when Amelia wasn't there.'

'Well, when she is there, just try to stay out of her way,' I suggested. 'You like Freya now, don't you, now you've got used to her?'

She nodded. I wanted to ask whether she ever actually spoke to Freya. But at the same time, I didn't want to make her feel uncomfortable if she really was still too shy to speak.

I decided to give it a little more time. Sure enough, by my second week back at work, things seemed to be settling down, Daisy wasn't asking to go back to the old house any more, and she even seemed a little happier about going to Whitegate House. The weather had been lovely, the girls were in the pool most days, and Daisy was indeed now swimming with only one armband on.

'Eventually she'll only be wearing it to give her confidence,' Kirsty said. 'Then I can gradually deflate it a little. That's what I did with Freya, until she got confident enough to stop wearing it.'

'I've been looking into booking her some lessons,' I said, 'but they all seem to be full.'

'Oh, there are after-school lessons held at the girls' school. Let me see if I can book Daisy in for September.'

'I'm not sure about that.' I felt awkward now. Amelia and Freya went to a private girls' school called Tudor Hall Academy, on the edge of town. I'd looked it up online, out of curiosity (well, OK, downright nosiness), and the fees were astronomical, even if it was set in a beautiful old mansion in acres of grounds, boasting every facility you could ever imagine. 'Perhaps if there's a phone number you could give me, for whoever runs the after-school lessons...' *If they're not too expensive.*

'Don't be silly, I'll look into it myself. I'm on the board of governors.'

*Of course you are*, I thought.

* * *

The next day, the weather was suddenly noticeably cooler, with a brisk wind and rain in the air. Even though the pool at Whitegate House was heated and under cover, Daisy told me, when we got home that afternoon, that she and Freya hadn't felt like swimming. Instead, Freya had asked Amelia if they could play on her Nintendo.

'And did she let you?' I asked. Daisy had never played on any kind of game console before, and I had no idea whether she was actually old enough. I felt a shiver of apprehension. I'd have to ask Kirsty whether the games Amelia was introducing her to were suitable for a six-year-old.

'Yes, but *she* had to play with us.'

'And was that fun?'

'No. Well, the game was fun, we had to choose a person – I was a girl in a yellow top and blue trousers – and we had to race each other, jumping over things.'

'That *sounds* fun.'

'But I didn't like Amelia playing with us. She was bossy. And she called me and Freya rude names.'

'Did she?' I felt my hackles rising. 'What sort of rude names?'

'She said I was stupid because I didn't know how to play the game, until Freya showed me. And she said me and Freya were pathetic. What's pathetic, Mummy?'

'I think she probably meant you weren't as good as her at

the game. But of course you wouldn't be, as she's a lot older than you. Don't worry about it – she shouldn't—'

'Me and Freya didn't want to play any more. But Kirsty said she's going to buy another Nintendo, for Freya, so then we won't have to ask Amelia to play.'

'That'll be good, then. Aren't you lucky, having all these exciting new things – a swimming pool, and Nintendo games?'

'I don't really want to have to go to the big house at all, though, Mummy,' she said with a huge sigh, as if the weight of the world were on her shoulders.

'Well, it'll soon be the weekend, then you can stay here with me. Then you'll be going to the holiday club for the next two weeks, remember.'

'Yay!' she said, smiling.

I smiled back at her, not wanting to spoil her happy mood. Nothing Kirsty could provide – no amount of swimming, or playing Nintendo games – could compete with seeing her old school friends. I'd already booked her into the holiday club at her old school, and paid for it in advance, before we knew we'd be moving. It wasn't really convenient to take her back there now, but as it happened, it coincided with Kirsty, Craig and the girls going away on holiday, so it was lucky I'd booked it. And Daisy was looking forward to seeing Jessica, her best friend.

But it wouldn't be long before she'd be starting at the new school and I knew she hadn't fully taken that on board yet. There was no point bringing the subject up until nearer the time: she had enough to get used to, for now.

## 5

'Don't worry, there are lots of Nintendo games suitable for her age,' Kirsty reassured me breezily when I dropped Daisy off again the following day. 'I told Amelia to make sure they chose one that was OK for the younger girls. Amelia probably found it boring! She plays more complicated ones with her friends, of course.' She smiled at me, before going on, 'Daisy's still so quiet while she's here, though. Like a little mouse. She talks to Craig, of course, but otherwise it's virtually impossible to get a word out of her. I know Freya can be overwhelming, but—'

'I know she can be a bit shy.' I was slightly irritated that Kirsty had moved the conversation on so quickly from the point I was trying to make about Amelia. 'She'll come round gradually. She talks all the time about Freya.' I checked my watch. I had to get going or I'd be late for work. 'But anyway, yes, I realise it might be frustrating for Amelia, playing with a six-year-old, especially one who's never played on a Nintendo before.'

'I'm sure she didn't mind.'

I was equally sure, of course, that she did mind – that she'd been annoyed with her sister, and even more so with Daisy. But I didn't really want to tell Kirsty that Daisy had complained to me about Amelia – it sounded petty. I knew kids had to sort out their own issues and disagreements, up to a point. But the balance of power here, Amelia being so much older, as well as being the elder daughter of the house and the owner of the games console, made what Daisy had described feel unkind, if not downright nasty. Together with the story of how she'd laughed at Daisy and called her a baby because she'd been nervous about the pool, it was weighing on my mind and beginning to make me dislike the girl. I told myself not to be ridiculous, that I was an adult and Amelia was just a twelve-year-old girl who was perhaps having her nose put out of joint by the incursion of another younger child in the house. But my maternal tiger instinct had been triggered and I was finding it difficult to rein it in.

'Can't you have a word with Craig?' Jackie suggested when I couldn't help telling her about it that afternoon. 'Amelia's not his daughter, so he's got no reason to be offended. Or to defend her.'

'Yes he has. She's the daughter of the woman he's chosen to move in with,' I pointed out, a little sourly.

'But surely he'll still be protective of his own child.'

'I don't know. He'd probably say I was making something out of nothing. And I suppose I probably am. Kids are sometimes unkind to each other, we all know that.'

'But Daisy's not used to mixing with older girls, is she? It's all right for Freya, she can laugh it off or stick up for herself because she's used to Amelia being the bossy big sister.'

'The miserable big sister, you mean. Honestly, I've never yet seen that girl smile. She slopes around the house with a face like thunder, snapping at Freya, answering her mother back, staring at me like I'm an intruder in her house, just for going to pick Daisy up.'

'She sounds very unhappy, Tash,' Jackie said gently.

'Yes, I know. You're probably right – after all, she lost her own father, didn't she? But, well, I don't want her making my daughter unhappy too.' I paused, then shook my head and added, 'But I suppose I'm being a bit judgemental, aren't I?'

'I don't blame you. Daisy is yours to protect. But you've got to keep the peace, really, haven't you? You need that arrangement. I hate to say it, but it sounds like Kirsty's being good.'

'In having Daisy for me, yes, she is. If you ignore the man-stealing.'

Jackie smiled. 'I know. It must be hard, love. And it's early days. Daisy's probably still finding it difficult being there, in their house, even if it is her daddy's home now. It's quite a big adjustment for her.'

'I know. You're right. As usual,' I said, giving her a grateful look.

I didn't have a mum, or a big sister, but I often felt like Jackie fulfilled that role for me. It really meant a lot, having someone older to talk to about my worries. When she eventually retired, I'd have to try to spend at least one day a week with her, to pour out everything I wanted her advice about.

'According to Craig, Daisy doesn't even speak to anyone except him while she's at their house. And Kirsty mentioned it herself this morning, too. She seemed a bit concerned.'

'She's shy, that's all. She'll come round.'

'I suppose so.' I smiled back at her, hesitating. I called Jackie my agony aunt. If I was going to tell anyone about my problem – the problem which was growing in seriousness every day, threatening to overwhelm me, giving me nightmares that made me wake up at night in a cold sweat of fear – it would be Jackie. She'd help me, she'd tell me what I needed to do. She'd understand, she wouldn't judge.

'Jackie,' I began, tentatively. 'I've been doing something, something really stupid—'

'Are you two going to stand there gossiping the whole afternoon?' Camel suddenly boomed from behind us, making me jump and turn away to pick up a towel, flustered into silence. 'Can't you at least make yourselves busy while you're waiting for your next clients?'

'Tell me later,' Jackie whispered while Camel stalked off and my next client appeared at the door.

But the moment had gone. I shook my head. 'It doesn't matter.'

* * *

I was tired by the end of the week. Work had been exhausting, with an unusual number of walk-ins prepared to sit and wait until we had a gap between appointments, which always made us feel anxious – like we wanted to rush our regular clients but knew we mustn't.

'Thank God it's Friday,' I said, stretching and yawning after I'd said goodbye to my last lady. 'If I had to ask one more person if they were doing anything nice at the weekend, I think I'd have thrown in the towel, literally.'

'No, you wouldn't,' Jackie teased me. 'You love your work.'

'Yes, I do, strangely,' I agreed.

'Well, you're lucky, at least you don't have to come in tomorrow.'

'I know.' I gave her a sympathetic smile. Camilla had agreed from the start that I could work on Mondays – one of the days Jackie had off – instead of doing Saturdays, otherwise I'd never have been able to take this job. And I was very aware that Saturday was their busiest day, so I had to be grateful.

* * *

'Did you have a good time?' I asked Daisy when I collected her from her first day at the holiday club.

'It was all right,' she said with a shrug.

'Only *all right*?' I teased her. I guessed she was probably tired – it had been a long day, beginning with an early start, for the drive back to our old village, and finishing with her being one of the last children to be collected, after I'd had to drive back again through the rush-hour traffic. 'I bet you enjoyed seeing Jessica and Ava, didn't you?'

'Jessica wasn't there. She *said* she'd be there, but Ava said she's gone on holiday to Greece with her mummy and daddy. Why can't *we* go on holiday, Mummy? I want to go on holiday with you and Daddy, like we did last year to Lansee-Rotten.'

'Lanzarote,' I said with a smile. 'Well, perhaps next year I'll be able to take you somewhere nice, but—'

'With Daddy too?' she persisted.

I sighed. This was never going to get easier, was it?

'No, sweetie. Daddy will be going away with Kirsty in future, won't he? They're away in Italy this week, you know that. But *I'll* take you away, I promise, one day when I've saved up some money, and meanwhile, don't forget Daddy promised to take you away at half term, to Center Parcs! Won't that be great?'

'No. I don't want to go. I don't want to go on holiday with Kirsty and Amelia and Freya. I want Daddy to come on holiday with *us*.'

She was starting to cry. We were walking to the car park but I stopped and pulled her into my arms.

'Oh, sweetie, I know that's what you'd like. So would I. But things don't always work out how we want them to, and that just isn't going to happen, OK? I'm sorry you're sad. It is sad sometimes when things change. But there will still be nice things to look forward to, and you'll love Center Parcs – you like playing with Freya—'

'But I don't want to go if Amelia goes.'

'I'm sure Amelia will leave you and Freya alone. She'll want to make friends of her own on holiday, friends her own age.'

'But Daddy won't want to play with me because he's got Kirsty and Amelia and Freya. And it's not fair, Mummy, because I've only got you, and you can't go on holiday until you've got some more money.'

'He *will* want to play with you,' I tried to tell her, but the lump in my throat was almost choking me.

*I've only got you.* Those words felt like knives to my heart. What were we doing to our precious daughter – what had *Craig* done to her? Swapping partners, as if it was of no more consequence than changing his clothes? Messing up her little life? For a moment, I actually hated him for what he'd done to us. He'd not only left us, he'd *benefited* from leaving us, and of course, I resented that, how could I not? Kirsty was wealthy, but that wealth wasn't his to exploit, not even to pay a higher level of maintenance to his own child. It was all very well him saying he needed to contribute his share of household costs and so on to Kirsty; I'd agreed – it had all sounded very fair and noble at the time, but not so much now, in the cold light of day, the icy-cold light of my own proximity to bankruptcy. I shivered, despite the warmth of the August afternoon. What was I going to do? What if I couldn't pay my next mortgage instalment? *Why* had I been such an idiot, getting myself into a situation I couldn't handle, getting myself deeper and deeper every day in my efforts to dig myself out? I was living from day to day, trying not to think about my problem until after Daisy was in bed, and spending every evening trying – and spectacularly failing – to put it right.

'Come on, let's get you home,' I said now to Daisy, wiping her tears and forcing myself to smile. 'I know you must have been disappointed that Jessica wasn't there today, but at least some of your other friends were, weren't they?'

'Yes. But Ava doesn't like me any more. She said she likes Harriet best and she said there's no point playing with me because I won't be going to that school now. And when we needed a partner, there were only boys left and I had to be Jake's partner and he's *horrible.*'

'Oh dear, you really didn't have a good day, did you?' I sympathised. 'But look, tomorrow will be different, I'm sure. There will be some different children there, and perhaps Jake won't be going tomorrow.'

There really wasn't much else I could say to cheer her up. The way things looked, she might have been happier going to Whitegate House than to the holiday club for these two weeks, after all – if it weren't for the fact that Craig and his new family were now on the Italian Riviera.

* * *

Over the course of those two weeks, though, I did manage to coax Daisy into going back to the holiday club every day, and apparently Ava and Harriet decided to like her again – in the carelessly cruel way of children, saying she could be their friend but only until the holiday club finished. If nothing else, it stopped her asking to invite them over to play, and I hoped that would encourage her to make new friends when she started at the new school.

There was going to be another hurdle to face then, too: Kirsty had told me, on the last day before they went on holiday, that she'd managed to *pull some strings* to reserve Daisy a place in the beginners' after-school swimming class, held at Amelia and Freya's school. I'd already looked at these online, so I knew the lessons were going to cost twice as much as I was originally planning to pay at Daisy's old school. But before I could even voice my concern, Kirsty told me very firmly that she was going to pay for them. Of course, I should have been grateful, but I wasn't; I was just offended that *she* was offering to pay – not Craig, Daisy's own father. Couldn't she, at least, have *pretended* it was coming out of his wallet? But the trouble was, of course, if I'd made more than the necessary pretend-polite gesture of refusal, I'd have either had to find the money myself – which would have been frankly impossible – or deny Daisy the opportunity. It was pretty hard to make a pretend-polite gesture of refusal and then a pretend-polite speech of gratitude while I was actually fuming inside.

Craig and I had been for a visit to Daisy's new school before moving house. It was a more modern building than her old school, and a lot bigger, with three classes across each year group. I'd wondered whether Daisy might find this a bit overwhelming. But Mr Frost, who'd be Daisy's class teacher, did indeed seem lovely.

'Do you like playing games?' he'd asked Daisy, and when she nodded, he enthused that this was great news, because he *loved* taking his class for games on Fridays, and they didn't just play with footballs or tennis balls – oh no, they played with hoops, skipping ropes, and all *sorts* of stuff!

Daisy had looked quite excited about this at first, but later she admitted she'd thought he meant games like Connect Four or Pop-Up Pirate, or even Nintendo games like the one she'd played with Freya. But I'd been quite touched by Mr Frost's almost childlike enthusiasm for his job, and I hoped she was going to enjoy being in his class. I wasn't getting ahead of myself, though. I knew going back to school after the six-week break was hard enough for most kids anyway, without the added anxiety involved in starting somewhere new.

Daisy's first day at the new school would be on a Tuesday, so on the Monday she went to play with Freya again. Amelia and Freya weren't starting back at their own school for another week, and Kirsty told me she was so glad to have Daisy there, because Freya had apparently been bouncing off the walls since they'd returned from their holiday in Italy.

I found out the reason for all the excitement when I collected Daisy at the end of the day.

'Mummy, guess what?' she squawked as I strapped her into her car seat. 'They're getting a doggy!'

'Are they?' I asked in surprise. 'Are you sure? Is that just what Freya told you?'

'No, Kirsty told me it too, and so did Daddy. It's a little baby puppy and they're getting it tomorrow. They're going to call it Max.'

'Well, that's a surprise, isn't it?'

I knew what was coming next, of course.

'Can we get a dog too, Mummy? Please? I really, really want a doggy, why can't we get one?'

I sighed. 'We've been through this already, haven't we, Daisy? You know why. The poor dog would be on its own all day.'

'It's not fair,' she said, pulling a face.

'Well, look, whenever you go to Daddy and Kirsty's house, you'll be able to see Max, won't you? If they're getting him tomorrow, you'll see him when you go there after school.'

'And will I be able to play with him?'

'I expect so. But that'll be up to Daddy and Kirsty. If he's only a baby, he'll probably need a lot of sleep, and he might be nervous about being in his new home. But at least you can see him. That's exciting, isn't it?'

'Yes,' she agreed, bouncing up and down in her seat as I started the engine for the drive home. 'I'm glad I'm going to the big house tomorrow, now. I can't wait.'

I hadn't expected to hear that, and it was such a relief to know she'd have something to look forward to after her first day at the new school that I took the opportunity to remind her that it would be Craig picking her up in the afternoon, not me.

'I know. I can't wait to go back to their house to see Max.'

And I drove home feeling an unexpected burst of gratitude to a little puppy I hadn't even met yet. It was so lovely to see Daisy so happy, so full of excitement, that I decided to stop worrying about her going to the big house from now on. She might feel a bit shy there, but she'd be OK. She was getting used to it gradually, and the dog was surely going to help.

## 6

Daisy was nervous, of course, the next morning when I laid out her new school uniform on her bed.

'I want to wear my other school clothes. The blue ones.'

'Well, for one thing, you've got too big for them now,' I said. 'And red is the colour for your new school.'

'I like blue,' she said sulkily, scowling at the red cardigan.

'Well, I think red suits you. I think you'll look extra nice in it. And it's more special, too. Lots of schools have blue uniforms, but not so many have red.'

'Freya says she has brown at her school. That sounds horrible,' she said, pulling a face.

'Well, there you are – you're lucky you haven't got brown, aren't you?'

She finally agreed to get dressed in the new uniform and somehow we were ready to leave on time for her first day. Mr Frost greeted us at the classroom door, welcoming Daisy with far more excitement than she was showing herself, and telling her he had *lots of good stuff* lined up for the children on their first day back. I thanked him and made my exit quickly. I knew this was the best way, knew that if I hung around, showing my own anxiety, I'd only make things more difficult for Daisy. But even so, I felt close to tears as I drove on to work. My baby girl was still so little, so young to be going through the difficulty of starting a new school. I thought of nothing else all day, watching the time, wondering what she was doing and whether she was settling down, whether she'd remember that Craig would be picking her up in the afternoon. I even started wondering whether Craig himself would remember, and considered whether I should message him a reminder, but I told myself to stop it. He'd sounded just as anxious as I was the previous day when I'd collected Daisy from his house, saying how much he hoped she'd settle at the new school and how he was looking forward to seeing her afterwards. He wouldn't forget. He might have stopped loving me, but he hadn't stopped loving his daughter.

\* \* \*

By the time I finished work I was so on edge I could barely breathe. I was ringing the doorbell at Whitegate House earlier than I'd ever managed before, and as I did, I heard the sound of yapping from inside, and remembered about the puppy. A door inside slammed shut and I heard Kirsty shout, 'Keep him in the kitchen while I open the front door!'

'Hi, Tasha,' she went on wearily as she opened the door. 'Come in, welcome to the madhouse. I don't know who's more excited, the puppy or the kids.'

'How's Daisy been?' I asked anxiously. I was far more concerned about my daughter than about the new puppy.

'Oh, she's fine. Daisy!' she yelled as she opened the kitchen door. 'Your mummy's here.'

A tiny scrap of black and white fur hurtled out of the kitchen towards me, followed by all three girls – Daisy and Freya almost tumbling over each other in their rush, Amelia following more slowly, looking as if she was trying to remain cool and aloof despite the circumstances.

'Max!' Freya screamed. 'Come here, come and get your squeaky toy.'

'All right, Freya, calm down, he's just coming to say hello to Daisy's mummy. Honestly, Tasha, I think the poor puppy's going to be exhausted; Freya hasn't stopped squealing at him since we picked him up. He's only a baby, Freya. He needs a rest.'

I bent down and rubbed the little dog's head, laughing at the way his tail swished madly backwards and forwards in his excitement.

'He's called Max, and he's a Border collie, and he's going to go to classes when he's big enough, to learn to do what he's told,' Freya shouted, jumping up and down in front of me.

'I think we might need to find some of those classes that work for little girls,' Kirsty said.

'Hey, some of us are trying to work in this madhouse.' Craig was laughing as he came out of his study. He gave me a smile. 'Pick-up went smoothly, Tash. Mr Frost seems like a nice guy. I wish we'd had jolly teachers like him when we were at school.'

I glanced at Daisy, who was too engrossed in fussing over Max with Freya to take any notice of our conversation, and asked quietly, 'Did she seem OK?'

'A bit subdued. But that's only to be expected, isn't it?'

'She's brightened up since she's been back here,' Kirsty said.

'Well, your timing couldn't have been better, with the puppy.'

'Oh, we decided some time ago to get one. We went to the breeder to choose Max earlier in the summer, but we obviously didn't want to collect him until we came back from Italy.'

'Of course.'

Daisy finally stopped playing with Max for long enough to look up at me and come for a hug.

'How was your day at school, sweetie?' I asked her.

She pulled a face. 'I didn't like it. Everybody had friends but I didn't.'

'Why don't you come to *my* school, Daisy? Then I'd be your friend!' Freya yelled at the top of her voice.

'Freya, calm down,' Kirsty said, shaking her head. 'Daisy wouldn't be in your class even if she did come to your school; she'd be in the year below you.'

To say nothing of the fact that I'd never in a million years have been able to afford to send her there. But Daisy, now she'd stopped playing with the puppy, suddenly looked so tired, I made our goodbyes quickly and headed home. She was so quiet in the car, I thought she'd fallen asleep, but when we pulled up outside our house I realised she'd been silently crying to herself.

'Oh, come here, sweetheart,' I said, helping her out of the car. 'Look, you'll soon make friends at your new school, I promise you. It'll be fine.'

'No it won't. Nobody talked to me. Nobody played with me at playtime. I didn't know where to sit at lunch because they were all sitting with their friends. Please let me go back to my old school, Mummy? *Please*?'

I pulled her towards me and let her cry for a few moments while I stroked her hair and wiped her tears.

'I can't do that, Daisy. I'm sorry. But it'll get easier, really it will. I know you probably feel shy, but if you try to talk to some of the children I'm sure they'll be nice to you.'

'They won't. They don't like me. If you won't let me go back to my old school, can I go to Freya's school instead?'

'No, I'm afraid not. It costs lots of money, more than I'll ever have. Come on, let's get you something to eat and drink, and put something fun on the TV for a little while, shall we? Tomorrow is another day.'

'Another horrid day,' she muttered tearfully, making me feel even worse. 'I wish you had lots of money, Mummy. It's not fair.'

There wasn't a lot I could say to that, was there? I told myself that I'd be sure to notice a gradual improvement in Daisy's mood as the week passed, but if anything, she became quieter and quieter each day on the subject of school, and only seemed happy when she talked about her time at Whitegate House. She didn't seem in the least upset any more about being taken back there by Craig every day after school; in fact she seemed to love the time she spent there every afternoon, playing with Freya and the puppy. She'd apparently got used by now to Freya's boisterousness, and when I asked her about Amelia, she just shrugged and said that Freya had told her to ignore her.

'What sort of things has she been saying, that you have to ignore?' I asked on the Friday evening when this was mentioned again.

Daisy shrugged. 'Stuff about Max. Like, she said I can't stroke him or play with him because he's not my dog, cos I'm not part of the family.'

Once again I felt my hackles rising.

'Yes, you are! You are, because your daddy lives there.'

'I know, but I'm not really, am I, Mummy, because I don't live there all the time like they do.'

'No, but you wouldn't want to, would you?' I felt bad for asking this, because I knew I was only hoping to reassure myself. And then I wished I hadn't asked, because she sat for a while, her head on one side, considering this before replying, 'No, not really, cos *you* don't live there, Mummy. But if you did, I would want to.'

Ouch! I swallowed back my surprise and disappointment, but I still couldn't help risking more, by asking, 'You'd like to live there? Even though Amelia sometimes says nasty things to you?'

'I know, and I don't like her, but me and Freya have to ignore her. That's what Kirsty says too.'

'So why would you like living there?'

She laughed, as if this was such a ridiculous question, it barely merited an answer.

'Because then I'd live with Max all the time. And with Daddy, and with Freya. And I'd be able to go in the swimming pool. And Freya's getting her Nintendo soon. And if I lived with them, I'd go to their school, wouldn't I, and I bet it's nicer than my one.'

I told myself to be pleased that Daisy was so much happier now about going to Whitegate House. It was a massive step forward, and I was glad she and Freya seemed to be getting on so well. It meant I could feel more relaxed, and less guilty, about working full time and having Craig collect her from school every day. And if she was managing to ignore Amelia's nasty little digs, instead of being upset by them, that was good too – wasn't it?

But whatever I told myself, *I* still couldn't ignore them. I was furious to think anyone might be saying spiteful things to my baby, and if Amelia really was being that nasty, I'd have preferred Kirsty to take action, rather than just telling Daisy to ignore her. Surely Amelia was old enough to know better, even if she was feeling resentful about having another younger child in the house. She ought to be told, and if it went on, maybe I should have another word with Craig about it.

But before I could think any more about that, we had Daisy's first swimming lesson, booked by Kirsty, at Tudor Hall Academy. The timing of the beginners' class meant I was going to have to take Daisy straight there after picking her up from Kirsty's.

'I don't want to go,' Daisy said, predictably. She was lingering in the kitchen at Whitegate House with Freya and the puppy, avoiding looking at me.

'I know it's a bit scary, going somewhere different, sweetie, but I'm sure you'll enjoy it,' I said in my pretend-excited voice.

'You're going to *my* school, Daisy,' Freya said. 'My school's really nice, and the swimming pool's warm – it's in, like, a glass building outside of the school, and you'll see all the tennis courts and stuff, and where we play games.'

'Will there be big girls there?' Daisy asked. Freya had already told her that the school was for girls of all ages, from four to eighteen, which Daisy had found both amazing and scary.

'Not in your swimming lesson,' Freya said. 'It's only for beginners, so they'll be, like, mostly your age or younger.'

'And it's not just for children from Freya's school anyway, Daise,' I reminded her. 'There might be children from *your* school there. Come on, quickly, or we'll be late.'

'All right,' she said, unwillingly. 'But if I don't like it, can I not go any more?'

'We'll see.'

The pictures of Tudor Hall on the internet really hadn't done it justice. Close up, the place was even more impressive. The swimming pool, which, as Freya had described, was outside the school, in its own glass-covered building, was beautiful and pristine.

Daisy's eyes were wide with wonder, and in the changing room she got into her costume quietly, without any further protest, while looking uncertainly at the other children, who, as Freya had predicted, all looked about the same age as her.

'That girl's in my class,' she whispered as a little dark-haired child stared at her across the changing room. 'Her name's Edie.'

'Well, that's nice, isn't it?' I encouraged her. Perhaps she'd finally make a friend from her new school now.

'No. She doesn't talk to me at school.'

But she continued to watch Edie, and – albeit reluctantly – followed her to sit by the side of the pool and wait for the teacher, while I went to watch from the seating area. The other children were all chatting to each other, while Daisy sat on the end of the bench, looking at the floor. I reminded myself that perhaps some of the others already knew each other, so it would inevitably take time for Daisy to feel included. But the teacher was young and very friendly – chatting to the children enthusiastically about how they'd all soon be good little swimmers but not to worry if they were nervous at first. She gave the children armbands and asked each of them in turn to show her what they could do – if anything – in the water. Some of the children couldn't swim at all yet, but when it was Daisy's turn she took off one armband and doggy-paddled right across the pool. Afterwards she was glowing from the teacher's praise.

'She said I'm probably ready to try without any armbands,'

she said proudly. 'Do you think I am ready, Mummy, or will I sink?'

'I'm sure your teacher will make sure you don't sink.'

'And she's going to teach us all how to do proper swimming strokes like Amelia and Freya do. One is called Crawl and one is called Best Stroke.'

'Breast stroke,' I said, smiling. 'Well, isn't that exciting. I'm glad you enjoyed your lesson.'

'And I like this school better than my one,' she said emphatically, looking around her at the gorgeous grounds and tennis courts as we walked back to the car. 'I really want to come to this one, Mummy.'

Oh dear.

I buckled her into the car, passed her a packet of crisps to take her mind off the subject of the school, and wondered if these lessons were going to be such a good idea after all.

## 7

'It sounds like things are settling down,' Jackie said during a quiet spell at work a week or so later. 'Daisy's not complaining so much now about going to Kirsty's place?'

'No, she's not. But in a funny way it bothers me just as much now, because she still talks about how Amelia's mean to her, scowls at her and mutters under her breath all the time. But Daisy insists it's OK because Kirsty keeps telling her to ignore it. I don't think that's the answer, though, is it? It worries me that Amelia might be being really unkind to her and nobody's picking her up on it.'

'What does Craig say?'

'Oh, he just defends Kirsty every time, of course.' I sighed, frustration making me shake my head and scowl, just as Camel came in from her lair at the back of the salon and snapped at us both to tidy things up. 'I feel so conflicted,' I went on quietly after she'd gone back. 'I lie awake at night steaming with anger about it all. Why is life so unfair? Why do I have to put up with this situation – letting my daughter go there every day, to her house, the house of the woman who stole my man? Why do I go along with this situation, Jack? Why do I have to be polite to her? I shouldn't even have to talk to her! Where's my pride? What's wrong with me?'

'There's nothing wrong with you,' she soothed me. 'You're going along with the situation because it's what's best for Daisy, and for you. You need to work, she needs to be somewhere safe while you're here, and she needs to be allowed to spend time with her father. The arrangement ticks all the boxes; there's no other option that could work so well, and you're being an amazing mother – putting your daughter first – by swallowing your pride and putting your hurt feelings aside, making an effort, being polite to Kirsty in return for her taking care of Daisy. I know how you must feel. Well, OK, I don't, but I can imagine. It must be so hard. And because you know you have to be polite to Kirsty, I think you're transferring all your resentment onto poor Amelia.'

'Poor Amelia?' I squawked. 'She's so rude! The other day she opened the door to me and all she said was, "Oh. It's you," before turning her back on me and walking away – leaving me to step inside and close the front door behind me. Even Kirsty complains to me about how badly behaved she is! I can't believe Daisy's managing to ignore all her taunts and insults, while she's still getting upset about the kids in her class at school.'

'She's being reassured about Amelia by Freya and Kirsty. But is she still no happier at school? I was hoping she'd have settled down a bit by now.'

'No, not really. I mean, she's getting used to it, but she's not happy. She hasn't made any friends. And she's still keeping on about wanting to go to Tudor Hall.'

'You'd better start doing the Lottery, then,' Jackie joked.

I shivered. This was just not funny. If Jackie knew – if I'd had the time, or the courage, to tell her – just how unfunny this was, considering my current circumstances of being so close to defaulting on my mortgage, she wouldn't joke about it.

'Things will get better, trust me,' Jackie said gently, seeing the look on my face.

But would they? Could they ever get better, now that I'd got myself into such a mess?

* * *

I found myself thinking about the conversation later that evening, at home. Daisy had, again, been complaining about her school and bemoaning the fact that Freya seemed to have fun at 'the school where I go swimming'. She was loving her swimming lessons, ignoring my repeated reminders that these weren't anything to do with Tudor Hall school, but run by an outside swimming coaching organisation. In her mind, it was all one: the lessons were good, the school looked good, Freya loved it there, so she would, too – if only I would stop being so mean and let her go there instead of her 'horrible new school' where, apparently, nobody liked her. I knew I had to be patient, that I should at least be pleased that she'd taken so well to the swimming lessons and that she and Freya had become good friends. But still, Daisy's comments about Amelia were getting to me. Almost every day, there was a mention of some meanness, some small act or word of spite that Daisy seemed to have more or less shrugged off, but still felt she had to tell me about. I hated to admit it, even to myself, but I was beginning to feel such a violent dislike of the girl that it was difficult to even look at her if she happened to slope moodily past me when I collected Daisy in the evenings. Sometimes I felt mean, remembering what Jackie had said about how unhappy she must be, so I would try to engage Amelia in conversation, only to be given a glare and a shrug and a few mumbled words to the effect that she would be fine if everybody would just leave her alone.

Finally, Daisy told me about an incident that I couldn't ignore.

'We took Max for a walk today,' she told me as I was driving her home.

'Did you? He's allowed to go out now, is he?'

'Yes,' Daisy said importantly. 'Kirsty said he'd had all his injections now so it was OK. We all went out together. But Freya and me weren't allowed to hold his lead yet. Only Kirsty, and then she let Amelia have a turn because she was sulking.'

*Of course she was*, I thought to myself. *So she gets what she wants.*

'And then Kirsty took hold of Max again because we had to cross a busy road. And Amelia sulked again and me and Freya laughed at her. And she pushed me into the road and got told off by Kirsty.'

'Amelia pushed you into the busy road?' I said, trying to control the fury in my voice. 'She deliberately pushed you?'

'Well, I was all right because Kirsty grabbed me before I fell over, Mummy, and she shouted at Amelia because she said she might have let go of Max while she grabbed me, and it was dangerous, but Amelia said it was an accident.'

'Was it an accident? Or do you think she did it on purpose?'

'I don't know. I thought it was on purpose, but Kirsty said, "All right, just be more careful, Amelia." So I suppose it was an accident but it felt like a push.'

OK, so I now had a definite reason to talk to Kirsty, and I wouldn't accept any excuses. Daisy didn't seem as bothered about this incident as I'd have expected – she was obviously prepared to accept Kirsty's opinion about it being an accident; after all, Kirsty was the adult. But if it felt like a push, I was almost certain it would have been a push. Everything I'd seen and heard of Amelia so far was leading me to believe she'd be capable of it.

\* \* \*

As it happened, Kirsty wanted to talk to me the following day when I collected Daisy, anyway.

'I just wanted to say, in case you've been worried about it, that Daisy seems to be gradually getting over her shyness with us now. I think the puppy has helped. It's like he's helped her find her confidence. She still doesn't talk to Amelia, which is understandable, but she chats away to Freya now as if they've known each other forever.'

'Ah, that's good to hear,' I said. 'I thought we'd get there eventually. But I'm sorry,' I went on, 'I don't like having to ask you this again, but are you sure Amelia isn't being spiteful to Daisy? She's told me Amelia might have pushed her into the road yesterday when you were all out with the dog.'

Kirsty sighed. 'I know. I didn't actually see how it happened, but yes, Daisy did stumble into the road for a second. Don't worry, I caught her before she fell, she was back on the pavement within two seconds. I did shout at Amelia, but to be fair, I can't be sure she actually pushed Daisy; it might have just been that they were jostling and got in each other's way. You know how it is, with three kids, all wanting to be closest to the dog.'

I didn't, but I could imagine. I wanted to say that if she found three kids and a dog too much to cope with, she shouldn't take all of them out together, but that felt a bit too critical, and what would I have done if she'd said OK, she'd better stop having Daisy?

'I won't take all of them out with me together again,' she said now, as if she was reading my mind. 'Amelia can stay at home. Or perhaps Craig can take Max for a walk when he goes to meet Daisy from school. Then she can have the puppy on her own for a little while on the way home.'

I smiled. I had to admit, this was a really nice idea.

'Daisy would love that,' I agreed. 'Thank you.'

'That's OK, Tasha,' she said. She looked at me sadly. 'I *am* sorry, you know.'

'About Amelia?' I asked.

'Well, that too. I know she's going through a difficult phase, being quite hostile, really. But don't worry, I'm watching the situation; I won't let her take her feelings out on Daisy. I've told Daisy to ignore her—'

'Yes, she's obviously taken that on board. I think she tries to avoid Amelia as much as she can.'

'Sensible girl,' Kirsty said ruefully. 'But no, what I actually meant was, I'm sorry about Craig. What's happened, with him and me. Especially the way he told you. I was so cross. I said he could have been kinder. I felt for you, I really did. And, well, I wish it could have been different, because you're a nice person and you didn't deserve this happening to you. But I do love him, you know.'

'So did I,' I couldn't help reminding her, and she looked back at me, her eyes so sad, the sympathy dripping off her, and I didn't know whether to admire her for making the effort, broaching the difficult subject that lay awkwardly between us, or just feel sickened by the hypocrisy, the attempt to cosy up to me from her position of superiority. After all, she'd won. She'd stolen Craig from me. She could afford to be magnanimous.

But she must have been good at it. Because I found myself melting under her sympathetic gaze, telling her it was OK, agreeing that we women had to stick together; after all, we were always the ones, weren't we, even in this day and age, who ended up with the kids and the shopping and all the chores?

It wasn't until I got home that I wondered how exactly I'd let that happen: that I'd laughed and let her cosy up to me as if we were now the best of friends and both in it together, when nothing could really have been further from the truth. I had to reluctantly admit that I was finding myself, these days, quite liking Kirsty. Perhaps, if we'd met some other way, we might have got on really well together. I'd prefer to have hated her, but she seemed to be making that difficult, and much as I resented it, I had to admit that the more I saw of her and Craig, the weaker he looked, and the more I could understand how easily she'd snared him.

## 8

Half term was approaching and Daisy was getting anxious about the forthcoming Center Parcs holiday. Kirsty must have been talking to her about it, because Daisy was coming home from Whitegate House with stories of how big the swimming pool would be, and how they could all get bikes there and go for rides, and there would be adventure golf, and boats, and den-building and baby owls, and she and Freya were going to play football. Then in the next moment she'd go suddenly quiet and say she wasn't really sure if she wanted to go.

'But it sounds so exciting,' I encouraged her. 'You'll have a lovely time.'

'But Mummy, I want *you* to come,' she said sadly. 'I don't want to go on holiday without you.'

'I can't come, sweetheart. It's Daddy's holiday with Kirsty, and with you and Freya and—'

'And I wish Amelia wasn't coming,' she put in before I could even mention her. 'Or her friend.'

'Her friend?' I looked at Daisy more closely. 'Is Amelia taking a friend on the holiday?'

'Yes. She said she didn't want to come, so Kirsty said she could bring her friend. And Daddy said that means we'll need two cars. Daddy will drive one with me and Freya, and Kirsty will drive the other one with Amelia and Grace, that's her friend, because otherwise we won't have room for our suitcases.'

'I see. And is Amelia happier about coming on the holiday now?'

'Yes. She laughed at Freya and said, "I'm bringing my best friend and you've just got to hang around with that baby." She meant me, Mummy. I'm not a baby, though, am I?'

'No, of course you're not. Amelia was just being mean.'

'That's what Freya said. She said she didn't care, anyway, because I'm *her* best friend.' Daisy smiled. 'Freya's my best friend too. I wish we went to the same school, Mummy.'

I sighed. I was glad Daisy was getting along so well with Freya, and that this helped her to brush off Amelia's nasty digs. But once again we were back on the subject of the school. It had been nearly half a term, and still she wasn't happy at her own school. Mr Frost had asked me for a phone chat one evening, and had told me he had concerns about her.

'Daisy never seems to speak to anyone,' he said quietly, sounding quite serious. 'I realise she's probably shy, but she doesn't even reply if they speak to her.'

'She tells me nobody talks to her at all,' I protested.

'Some of the children have tried. I've seen them, heard them. But Daisy just looks down at her feet and says nothing. I've given her quite a bit of time, as I thought it was just shyness and that she'd settle down, but I thought maybe I should let you know. Is everything all right at home, for her?'

'Well, as you know, Daisy's father and I are separated, but she goes to his house after school every day, and I think she's settled down well there now. She's always a bit quiet when she doesn't know people: apparently she didn't talk much there at first, but now she seems to be fine. Is there anything I can do to help her settle at school? Should I invite one or two of the other children to play at the weekend, do you think?'

'I'm not sure that would be a good idea. There's nobody yet that I can really suggest – unfortunately, although I have tried to encourage the children to be kind to anyone new, they do tend to give up trying if they don't get a response. They will probably have assumed that Daisy wants to be left alone.'

'But she's always complaining that nobody speaks to her and nobody likes her.' I paused, then added, 'Does she talk to you?'

'If I ask her a question, she'll respond, but only in a whisper, looking at the floor. I was trying to encourage her to speak by addressing her quite a lot in class, but I'm beginning to realise I might have been making things worse for her, as she was obviously finding it really difficult to reply, even in a whisper.'

'She's whispering?' I repeated.

'Only if she has to. Otherwise – nothing. Just silence. It's interesting she was silent at her father's house at first, too.'

'But not now,' I insisted, 'so hopefully the same will happen at school.'

'OK. Well, I thought I should just check in with you. I did wonder whether you'd feel you might perhaps, if Daisy doesn't improve, think about getting her some help.'

'What do you mean? What sort of help?'

'From a doctor. Or some kind of therapist. I haven't had a child with this level of problem myself before, but one of the other teachers here has had a child in their class who was literally unable to speak due to severe anxiety. And, well, that child has gone on to do well, with therapy.'

'Therapy?' I heard myself squawk. This was all so sudden. I was struggling to take it in. *This level of problem?* Did he really think it was that serious? I felt a shiver of anxiety run down my spine. He thought there was something actually wrong with my daughter. 'But surely she's just shy. I've always assumed she'd grow out of it.'

'And I hope that happens, too. But I think it might be worth getting an opinion, that's all. It's quite extreme for a child not to say a single word to anyone for nearly half a term. And I don't think she'd even have responded to me, if she wasn't afraid not to. When she's whispered to me, it's sounded almost painful. Like it was hurting her to even try.'

'She hasn't told me any of this,' I protested, thinking with a sinking heart about Daisy's sad little face when she told me how excluded she felt. 'Just that nobody speaks to her and nobody likes her.'

'She probably doesn't want to worry you. Or she might actually be embarrassed for you to find out. If she really can't help it, she might be feeling awkward and upset, thinking it's her own fault.'

'This is all a bit of a shock to me. I need to think about it, and talk to her father.' My head was spinning. Surely Mr Frost was just being over-zealous, imagining every quiet child had a problem just because there'd been a child like it in another class? Surely this was just shyness and anxiety?

'Of course. But I thought it was important to let you know how serious I think this appears to be. You may not want to tell Daisy what we've discussed, for the moment, of course.'

'Of course. Well, thank you.'

I hung up and stared at the wall for a moment, feeling

stunned. Daisy wasn't talking at school – not *at all*? I still wanted desperately to believe she was just feeling shy, and unhappy. She'd told me often enough, after all, how sad she was that nobody spoke to her, so it would have become difficult for her to keep trying. And at least Mr Frost said she did respond to him, even if only in a whisper. She was probably embarrassed to speak out loud if the other children all stared at her, as she claimed. I decided to talk to Craig about it the next day. He collected her from school every day so he might have more idea whether there was any truth to this, any real cause for concern.

* * *

The next day, though, things took a different turn. Daisy seemed happy and excited when I arrived at Whitegate House to collect her.

'Mummy, Kirsty wants to ask you something,' she said, her eyes shining. 'She says I can come and—'

'Hey, Daisy, I said let me talk to Mummy about it first,' Kirsty said, laughing as she came up behind her. 'Girls, go and play with Max again, would you, while I talk to Tasha?'

She shook her head, smiling, as they ran off after the puppy.

'Sorry, Tasha – they're both so excited. I asked Daisy if she thought she might like to stay one night for a sleepover with Freya. Perhaps on Friday? I thought it would give you a break, and more to the point, it would be good for Daisy to do this before we go off to Center Parcs. I wasn't sure if she's ever spent a night away from you yet?'

'No, she hasn't,' I confirmed. I'd been a little bit anxious about this, and had planned to warn Craig that, since he'd left,

Daisy had become more clingy to me, and that he'd have to make sure he spent plenty of time with her during the week away, comforting her if necessary. 'I suppose that would be a good idea. I don't know whether she'll be upset, though, when it comes to it.'

'Well, Craig and I will both be here to look after her, but honestly, Tasha, she seems so excited about it, and so does Freya. They really are like best buddies already, you know. It's so nice to see, especially as I was quite worried at first, when Daisy was too shy to even speak to her.'

'Yes, it is,' I agreed. And I found myself adding, 'And especially as Daisy's having such trouble making friends at the new school.'

To say nothing of the teacher thinking there was something wrong with her.

'Is she? Oh, poor little Daisy, I'm sorry to hear that. Would you and Craig ever consider sending her to Tudor Hall instead? It's such a wonderful school; Amelia and Freya both love it there, and—'

'No,' I interrupted her. I was already bristling at the 'poor little Daisy', wishing Kirsty wouldn't keep categorising my daughter in that way – however true it might feel at the moment – without her adding fuel to the fire of my irritation by bringing up Tudor Hall. It was bad enough that Daisy kept on about it every week when I took her to the swimming lessons. 'No, that's completely out of the question, I'm afraid.'

She looked back at me sadly, her head on one side.

'I know the fees are a little steep, but perhaps if I were to offer to contribute? After all, Daisy's practically my own daughter now, really.'

'No, she's not,' I retorted sharply.

I was properly offended now, almost to the point of calling

Daisy and walking straight out – forget the offer of a bloody sleepover. But Kirsty had placed a hand on my arm, shaking her head, actually blushing.

'Oh, Tasha, I'm sorry, that was so tactless of me, so offensive to you. Please forgive me; I didn't mean it quite the way it sounded. What I meant is that Daisy is obviously *Craig's* daughter, and as Craig and I are together now, I'm trying my best to treat her the same as I treat my own daughters. Does that make sense? I know she's yours, she'll always be yours, nothing can change that, I promise you. But I really do want her to feel loved and wanted here in our house, too. And she and Freya have become so close.'

'I know they have,' I relented, softening. I couldn't deny Kirsty had been good to Daisy, and helpful to me, too. I couldn't deny, either, that despite everything I actually quite liked her; I liked the apparently genuine warmth of her apology, the fact that she'd been so quick to admit her mistake in her choice of words. 'But please don't mention Tudor Hall again. I've told Daisy it's not going to happen.'

'Fair enough. Daisy's your daughter, and it's only for you and Craig to make these decisions.' She smiled now. 'But will you let her stay overnight on Friday? I think Freya will have a nervous breakdown if you say no.'

I laughed, and the tension was eased. 'Yes, of course. Thank you, I'm sure Daisy will love that.' I paused, remembering the other matter, which had been playing heavily on my mind. 'Meanwhile, I need to have a quick word with Craig, if he's available.'

'Of course.' She shouted for Craig. 'Is everything all right, Tasha? You look worried.'

'It's about Daisy. But I need to ask Craig what he thinks.'

'Of course,' she agreed again. 'Why don't you go in his study. I'll keep the girls away while you talk.'

I opened the door to Craig's study and peered around it cautiously, in case he was mid phone call, but he was sitting back in his swivel chair, looking up almost guiltily, making me think that he'd possibly been playing a game on his laptop.

'What is it?' he asked warily, as I closed the study door behind us.

I started to describe the conversation with Mr Frost, and his frown deepened as he struggled to follow me.

'He thinks she doesn't talk – not at all?'

'Only if he asks her a direct question. And then she answers in a whisper, apparently. I don't know if I can believe it, to be honest, but it really took me aback. How does she seem when you pick her up?'

'Quiet,' he concedes. 'But she always tells me the other kids don't speak to *her*. So I suppose it's obvious she doesn't talk – she's probably given up trying.'

'That's exactly what I thought. But Mr Frost thinks it's the other way around: that the other children have given up on her because *she* doesn't talk. And he says he's now avoiding asking her questions so that she doesn't have to even whisper.'

'She's just being shy. She's perfectly fine here, with us, although...' He hesitated for a moment, looking at me thoughtfully.

'What?' I said.

'Well, it's just that she *was* very quiet when she first started coming here. She didn't talk to Kirsty, or even Freya, not even to respond if they spoke to her. But she soon got over it. She was just shy,' he added with more conviction. 'That's nothing to worry about. She needs to get more confidence with the kids at school.'

'Does she talk to Amelia?' I asked him.

'No, I suppose not. But that's hardly surprising. Amelia scares the life out of her.'

'Yes.'

We looked at each other in silence for a moment.

'Mr Frost thinks I should talk to a doctor or someone,' I said.

'Rubbish. There's nothing wrong with Daisy. What, does he think she *can't* talk? That's nonsense – she's a right little chatterbox.'

'Yes,' I agreed again. 'So what do you think I should do?'

Why was I even asking him? I'd made all the decisions for Daisy since he'd walked out on me. Yes, he was still her father, I knew he still cared about her, but what difference would it make to his life, really, whether I decided to follow Mr Frost's advice or not? When Daisy was out of his sight, she was out of his mind. The uncomfortable truth was that I really didn't know what to do. I didn't want to make Daisy any more upset about school than she was already, by treating her as if she had some kind of condition that needed doctors' involvement, when I was pretty sure she just needed to make one friend, someone who'd bear with her shyness and give her a chance to find her feet in the new environment. But what if I was wrong, and Mr Frost was right?

'Ignore him,' Craig said firmly. 'As long as she's doing OK with her reading and writing and everything, why worry about it?'

I nodded. 'OK.'

Afterwards, I realised why I'd bothered to discuss it with Craig at all. I wanted to be able to blame him if it turned out to be the wrong decision.

\* \* \*

I told Daisy, on the way home, that I'd agreed to her having a sleepover with Freya, and it was lovely to see her excitement.

'It means you won't see me from when I drop you at school on Friday morning until I pick you up on Saturday,' I warned her.

'I know, but it's all right, because I'll be with Daddy, and Freya, and Kirsty,' she said. 'And Freya said we can play on her new Nintendo because she's getting it this week.'

'Wow, that'll be good, then,' I agreed, smiling.

But when Friday arrived, I went home from work feeling completely lost. I ate a lazy microwave dinner in front of the TV and then spent the rest of the evening desperately trying – and failing yet again – to get myself on top of my finances, before going to bed early and crying myself to sleep. How was I ever going to get myself out of trouble? The only possibility I could think of would be to take on some extra work, and how could I do that? I was already working full time from Monday to Friday. And Saturdays were out of the question, obviously. Or... were they?

## 9

I was expecting Daisy to be tired – shattered – when I arrived at Whitegate House to pick her up after her sleepover, but in fact she was still on a high, bouncing down the stairs and into my arms, grinning from ear to ear.

'Did you have a lovely time?' I asked, pulling her close for a hug.

'Yes!' she squealed. 'We played on Freya's Nintendo all the time, and I'm getting better at the games, and guess what, we had a pizza for tea but not from the shop, Kirsty made them herself and cooked them in a pizza oven! And we could choose what we had on them, and I had ham and pineapple and I didn't even know I liked pineapple but I did, it was yummy, and then we had ice cream, it was mint choc chip, my favourite, and then—'

'Hey, all right, slow down!' I said. Kirsty and I were both laughing, and Freya was jumping up and down behind her, trying to get her own comments in about the pizzas and the ice cream. 'It sounds like you had a brilliant time, girls. Daisy, you'd better thank Kirsty and Daddy very, very much for letting you have such a nice evening. Thank you, Kirsty,' I added. 'I hope you're not too exhausted.'

'No, they were fine – they kept each other amused the whole time,' she said, smiling as Daisy rushed off to find Craig and say goodbye to him, with Freya running behind her. When they came back, they had their arms around each other and were looking at each other mournfully.

'I don't want Daisy to go home,' Freya said.

'Can Freya come back and stay with me at our house, Mummy?' Daisy asked. She seemed to have, overnight, become as loud and excitable as Freya – it must have been rubbing off on her. How could Mr Frost possibly think she had a problem talking? If he saw her now, he'd have laughed at his own suggestion.

'Perhaps another time,' I said, picturing the state of my house – the piles of laundry and ironing, the hoover abandoned in the middle of the hallway because I'd planned to do some housework the previous evening while Daisy was out, but instead had spent the whole time trying to do something about my financial situation. 'Anyway, you'll see her after school on Monday and you're both going to Center Parcs next weekend, aren't you?'

'Yay!' both girls shouted together. 'We can't wait!'

I was just about to say how pleased I was that they were both so excited about the holiday, when Amelia suddenly appeared from the lounge, wearing her usual sullen expression, scowling at me as well as the two younger girls. I made a point of saying hello to her and asking how she was, but got an angry glare in response.

'Amelia, please don't be so rude to Tasha,' Kirsty reprimanded her, but Amelia turned to her in fury.

'I'm not rude, you're rude!' she shouted at her mother, red

with anger – or was she red from the humiliation of being told off in front of me? 'I know you hate me, Mum. I wish my dad was still here; he was the only one who cared about me. He was lovely, and kind, and gentle, and he shouldn't have died!'

Daisy was looking at me with wide eyes, as Amelia stomped off upstairs.

'I'm so sorry about that,' Kirsty said quietly. 'As you can see, she has these tantrums sometimes—'

'She must miss her father terribly,' was all I could manage to say. I did, obviously, feel sorry for her, having heard this stream of total angst, but could that really excuse the way she was talking to her mother? It was beginning to sound to me as if Amelia was the child who needed therapy, rather than Daisy.

On the way home, I asked Daisy how Amelia had been with her and Freya.

She shrugged. 'She was horrible to us but we don't care.'

'How was she horrible? What did she do?'

'She kept coming in to Freya's room to spy on us playing on the Nintendo, and laughed at us because she said we were rubbish at the game. But we don't care, Mummy, because she was just being horrible and Freya says she was jealous because she didn't have a friend round. *And* Amelia said she doesn't want me to go to Center Parcs with them because I'm a baby. I'm not a baby, am I, Mummy, because I can swim now, almost as much as Freya, and I'm going to swim right across the pool at Center Parcs.'

'Good for you. Of course you're not a baby.'

'Anyway, me and Freya don't care. Freya's my best friend forever. And she said I'm her best friend forever too.'

'Well, I'm really pleased that you get on so well together.'

Although I was glad Daisy seemed not to be letting Amelia intimidate her too much any more, I still felt irritated at the thought of the older girl making spiteful comments. And I wondered if Daisy still felt too shy to talk to her. Well, I couldn't blame her for that. Amelia was obviously unhappy and perhaps felt left out, with the two younger ones spending so much time together and becoming such good friends. And it was more obvious to me now than ever, how much she missed her father. But it didn't excuse her nastiness. I just hoped that on the holiday, she'd spend all her time with her own friend and leave the little ones in peace.

* * *

That Monday at work, before the first client even arrived, Camel came into the salon looking very self-important.

'Listen, ladies. You have a new stylist joining you all today,' she announced. By *all*, she could only have meant me and Paige, as it was one of Jackie's days off. 'His name is—' The bell over the door pinged and she coloured slightly as she went on, 'Ah, hello, Lee. This is our new stylist, ladies – Lee Fellows. He'll be working here on Mondays, Wednesdays and Fridays until the end of next month, and from then on, after Jackie retires, he'll be full time.'

I'd felt my eyes widen in surprise as soon as Lee had walked in; he was probably in his mid-thirties, tall, muscular and extremely good-looking, with a smile to melt... well, the heart of anyone whose heart hadn't already been smashed to smithereens. I noticed Paige simpering a little as she said hello to him, and even Camel managed what passed for a smile. But what had actually made my jaw drop was the last part of Camel's little speech: *at the end of next month, after Jackie retires.*

'Jackie's retiring?' I gasped, still staring at Lee, who was trying to smile at me and looking a little uncomfortable now.

'Yes, as you know perfectly well, Tasha.' She made no attempt to hide the irritation in her voice. 'She always planned to retire before the end of this year; she's already stayed longer than she intended.'

'I know. But it's only...'

I stuttered to a stop. It was nearly the end of October. By the time Lee had worked here until the end of next month, we'd be getting close to December. Of course Jackie was going to retire. She'd been saying so for ages; I just hadn't really wanted to believe it.

'Right,' I said faintly. I felt a little bit sick. I was going to miss Jackie so much. She was the only person I could really talk to, these days, apart from...

And I just stopped myself in time; was I really going to say *apart from Kirsty*?

'Hello, Lee,' I said, belatedly pulling myself together and making an effort. 'Nice to meet you. I'm Tasha.'

'Hi, Tasha,' he said. His voice was almost as sexy as his appearance, not that I noticed, in the slightest. He turned, immediately, of course, to Paige, who was less than half my age, probably almost half my dress size, and was simpering at him from her position behind the sinks, announcing her name and classing herself as *a trainee at the moment*, as if it was merely a temporary inconvenience that she wasn't fully qualified yet.

I waited for a break between clients to go into the back office to talk to Camel.

'Camilla, I was going to ask you something today,' I said, trying to sound polite and pleasant.

'What?' she retorted – neither pleasantly nor politely. 'You can't take any time off. We need a full complement between now and Christmas. That's why I've started Lee.'

'I know. It's not that. It's just, I wondered, if I can get the childcare sorted, whether I can work on Saturdays sometimes.'

She looked up sharply. 'I thought you couldn't – not ever, you said. That's why Jackie's had to do Saturdays, that's why I've started Lee early, as much as anything else to help out on Saturdays because it's our busiest day, our busiest time of year.'

'I didn't know you were taking someone else on. I thought you might be glad to have me here on a Saturday sometimes.'

'I might have been. But there's no need now.' She glanced out through the salon to the outside door. 'I think your next client's here.'

'Would you at least consider it?' I asked hurriedly. I'd been so sure she'd say yes, I'd planned to talk to Kirsty about it this evening.

She sighed. 'I might have done, after Jackie retires, if you wanted to work *every* Saturday. But I've decided to take on a Saturday girl to work with Lee, instead. I can't afford to pay for an extra stylist, just on the odd occasion that you might find yourself available. I need someone reliable. It's not enough just having one stylist here, plus a trainee, on our busiest day. I'm having to turn clients away, and it'd be no help at all to have you turn up just when you feel like it. I can't plan appointments that way.'

'Oh, but surely—' I started to squawk, but Camel was staring at me pointedly, gesturing to the window in her office which overlooked the salon. I'd wanted to argue the point, to try to make her see that I'd be more help to her than a Saturday girl who didn't know our clients or have any loyalty, but it obviously wasn't the right time. Perhaps I could try to work on her again later, if I got the chance, but it sounded as if she'd already made up her mind to advertise for a Saturday girl.

I turned to go out to greet Mrs Atkins, my wet-cut-and-blow-dry lady, who was already at the sink waiting for Paige to get the water to the right temperature for her wash. I pasted on a smile and throughout the morning managed to keep up the expected level of chat, responding as well as I could to Lee's new-boy polite conversation. During my lunch break, I went outside where I couldn't be overheard, and called Jackie.

'Camel did tell me she was going to take someone new on,' she admitted, 'but I didn't realise it would be this soon, or I'd have mentioned it to you. But to be honest, I had no idea you were thinking of working Saturdays. What would you do about Daisy? Have Kirsty and Craig said they'd have her?'

'I haven't asked yet, but I was hoping they might. I didn't want to ask them to have her *every* Saturday,' I added, suddenly consumed by sadness at the thought of how much I'd have missed spending every Saturday with my little girl, and how upset she might have been about it. 'Well, it isn't going to happen now, anyway.'

'Perhaps it's for the best,' Jackie said gently. 'Although I'd be happy to talk to Camel about it, if you wanted me to? Try to get her to change her mind?'

'Thanks, but it'd be a waste of time. I think she's made up her mind to hire a Saturday girl.'

I couldn't help feeling deflated. My new plan for trying to get myself out of my difficulties had failed at the first hurdle, before I'd even consulted Craig or Kirsty about it. And the method I'd been trying up till now had only got me further into trouble. If I asked Craig for more money, he'd want to know why I was struggling so badly – and I couldn't tell him. I couldn't tell anyone what I'd been doing. I was too ashamed.

## 10

Daisy was still looking unhappy each time I dropped her off at school, and continuing to tell me nobody liked her, nobody played with her, and nobody talked to her.

'I sit on a bench on my own in the playground every day,' she said mournfully. 'Nobody wants to talk to me.'

I didn't want to ask her directly whether she actually tried speaking to them. I told myself I wouldn't because Mr Frost had advised me not to. But hadn't I discounted Mr Frost's advice anyway? Was I, really, more worried that Daisy might admit she didn't speak – and I'd have to start treating his worries seriously?

He finally called me again the following day, asking whether I'd taken his advice to discuss Daisy with our doctor.

'Not yet,' I prevaricated. 'I'm hoping things will improve, to be honest. Her father reminded me that she was completely silent at first when she visited his new home and new family. But because they were so nice to her' – I was mentally excluding Amelia here, of course – 'she quickly found her voice.'

I knew what I was implying: that if only the other children in the class would be nice to Daisy, she'd start talking to them, too. I believed it, anyway; it was what I was holding on to, what was keeping me from panicking about the situation.

'That's interesting,' he said. 'It suggests that Daisy has a tendency to this... mutism, if she's unsure or upset, doesn't it? Not just at school.'

*Mutism*? I took exception to the word. What was he implying, here? That my child was dumb? No, she was just shy! An image of my *shy* little girl, chasing around the house with Freya and the dog, squealing and laughing, came into my head and I quickly dismissed it. That was different.

'She'll be OK. She's only unsure and upset, at school,' I said pointedly.

He was silent for a moment. Then he went on. 'Well, look, I've got one idea that might help Daisy. There's another new girl starting in my class after half term; her mother tells me she's shy too. I'll sit her next to Daisy and encourage Daisy to show her around and help her to settle in. As she won't know anyone else, they might strike up a friendship, and that might encourage Daisy to talk.'

'Thank you. Yes, that might be a good plan,' I agreed.

I kept it to myself; I wanted Daisy to have a surprise, something that might make her feel better when she returned to school after her Center Parcs holiday. The fact that she was looking forward to this so much – more than I'd dared to hope – was helping to keep the atmosphere less tense during that final week at school.

'It's going to be *amazing*,' she kept saying, her voice rising to a Freya-type shriek as she repeated over and over the various exciting things they were going to be doing, and every morning she announced how many days were left until Saturday.

\* \* \*

'I've been thinking,' Jackie said when we both arrived at work the next morning. 'Instead of trying to get Camel to give you extra work, how about taking on a few home-hairdressing clients? You could do Saturdays, if Kirsty would have Daisy for a few hours – or if you think Daisy might be OK staying at home with you while you worked? Or you could even do a client or two in the evening, after she's in bed, couldn't you? If your lighting's good enough at home?'

I stared at her, totally nonplussed for a moment.

'That's never occurred to me,' I admitted. 'But how would I go about it? I mean, I'd have to buy everything myself.'

'Well, yes, but surely only a hair-cutting kit and a hairdryer? And after the initial outlay, that'd be it. All profit.'

'What about all the shampoos and bleaching agents and dyes?'

'OK, they'd come out of your profits too. You'd have to work out your prices to take account of that. And there might be some rules, as you'd be running a business from home. You'd be self-employed, as well as being an employee here.'

'I don't know how that works,' I admitted, filled with panic just at the thought of it.

'Well, no. You'd have to look into it. Google it!' she added cheerfully. 'Anyway, it's just an idea.'

'Yes, you're right, thanks, it's something to think about. Or I could do mobile hairdressing. Lots of older clients might like someone going to their own homes. But I suppose that's self-employed too, and I'd have to sort out my own tax and stuff.'

The thought of having to be responsible for things like this, when I was already struggling to get control of my finances, was enough to put me off completely. As it happened, my first client turned up just then, and we didn't really get the chance to discuss it any further, but the following day I was working with Lee again, and mentioned it to him, thinking he might know more about it.

'I did mobile work for a while,' he said breezily. 'And yes, you'd be partly self-employed.'

'Right,' I said. Well, that was that, then. I couldn't cope with that – I knew I couldn't trust myself to pay my own tax – put money aside for it, or find the money to pay it when it was due. I was struggling now, just finding the money to survive every month.

'It really isn't worth the stress, just for an occasional Saturday.'

'Might be worth looking into it, though,' he said. 'In case you ever change your mind. Mobile hairdressing sounds like a good idea. It might work out better for you to do that full time, while you've got a little kid to consider, rather than working here. You could sort out your own hours.'

I shrugged and turned away to prepare for my first client. To be honest, I needed extra work to top up my income from the salon, not to replace it. I needed more money, not less. I felt the familiar panic rising up inside me as I thought about the bills waiting to be paid, the two credit cards already maxed out, the little economies I'd been trying to make, to try to tide me over until...

Until what? My good fairy waved her magic wand and made everything all right? It wasn't going to happen. I was the one who'd got myself and my daughter into this dire situation, and I was the one who'd have to get us out of it.

* * *

On the Friday evening, Daisy was quiet in the car going home from Whitegate House, and when I asked her if everything was all right, she asked in a little voice whether I'd miss her while she was away.

'Of course I will,' I assured her, feeling a pang in my heart just at the thought of the seven long, lonely evenings ahead of me, wondering what my baby would be doing, whether she'd be sad without me – and whether Amelia was bothering her or upsetting her. 'I'll miss you lots and lots, but I'll know you'll be having a lovely time. And I'll be looking forward to you coming home again.'

'I wish you were coming too, Mummy.'

'So do I, sweetie, but I can't,' I said firmly. 'It's Daddy's special time with you; he'll be looking forward to spending a whole week with you.'

'He spends more time with Freya and Amelia than he does with me,' she said sadly – and then, before I'd had time to come up with a response to this, she went on, 'Did you know, Max has to go on a holiday too? He's not coming with us, he's going to a place called Kennels, and Kirsty says it's like a Center Parcs for dogs.'

'Wow, he's a lucky little dog, then, isn't he?' I said, laughing.

It felt odd later – almost painful – helping her to pack her little suitcase, imagining her unpacking it again when they arrived at the resort, wondering if she'd feel lost and over-whelmed, hoping Craig was going to step up to reassure her and keep her safe and happy all week. A whole week without me.

'You will look after her, won't you?' I asked him when I took her back to Whitegate House in the morning and watched her run straight in to squeal with Freya. Kirsty had apparently gone to take Max to the kennels. 'She's never been away from me before.'

'I know,' he said, looking puzzled by my concern. 'But she'll be with me. I'm still her father,' he added a little tersely.

'I know. But you've got others to look after now, too.'

'She'll be fine, Tash,' he said with exaggerated patience. 'We'll all be looking after her.'

'Well, just make sure one of you is always watching her in the swimming pool. She doesn't swim as well as the other girls, remember. And don't let her wander off with Freya on their own – they're so excitable, and they're both still so little. And...' I hesitated. 'Well, I'm sorry, but I'm going to say it: I presume you won't let Amelia look after her.'

'What? Of course not. Amelia and Grace will want to go off on their own; the last thing they'll want to do is hang around with the younger ones. What's your problem with Amelia, Tasha? I know she can be sulky, but honestly, she's still just a kid. Even Daisy's learnt to ignore her moods.'

'I don't care about her moods, unless they impact on Daisy, but the fact is, they do, Craig. Kirsty admits it. She's been downright nasty to Daisy at times, and did you hear about her pushing Daisy into the road? What if Kirsty hadn't grabbed her so quickly? What if a car had been coming?'

He sighed. 'Amelia said it was an accident. They were fighting over who held the dog's lead. It won't happen again. Anyway, I take Max with me when I meet Daisy from school, so she has a turn with him on her own.'

'I know, and that's nice. It's just, look, she's only six, we need to protect her around older kids. She can't be expected to stand up to a twelve-year-old. I don't want her being bullied.'

'Nor do I.' He gave me an exasperated look. 'But I also don't want her to be turned into a little princess, being protected against every normal little knock she might experience, every little taunt or tease she gets. It's all part of family life.'

I turned away from him, my face flaring hot with annoyance, stifling the urge to swear at him.

*All part of family life.* He couldn't have chosen a more hurtful phrase to fling at me. Daisy was part of his family now, he was saying: part of his new little empire at Whitegate House – she wasn't just mine, or even his and mine any more. What was worse, I was beginning to feel like that was even how Daisy was seeing herself. I was just boring old Mummy who cuddled her when she was upset, tucked her into bed, and took her to the school she hated, instead of the wonderful school her best friend and new *sister* Freya went to. Daisy was coping with the aggression and menace from Amelia, Craig was implying, because she was just a moody big sister to her. She put up with it, so why couldn't I?

Well, perhaps I couldn't because I was the one person here who wasn't part of this supposedly idyllic family circle. I was the one looking at them all from the outside, without wearing the rosy-coloured spectacles of smug superiority. To say nothing of being the only one who was struggling to make ends meet in a tiny run-down house on the other side of town, when it wasn't even me who'd crashed and burned our previously happy relationship. In fact, it was me who'd bent over backwards to accommodate this happy bloody family set-up, and I was beginning to wonder why I'd ever agreed to it. Quite apart from the fact that I was Daisy's mother – the one who'd given birth to her, and who had struggled with night feeds, horrible nappies, colic and sickness, colds and coughs, and measles when she was still a baby, too young to have been vaccinated against it and I was terrified she'd die.

All of this while he trotted off every day to his office, where unbeknown to me, he was eyeing up his boss and planning how to seduce her and get himself installed in her mansion as her toy boy.

Well, I wasn't going to put up with it, this condescending way of talking to me, the mother of his child. I wasn't going to be patted on the head and told to be quiet and be a good girl. Whitegate House was *not* going to swallow up my daughter and take her away from me, and Miss Amelia was not going to get away with hurting her, not if I had anything to do with it.

'Are you all right, Tasha?' said a voice behind me, making me jump and lose my train of thought for a moment. It was Kirsty, back from the kennels.

'Oh, yes, I'm fine, thanks,' I said automatically, instantly forgetting all my fighting talk, conditioned from birth, like us all, to be endlessly, boringly, polite. I swallowed, looked back at her, and shook my head. 'Actually, no, I'm not, really. I'm feeling a bit—'

Embarrassingly, tears came to my eyes, and I turned away, trying to hide them.

'Oh, come here, love,' she said, putting an arm around me. 'I know you're going to miss Daisy. I've felt just the same whenever Amelia or Freya has gone away on a school holiday. Come on, why don't we get Daisy downstairs so you can give her another quick cuddle before we go – then you can wait and wave her goodbye as we drive off. She's going to be fine, honestly; she'll have a lovely time and we'll look after her just like you would – won't we, Craig?'

'Of course,' he said obediently, smiling at her meekly. The creep. Why did I ever think I still loved him?

'Daisy!' Kirsty hollered. 'Come down and see your mummy for the last five minutes before we go.'

Footsteps thundered down the stairs as Daisy and Freya jostled each other, squealing and laughing, to the bottom.

'I thought you'd gone already, Mummy,' Daisy said, looking surprised.

*But we haven't said goodbye,* I wanted to scream. Wouldn't she even have realised? Wouldn't she even have cared? She ran into my arms for a cuddle and I stroked her silky blonde hair, kissed her on both cheeks and told her, forcing a happy-mummy smile, to have a lovely time and be a good girl for her daddy and Kirsty.

'OK, I will! Bye, Mummy!' she squealed, running out of my arms and chasing after Freya again without a backward look.

I should have been reassured – grateful – that she was so happy, that she wasn't going to be upset without me. I was. But just as Daisy had broken away from me, Amelia had walked past with her usual downturned mouth and sullen face, and for a moment I'd been sure she was about to elbow Daisy out of the way. She'd glanced up, seen me standing there, gone a bit red and asked in an almost aggressive tone, 'What's the matter? What've I done now?' before stepping to the side to let the two younger girls past, giving me a smirk as she walked off.

'Be careful, girls,' Kirsty called after them lightly. 'You'd better calm down a bit or someone's going to get hurt.'

Yes, I thought – and I knew which of them it would be.

I turned down Kirsty's offer to wait to wave them off. She smiled and agreed, assuming I thought it would make me upset again. But mostly, it was because if I stayed there any longer, I'd be tempted to grab hold of Daisy and carry her back to my car and take her safely home with me, away from that spiteful, moody girl. And if I was honest, it was also because I couldn't bear to see them glide off in their twin Mercedes with their personalised number plates – the perfect blended family,

off on another holiday – happy, smiling, pleased to bits with
themselves and their perfect lifestyle. While I set off home in
my beaten-up old Corsa, with its dodgy clutch and its exhaust
coughing behind me up the road – home to my washing, my
little girl's empty bed, my debts and my haul of massive regrets.
Not *all* of it was my fault.

## 11

I felt lost. It was still just the first day, and already I was wishing the hours away. Craig had promised he'd send me a text to say they'd arrived safely; I hadn't heard anything yet but I guessed they were probably still on the road. It was a Saturday, the traffic would be busy, and he'd have stopped halfway to give the kids a break and a drink. I was glad Amelia and her friend were in a separate car; I wouldn't have liked the idea of Daisy perhaps having to share a back seat with Amelia. That girl still gave me the creeps; she glowered at me every time she saw me, as if it was *my* fault her mother had decided to steal Craig from me. I still didn't trust her around Daisy, however much Daisy told me she was managing to ignore her, and however much Kirsty and Craig both said she was just at a difficult age, missing her father, or going through a stroppy-teenager phase.

Once the washing was up to date, the housework was done, and I'd finally had the message from Craig to say they'd arrived safely and that he'd share pictures of everything Daisy got up to during the week, I felt even more at a loss, so I decided to go into town for some shopping. With only me at home, and just about enough food in the fridge to last me the week, I didn't really need much, but when you're bored, it's easy to mooch around the shelves, distracting yourself by looking at items you don't really need. I'd put some ridiculously unnecessary items in my basket before I could stop myself, and instead of abandoning them or putting them back on the shelves, I shrugged to myself and paid for everything on the credit card before suddenly remembering that I was broke, and that I'd already reached the limit of my credit. The payment went through, and I assumed my minimum payment must have just been automatically made... but when, after leaving the shop, I checked my account, I found the card company had increased my credit limit.

Instead of thinking myself lucky that I'd got away with buying a few luxuries for once and being determined not to risk it again, I celebrated by having tea and cake in one of my favourite cafés, and followed up with buying a dress I'd had my eye on in Next. On the way home, I castigated myself for my stupid recklessness. What was the matter with me? I was never normally careless with my spending. My credit card was now maxed out again already, and my monthly payment would be higher. I obviously should have kept that extra credit for anything urgent that might crop up. Now I was going to have to return the dress, and economise ruthlessly for the rest of the week. And I had bills I still hadn't paid. There was only one thing for it: I'd have to have one last attempt to improve my situation, the only way I knew – the way that had already done nothing but get me into more and more trouble and despair.

\* \* \*

'What's up, Tash?' Jackie asked me the next time we were at work together. It was Tuesday, and during the previous couple of days I'd tried to keep busy but felt like I was sinking further and further into despondency. 'Are you missing Daisy?'

'Of course,' I said, shrugging.

'Have you heard from her, or from Craig, at least?'

'Yes. He's sent me some photos. Look.' I opened my phone and showed her the latest picture, of Daisy and Freya on little bikes, their grins almost as big as their helmets.

'Aw, she looks really happy. Don't worry, I bet she's having a great time.' She paused and looked at my face. 'But you're not happy, are you? You must feel completely lost without her.'

'Yes.' I sighed. 'I've been spending some time, while Daisy's away, looking into how to set myself up to do some mobile hairdressing.'

'Oh, I thought you'd decided against it?'

'I had. Mostly because Lee put me off.' I pulled a face. I still wasn't 100 per cent sure about Lee. He seemed friendly enough – but sometimes I felt like his questions went beyond friendliness and verged on nosiness. Since discussing the mobile hairdressing idea with him, he'd brought it up again several times, asking whether I'd made any decisions yet, asking why I was considering it – all questions that I found frankly too intrusive, considering the short time we'd known each other.

'Anyway, I think I will definitely have to decide against it,' I went on. 'I can't afford it, Jack – paying for the equipment and the insurance and everything.'

'Wouldn't Craig help you out with that, if you asked him? Now he's got himself set up so nicely with his rich woman?'

I shook my head fiercely. 'No. I'm not asking him for anything other than what he pays me for Daisy.'

'Well, I admire you for that, up to a point. But don't let

pride get in the way of achieving your ambitions, will you? He should be helping you.'

I just shook my head again. There was no way I was going to go crawling to Craig, asking for money. No way was he going to find out what a state I'd got myself into. It was bad enough that Kirsty was paying for Daisy's swimming lessons, bad enough that I hadn't contributed a penny towards this holiday they'd taken her on – or even offered to. Perhaps it was stupid pride, but I felt like it was one thing them spending their money on Daisy, and totally something else to ask them to help *me*.

'No,' I said again. 'Besides, I really don't think it's worth me going to all that trouble, just to possibly get an occasional client on an occasional Saturday when Kirsty and Craig might, or might not, be able to have Daisy.'

'I suppose not.' She looked at me, her head on one side. 'But if you really want – or need – to earn more money, why not ask if they can have Daisy every Saturday, and get in quickly to ask Camel if you can work here instead of her getting a Saturday girl, before she puts the advert out?'

'They'd never agree to that.' Then I hesitated. Would they? But even if they did, would I *want* to leave Daisy with them every weekend?

I struggled with my own indecision for the rest of that week, along with my struggle to survive each day without my daughter. My financial situation was so dire now that I really did need to do something drastic. But sending Daisy to White-gate House every single Saturday still seemed a stretch too far.

* * *

I was on edge all afternoon on the day Daisy was due to arrive home, and had my shoes on and the car key in my hand ready to rush out and collect her as soon as I received the text to say they were nearly back. I drove there in a state of such excitement that I almost ran into the back of Craig's Mercedes on their driveway.

'How has she been?' I gasped when Kirsty opened the door.

She laughed. 'Absolutely fine, Tasha. We'd have told you if she wasn't. They've had a brilliant time together – she didn't want to come home.' She stopped, obviously embarrassed by her own tactlessness. 'Apart from wanting to see you, of course,' she added quickly.

'Where is she? She must be tired – and so must you be, having four kids for the whole week. I'll take her straight home. I can't thank you enough—'

'Not at all. Craig and I have had a great time; we hardly saw Amelia and Grace, of course, and the two younger ones were as good as gold, they loved it all. Honestly, Tasha, Daisy's been amazing, she had a go at everything and her swimming's come on in leaps and bounds.'

'Oh, that's great. I'm so glad it all went well. I'll take her off your hands now, then,' I said, trying to make a joke of it but actually just desperate to put my arms around my little girl and have her safely back at home with me.

'She's upstairs with Freya, of course. I'll give her a shout, but the two of them seem to go deaf when it comes to parting company from each other. We call them the terrible twins – anyone would think they were actual sisters. Look, why don't you come in and have a cup of tea with us while we wait for them to come down?'

'Thank you, but if it's all the same to you, I'd rather take her home now,' I said firmly. I was feeling more than a little bit miffed by the implication that Daisy might not want to come home, to say nothing of the talk about sisters. She couldn't have undermined my confidence in my relationship with my daughter much more if she'd tried.

But then I remembered: during the last couple of days, I'd finally decided to talk to her about the idea of working Saturdays. In my excitement about seeing Daisy again I'd almost forgotten, but in fact it was pretty urgent that I brought up the subject as quickly as possible, before Camel took somebody else on. 'Um, but before you call her down, I do have something I need to talk to you both about. Would you prefer I call you – tomorrow, maybe? – rather than bother you now, when you've just arrived home?'

'No, it's fine. Craig's gone to take Grace home with Amelia, but whatever it is, I'm sure we girls can sort it out between us,' she said brightly. 'Come and sit down in the kitchen for a moment, at least, won't you, while we talk? I'm sure Daisy and Freya will be pleased to have another ten minutes together.'

We sat down at the huge oak table in her kitchen, and I spilt it all out – well, not about my financial situation, of course, but just the fact that I really needed to work Saturdays.

'I know it's a big ask,' I said, 'and you'll want to talk it over with Craig, and you'll probably say no because after all, you probably have things to do on Saturdays and it's a huge imposition when you already have Daisy every day after school—'

'Not at all,' she said firmly without a moment's hesitation. 'Honestly, Tasha, Daisy's part of our family now, and one more child makes no difference whatsoever. In fact, the only difference she'll make is that Freya will be much happier on Saturdays and we won't have to be continually finding her things to do. So absolutely, I don't have to ask Craig – he leaves all these things to me – and there's no decision to be made. We'd love to have Daisy here every Saturday. As soon as you're ready to start.'

I should have been really grateful. Correction: I was really grateful, of course. But all I could think about, when I'd finally prised a reluctant Daisy away from her best friend – or sister, as we now seemed to be calling her – and drove her home, happy but almost too tired to talk to me much about her 'best holiday ever', was Kirsty's first sentence in her response: *Daisy's part of our family now.* She wasn't. And I didn't want her to be!

## 12

Unfortunately, Daisy wasn't as happy to be home as I was to have her back. I was disappointed, of course, but I had to plaster on a smile and pretend to be sympathetic while she complained about being separated from her 'sister'.

'You'll see each other again tomorrow, after school,' I said, forcing a smile while my heart was breaking. Hadn't Daisy missed me at all? Wasn't she at least pleased to see me?

'That's ages away,' she said mournfully. 'I wish I could go to Freya's school. So does Freya. At least then we'd see each other at dinner time. Please, Mummy, please can I go to—'

'No, I'm sorry, you can't,' I said firmly. 'But how would you like to go and play with Freya every Saturday, soon?'

'Really?' Her eyes lit up. 'Every Saturday? Yay!'

So that was settled, then. So much for my fear that she'd be unhappy about it. When I tried to talk to her about what she'd enjoyed most about the holiday, all she could come up with was 'being with Freya all the time'.

It wasn't until bedtime that she finally began to open up and tell me more. Apparently she'd liked all the activities – as

Kirsty had said, nothing had worried her; she'd tried every-thing and had been almost as good as Freya at most things, even jumping into the swimming pool and going on the zip wire.

'Was there anything you didn't like?' I asked.

She thought about this for a moment, her head on one side, before finally allowing that she hadn't much liked it when Amelia had pushed her into the pool.

'She did what?' I sat up straight on her bed, where she was snuggled down waiting for her story.

'She pushed me, and I fell in the water. It was the deep end, too, because me and Freya were just walking down the side of the pool. It was all right, though, Mummy, because Kirsty and Daddy were in the water and Daddy saw me fall in and swam over to get me, and I was already coming back up to the top, and he grabbed me and brought me over to the edge.'

'You must have been really frightened. What did Daddy say? Did he know Amelia pushed you?'

I was almost on the point of grabbing my phone and calling him, right that minute, to demand he or Kirsty did something about this, and I mean something serious, like banning that girl from being anywhere near my daughter, ever again.

But Daisy just shrugged. 'I did feel a bit scared when she pushed me and I felt myself going over the edge. But it was OK. Daddy held onto me and helped me get out of the water. He didn't know she pushed me, Mummy, he thought I just fell in. So I didn't say anything because I didn't want to be a tell-tale. I just stayed away from her for the rest of the week.'

'No, listen, Daisy,' I said, pulling her into my arms. 'It's not being a tell-tale when it's something as serious as this. Daddy and Kirsty need to know, because Amelia's much bigger than you, and if you're absolutely sure she pushed you – that it wasn't an accident—'

'It wasn't, Mummy, I am sure, because she was walking behind me and she walked faster. Then I felt her push me.'

'Was there a lifeguard at the pool?' I asked. My voice was shaking. I had to take a couple of breaths to try to control it.

'Yes, but I don't think he saw her push me, he was watching some other people in the pool. But he saw me fall in, and saw Daddy getting me out of the water, and he asked if I was OK and I said yes.'

'Oh, baby, you really should have told Daddy. Where was Amelia when you came out of the water?'

'She'd walked off with Grace by then. She didn't look back to see if I was all right.'

That said it all, really, didn't it? My fury was rising up to choke me by now.

As soon as Daisy was asleep, I called Craig, and repeated everything Daisy had told me.

'Well, that wasn't what she told me at the time,' he objected. 'Are you sure she's not just saying this now to get Amelia into trouble?'

So now he believed his girlfriend's daughter rather than his own.

'I'm quite sure,' I insisted. 'In fact, she says the reason she didn't say anything about being pushed was that she *didn't* want to get Amelia into trouble. Didn't want to tell tales, as she put it.'

'But she seemed OK, she wasn't even crying or anything when I helped her out of the water. She told me it was an accident. And Amelia wasn't anywhere near her.'

'No, because she'd walked off – quickly, I imagine – and didn't look back. Craig, I'm not going to argue about this. It happened, I believe Daisy completely. Amelia pushed her, she knew what she was doing. There's something wrong with that girl.'

'Oh, come on! Even if Daisy did feel Amelia push her, I bet it was just a bit of playful stuff between them—'

'Playful? Daisy doesn't *play* with Amelia, she avoids her like the plague! You're in denial about this, obviously. I'm going to have to talk to Kirsty again, if you won't. She knows Amelia's been playing up recently – she admits it. Is she there? Put her on the phone.'

'No, all right.' I heard him sigh. 'Look, I'll have a word with Kirsty, and perhaps we'll both talk to Amelia. OK? But I still think Daisy's probably just being over-sensitive.'

I hung up, furious. *Over-sensitive?* I wondered how sensitive he'd feel himself if someone came up behind him and pushed him in at the deep end. This was our six-year-old we were talking about. What if he hadn't got to her in time? What if the lifeguard hadn't seen? It didn't bear thinking about: OK, she was having swimming lessons now, but it was far too early for her to be in the deep end of the pool.

But the worst thing about it all was that I couldn't even threaten to keep her away from Whitegate House. I couldn't do the one thing for my daughter that would guarantee her safety, because without Kirsty, without Whitegate House, I wouldn't be able to work full time, let alone start working Saturdays. And I'd never be able to get myself out of the mess I was in.

\* \* \*

Getting my Saturday work guaranteed was my priority now. I didn't waste any time telling Camel that I was now going to be available.

'I've got childcare sorted,' I assured her. 'And I don't think you've advertised yet for a new girl, have you?'

'I've just written out the advert,' she said.

'Well, now you won't have to bother with it. I'm going to be available. My daughter's father and his partner are definitely going to look after her every Saturday. And you know I'm good and reliable, whereas if you take on a new girl, she might not be.'

'She might also come cheaper than you, though,' Camel said drily. But I could see she was wavering. 'Leave it with me. I'll think about it.'

*Don't do me any favours,* I thought, seething to myself as I started work on my next client's grey roots. Lee was looking at me sympathetically and I wondered if he'd overheard. But he didn't say anything until we both had a few free moments between clients, just before my lunch break.

'It'll be good if you get to work Saturdays with me,' he said. 'I've had experience before of working with Saturday girls. They're not always committed to the job, not as reliable as someone whose whole career is based here.'

'I worked as a Saturday girl myself, actually,' I said, feeling a bit offended. 'When my daughter was a baby.'

'Sorry. I didn't mean—' He coloured slightly. 'Well, what I meant was—'

But I'd turned away, going to look in the appointments book to see who I had booked in during the afternoon, before heading out of the salon to the square opposite where I often liked to eat my sandwich in the sunshine. *Typical of a man,* I thought to myself disparagingly. *Always ready to criticise those women who might not be as fully committed to a job as they are, without stopping to consider the reason why. And it's usually child-care – that thing they don't often want to know about.*

But at least I had good news the following day, when Camel told me she'd decided in my favour. There wasn't going to be a new Saturday girl; I would be working every week after Jackie had left. I told Kirsty and Craig as soon as I went to collect Daisy.

'We're very happy to be having her,' Craig confirmed. 'She keeps Freya quiet – well, perhaps not quiet, but happy, at least.'

'Yes, it's absolutely fine with us,' Kirsty agreed. 'Have you told Daisy yet that it's definite?'

'No. I'll tell her when we get home,' I said with a sigh. This really wasn't what I would have chosen to do at all, especially not since the latest worry about Amelia.

'I've spoken to Amelia,' Kirsty said, as if she'd read my thoughts. 'And I've warned her to stay right away from Daisy, all the time.'

'You have?' I asked, surprised.

'Yes. She always protests that she hasn't done anything to hurt her, but the fact is, Daisy's obviously nervous of her, so it's best if she just leaves her and Freya alone.'

'She still maintains it was an accident, at the pool,' Craig put in. 'She did admit there was a kind of tussle, but she says Daisy just fell in, and she walked away because she was scared she'd get the blame.'

'I've told her, she really should have, at the very least, shouted to the lifeguard, or even jumped in herself. She's done a lifesaving course, for heaven's sake,' Kirsty added.

'Well, Daisy's convinced it was deliberate.' I sighed. What else could I say? She was obviously going to stand by her daughter, even though I was sure Amelia was lying. It was all very well Kirsty defending her, but Amelia had now tried pushing Daisy into a road and a swimming pool – what was going to come next?

'I'll watch her more closely,' Kirsty promised. 'I don't blame you for being protective – my two are bigger and more boisterous than poor little Daisy, but she still seems happy to come here. She's adapted so well to all the changes in her life, bless her, hasn't she?'

I nodded slowly. I couldn't agree that Daisy had adapted well to all of the changes – she still complained every day about the new school, and I was obviously concerned about Mr Frost's theory that she had some kind of problem speaking. But it was nevertheless true she had fitted into the routine of coming to Whitegate House amazingly well, considering how wary she obviously still was of Amelia. And the problem was, of course, that I was now fully committed to continuing to let her come here. I'd just agreed to bring her here every Saturday for the whole day – I'd committed myself to it, I needed to do it, I had no other option. I had to be grateful to Kirsty, however much I resented it. And I did. I did resent it – the necessity of bringing Daisy here, to be cared for by my ex's new partner, to be pitied by her because she knew I needed the money, looked down on by her because Craig left me for her.

'I'm sorry, Tasha,' Kirsty said suddenly, putting a hand on my arm and looking into my eyes, her expression one of sadness and sympathy.

'Well, it was Amelia's fault, not yours,' I said without much grace.

'But I mean, I'm sorry for everything,' she said softly. And to my surprise, I found myself being pulled into her arms. 'If there's ever anything I can do to help you – in any way – you must always let me know. We women have to help each other, don't we? We can't rely on men.'

To say I was taken aback would be an understatement. Had there been a cooling off between her and Craig? Was she getting tired of him? Would she, perhaps, even send him back to me – and if she did, would I *take* him back? I wasn't sure any more. The love I'd been so sure I still felt for him had been steadily evaporating as I'd seen how completely useless he often seemed, looking, as I was now, from the outside of a relationship. But no, it had looked like genuine sympathy, actual caring, in Kirsty's eyes. Perhaps she was right that we needed to be on the same side, to work together to make the best of this situation. And I realised I would take her up on it, I would ask for her help if I needed it – I'd already done so, hadn't I, in asking for the Saturdays. I was pretty sure she didn't mean financial help. I couldn't come right out and ask her for money – I just couldn't, it would feel so demeaning. If I got desperate enough, if I couldn't get things back on track myself, I'd have to talk to Craig.

But I knew I'd do anything to avoid that. And it had far more to do with my pride and my embarrassment than caring about his fear of taking advantage of his girlfriend's wealth. If it did ever come to it, I'd have to insist he swallowed his pride and asked Kirsty himself for more money so that he could help me out. She would, I was sure of it, now. But I'd try anything else I could, first – however desperate.

## 13

As he'd promised, Mr Frost had changed some of the children's places in the classroom after the half-term holiday, and sat a new little girl next to Daisy. He told me this child, Isabella, who liked to be called Izzie, was also quiet and a bit shy. I waited until Daisy had been back at school for a couple of days, and when she hadn't mentioned Izzie yet, I asked her what she thought of her.

'She doesn't talk to me,' she said. 'She doesn't like me.'

'How do you know she doesn't like you,' I asked gently, 'if she doesn't speak to you? She might just be shy.'

'Some of the other children are mean to her, like they are to me. So she doesn't speak to anyone. Like I don't.'

I felt my breath catch in my throat. Daisy was admitting she didn't speak to anyone. But she was blaming the other children. Could this be all it was, that she didn't speak to the other kids because they'd been mean to her?

'So you and Izzie could be friends together, couldn't you? Then you'd both feel better,' I suggested.

'No.' Daisy shrugged. 'She doesn't like me.'

I almost suggested that we invited Izzie over to play, but I felt, instinctively, that I needed to give it time. Was it actually going to be helpful at all, though, to have two quiet, shy new girls, who were apparently unpopular with the rest of the class, sitting next to each other and expect them to become friends out of desperation? If only. Daisy was now pretty much coasting through her school days, putting up with what seemed to be a miserable time, only because she looked forward so much to going to play with Freya at the end of every day. And it didn't help that her teacher seemed convinced there was something wrong with her. I suddenly decided I needed to be more proactive here. If Mr Frost was concerned enough to have spoken to me, twice now, about Daisy being silent in class, I should be taking it seriously. I still felt pretty sure he was wrong about Daisy having a real problem, but he was right that I should stop burying my head in the sand and hoping the issue would go away. I owed it to Daisy to do everything I could, and reassure myself at the same time. I decided I'd try to talk more seriously to Daisy about it, to impress upon her that we only wanted her to be happy and that she must tell me if she had a real difficulty with talking. And I decided, too, that if I didn't get anywhere, and if there was still no improvement, I'd call the doctor's during December, to book an appointment.

* * *

I was due to start working Saturdays on the first weekend in December. Jackie had two weeks left at work and admitted she was now looking forward to her well-earned retirement. She was planning a farewell meal for all the staff on the evening of her last day so I mentioned this to Kirsty, and of course she immediately offered to have Daisy to stay overnight again with Freya.

'It'll do you good to have a night out with your friends,' she said. I had to restrain my instinctive feeling that I was being patronised, because of course, I was grateful.

'I'm going to miss you,' I said to Jackie while we were getting the salon ready to welcome our first clients of the day.

'Ah, I'll miss you too, love. But we'll make plans to see each other sometimes to have a good catch-up. I know it's hard for you to get out, but I can come to you for an evening now and then. Dave and I will be sick of the sight of each other within a month, now we're going to be together all the time.'

I laughed. I couldn't imagine that. When Craig and I had been together, I never got bored with spending time with him. We hardly ever argued, either. That was what made it even harder to accept that he wanted to be with someone else.

'Anyway, it's not like you'll be on your own,' she added, turning to indicate Paige, who was folding towels at the back of the salon, quietly and sulkily, as if the job was beneath her. 'And Lee seems a nice guy. He's really friendly, isn't he?'

'Hmm,' I said in response. 'He seems OK, but considering how new he is, I think he can be a bit too keen to give out his advice. He even suggested to Camel the other day that we should try a different brand of dye from our usual one. She didn't even take offence – she acted like she was impressed. There was something a bit creepy about it.'

'It sounds like he was just trying to be helpful,' she said.

I shrugged. 'OK, I'm probably just imagining it, being para-noid. Ignore me.'

We didn't have time to discuss it any more, anyway, and frankly I had other things to worry about. But it didn't change how I felt. Perhaps I'd just become generally less trustful of men.

\* \* \*

That Monday, when I was collecting Daisy from Whitegate House, Kirsty asked if I'd be able to do her and Craig a favour.

'Well, of course, if I can,' I said a little guardedly.

'We've been invited to a wedding reception, this coming Saturday. No kids allowed, not that we'd want to take them anyway! It's somebody from the company, and I've said we'd go. So I wondered...' She gave me a smile. 'Of course, if you're busy, we'd completely understand.'

'Of course, that's fine,' I said. 'I'd be happy to have Freya for the night.'

'And Amelia,' she said. 'I know she's nearly thirteen, but that's still too young to leave her at home on her own at night. Especially as she can be a bit... well, you know.'

I did know. And I didn't really fancy having her for the night, either – but again, I couldn't really say no.

'Sure.' I frowned, thinking about the logistics. 'Um, but I've only got two bedrooms, and Daisy's room is quite small; someone would have to sleep on the sofa—'

'Oh no, sorry, I should have said: you'll have to come here, if that's all right with you? Because of the puppy, you see? We can't leave *him* on his own yet, either. Obviously you'll bring Daisy with you. And you'd have one of the guest rooms, of course, because I suspect we might be quite late back. Would you mind terribly?'

'Oh!' I blinked in surprise. Of course, I should have realised this was what she was getting at. 'Well, no, I wouldn't mind – that'd be fine.'

It would actually be perfect, of course. I had to try to keep the grin off my face. A whole evening spent in their luxurious home, watching their huge TV, and then a whole night in one of their bedrooms, which I could only presume was as luxurious as the rest of the house. What was not to like about it?

'Then, the following Saturday we'll be having Daisy for the night for you,' she went on. 'So you'll be able to dress up and go out and have fun yourself.'

'Oh, it's only a meal with the others from work,' I said, a little dismissively. 'My friend is retiring, so I'm actually a bit sad about it. I'll miss her.'

I had no idea why I was confiding in Kirsty. Anyone would think she was my friend. But then I saw the sympathetic expression on her face and my heart suddenly lurched with the realisation that perhaps, actually, I'd begun to think of her – almost – as just that. A friend, despite the fact that I'd started off by hating her guts for stealing my man. How was that possible? What was wrong with me – where was my pride? Was I really so easily won round by the odd kind word or gesture from someone who, let's face it, could afford to be as magnanimous as she liked, who could be relaxed and carefree and give all her time and energy to cultivating a caring nature because it seemed she had everything she wanted and hardly anything else to do? Well, yes, it seemed I was. And perhaps it was because Craig couldn't care less about me any more and, frankly, there was nobody else in my life who did care, apart from Jackie, and soon I'd hardly ever see her any more. If I was going to have someone on my side, it might as well be a millionaire.

'Would you like a cup of tea while you wait for Daisy?' she asked. 'Craig's busy, and Amelia went to Grace's house straight from school. Daisy and Freya are, as usual, busy with their own secret games upstairs – they won't surface until I tell Daisy you're here and ready to take her home. So I feel kind of redundant.'

I took a breath, and then nodded. 'Thank you. Yes, that'd be nice, actually.'

She led the way into her kitchen, where she filled the kettle and put it to boil on the Aga. 'Would you like some short-bread?' She took a very fancy tin out of her cupboard. 'Sit yourself down, dear. Earl Grey or English Breakfast?'

I should have felt offended by the *dear*. It made me feel about seventy, despite the fact that she was a few years older than me. But I sank into one of the expensive-looking easy chairs in what she referred to as the nook off the kitchen ('No point going all the way across to the lounge just for a quick cuppa, is there? Let's just rough it, in the nook out here.') and closed my eyes for a moment, letting all the tension, all the worries about work, and money, and Daisy, slide to the back of my brain. Here was somebody who – for whatever peculiar reason of her own, perhaps simply to make herself feel better about stealing Craig from me – seemed to want to be friends. In the circumstances, I might as well grin and bear it. I bit into a piece of glorious shortbread and smiled at Kirsty as she returned with two proper china cups and saucers on a little tray and set them down on the fancy little table between our chairs.

'So how is Daisy settling into the new school now?' she asked after a few minutes.

I sighed. 'Still not well, unfortunately. Has Craig told you what Mr Frost says – that she doesn't talk at all while she's at school, and he thinks she might have something wrong with her – a kind of mutism?'

'What? No, he hasn't mentioned that. Mutism? Really?'

There was a sudden shriek of laughter from upstairs, and she raised her eyebrows at me. 'That doesn't sound like somebody who can't speak!'

'I know. It seems ridiculous. Of course, he's never heard the way she chatters while she's outside of school. But he says she only responds to him in whispers if she has to, and she looks so uncomfortable about it, he's stopped asking her questions. And she never speaks to the other children at all.'

'So what is he suggesting you do?'

'Take her to the doctor's. But Craig says it's nonsense, and I find it hard to believe myself. I'm worried about her not settling down, though. Mr Frost has sat her next to a new girl now, who's shy too, hoping they might bond. But all I can envisage is them sitting together in silence.'

'Oh, dear – poor little Daisy. And poor you, having all this worry.' She touched my arm, looking genuinely sympathetic.

'Sorry, I didn't mean to pour all that out, but it's playing on my mind.'

'Of course. And you must feel free to talk to me, any time anything's worrying you. I'm *so* glad we're getting along so well together,' she said, her watery blue eyes looking earnestly into mine. 'I've felt so bad for so long about... our situation. I wanted you to know I'd never have wished to hurt you, Tasha, or poor little Daisy. Craig handled everything so badly. You know how useless men are at this sort of thing. My late husband was no better, in some ways. Sometimes I used to wonder if it was even worth talking to him – he never seemed to listen to me.' She sighed, looking a bit guilty, then added, 'He ran the business superbly of course, but at home he was a quiet man, very easy-going, always lost in his own world. Obviously it was awful when he passed away, but—'

'I can imagine,' I sympathised. 'It must have been terrible for you.'

'Yes, it was – and for the children, too, of course. Amelia in particular adored him. So I know how it feels, being suddenly left on your own, and I wouldn't have wanted to inflict that on another woman. I truly am sorry, and if there's anything I can do to help you, any time, you only have to ask, you know? Just ask.'

I found myself wondering, ruefully, how she'd react if I said I could do with at least a couple of grand, to start with, to pay off some of my debts, if I added that I'd like not to have to work full time, let alone on Saturdays, and that I'd like never to have to worry where the next mortgage payment was going to come from. But of course, I didn't say any of that. I just smiled, thanked her, and promised I'd remember to ask her if I needed her help with anything.

And at that point, I gave in to the realisation that, against my better judgement, I'd found myself actually *liking* the woman who stole my husband – quite possibly liking her a lot more than I now liked him.

**\* \* \***

'I'm having another sleepover at the big house?' Daisy squawked when I told her the news that evening. She did a little dance of delight. 'I can't wait. I *love* going to Daddy's for a sleepover, me and Freya sleep in her room together, she's got bunk beds and last time she slept on the top one but she said next time I can sleep on the top one. I can't *wait!*' she said again, hugging herself.

'Good.' I smiled, although inside I was hurting, just a little bit, about how excited she seemed to get about going away from our home. I hadn't told her yet that I was going too, but when I did, she looked totally nonplussed.

'What, are you having a sleepover with Kirsty?' she asked, frowning. And then, her eyes widening, 'Or with Daddy?'

'No!' I managed to laugh. 'No, I'll be in a bedroom on my own. Daddy and Kirsty are going out, so I'm going to look after Freya and Amelia. And Max.'

'And me?' she said, looking puzzled.

'Of course – and you.' I gave her a hug. 'And then, next Saturday, you'll be going there again—'

She let out a whoop of excitement.

'—because *I'll* be going out, with my friends from work. So that time, it'll be Kirsty looking after you. And Daddy,' I added, although to be honest I was beginning to wonder if Craig had any input whatsoever in supervising his daughter when she was there.

'Yay! I like Kirsty looking after me.'

This time the hurt was like a blade to my heart. I swallowed. I mustn't react. I was an adult, Daisy was just a little child – she hadn't meant anything by it, I shouldn't be reading anything into it.

I was an adult, yes, but the point was, I was also a mother. I couldn't help it.

'What – better than you like me looking after you?' I tried to smile, and gave a little laugh as I said it, to try to fool her, or fool myself, that I wasn't hurt.

And she looked back at me thoughtfully, her head on one side.

'Well, kind of. Because we do fun things with Kirsty. She plays games with us and lets us do painting, and we go for walks with Max, and sometimes she helps us do cooking, like when we made gingerbread men. She isn't always busy like you.'

Ouch. I sat down on her little bed and pulled her into my arms, resting my chin on the top of her head. She smelt of strawberry shampoo, her breath smelt of her toothpaste, she was warm and soft and beautiful and I loved her so much – more than I'd ever realised, before I gave birth to her, that it was possible to love anyone – and I'd never imagined her words could hurt me so much. Because, of course, it was true: I was always busy. I was always rushing her off to school, rushing her home from Kirsty's to give her something to eat and get her ready for bed, rushing to do the shopping and the housework and the washing at weekends. And it was only going to get worse when I had to work Saturdays too. But she wouldn't mind, because she'd be enjoying herself at Whitegate House, with Freya, and Such-Fun Kirsty.

'I'm sorry. I'll try to make more time for you, sweetheart,' I said softly, promising myself that I'd try to keep Sundays just for us, to do special things together. I'd do my shopping online, have it delivered in the evenings after she was in bed, and never forget half of the things I needed, in future, so that I wouldn't have to dash out to Tesco so often. I'd get organised. If I did all my chores in the evenings, it might stop the temptation to do what I'd been doing, getting myself into worse financial straits. I'd manage somehow.

'Don't worry, Mummy,' Daisy said, interrupting my thoughts, turning to look up at me with her big blue eyes. 'I don't mind that you're always busy, because I have lots of fun when I go to the big house anyway, so I don't need to have fun at home as well, do I?'

## 14

'You're taking it too personally,' Jackie said when I found myself confiding in her again as we both arrived early at the salon on Tuesday. 'I can understand how you feel, but sorry, love – that's kids for you. They take their own parents, and their own home, for granted because you're always going to be there for them. They know that, they trust you, and OK, perhaps compared with going to other people's homes it's a little boring sometimes but they feel secure with you for that reason – home never changes, *you* never change. She feels safe with you but it's not necessarily exciting.'

'That's my fault, because I haven't got time to make it exciting.'

'No. Her security at home is tied up with the sameness of it. Excitement always has a hint of danger to it: kids would get stressed if they lived with that all the time.' She looked at me thoughtfully as she shrugged off her coat. 'You said she's still wary of... what's her name? Amelia.'

'Yes. So am I.'

'But she's learnt to live with that, because of all the fun she has there. But if home were to be like that – with the wariness, the hint of anxiety, always there in the background as well as the excitement – it wouldn't be fun for her. She comes home to you to relax, and drop her guard, because she feels safe with you.'

I nodded, slowly. 'How did you get to be so wise?' I muttered.

'By living to sixty-seven,' she chuckled.

I thought about Jackie's sensible words during the rest of the day, while we were working, and while I was eating my lunch in the room at the back – it was too cold to sit outside now, even on sunny days, and I couldn't afford to go to a café, so I had to sit in the only free chair back there, eating my sandwich and scrolling through my phone for something to do while listening to Camel muttering over the accounts at her desk. I knew Jackie was right; I was grateful to her for spelling out exactly what I'd needed to hear. But I still found it hard to put those words of my daughter's out of my mind: *We do fun things with Kirsty. She isn't always busy like you.*

\* \* \*

It was Saturday all too soon; Daisy was out of bed, running into my room earlier than ever, asking what time we were going to the big house.

'Not until this afternoon,' I said, pulling her into bed beside me. I thought about the pile of ironing I'd promised myself I'd do the previous evening, but hadn't – and wished fervently I had, because instead I'd given in to my usual temptation and now my heart sank at the memory of how that had turned out. I put the ironing firmly out of my mind again. It could wait. 'What would you like to do this morning?'

'Can we do some cooking, Mummy? Like me and Freya do with Kirsty? Can we make gingerbread men?'

I sighed. I didn't have a gingerbread-man-shaped cutter. Come to that, I didn't have any ginger. And probably not whatever else I'd need to make them. I had a quick mental stockcheck of my food cupboards and remembered there was some ready-rolled pastry somewhere in the freezer that I could thaw out quickly in the microwave.

'How about jam tarts?' I suggested. 'We could take them with us and share them with Freya. And Amelia,' I added quickly.

'Yay! Jam tarts, I *love* jam tarts, we never make them, do we, Mummy? Come on Mummy, get up, let's make the jam tarts now.'

She tugged at the duvet and I pulled it back again, laughing.

'OK, OK, let's have breakfast first, and get dressed, shall we?' I looked at the time on my phone and groaned. 'It's still very early, Daise. Wouldn't you like to get a book and come back here while I read you a story first?'

'No. Let's have breakfast and then make the jam tarts.'

'All right, bossy-boots.' I hauled myself out of bed, yawning. At least she was excited, for once, about doing something with me at home.

* * *

We arrived at Whitegate House at about half past four, Daisy clutching the tin holding ten jam tarts – we'd made a dozen but she'd already eaten two – while I carried our overnight bag.

'Come in, come in – Freya's in the garden, Daisy.' Kirsty

welcomed us as the puppy yelped and danced around our feet in excitement. 'Go out and find her – but don't forget to stay away from the end, where the rose bushes are. Freya pricked her finger again the other day,' she added to me, sighing. 'I'm so tired of telling her not to go near them. But thank goodness you're here, she's been driving me mad all day, asking when you're coming.' She leant over to give me a kiss on the cheek. 'Thank you so much for doing this.'

I took off my coat and as I hung it up, and before I'd even turned round again, the two girls had raced back inside together, thrown off their shoes and run straight upstairs to Freya's room.

Kirsty laughed. 'Where do they get their energy from? Please, just go through and help yourself to whatever you want – tea, coffee, or put the TV on, just make yourself at home. Oh, I'll take your bag upstairs for you; I'm going up to have a shower and get myself ready. You'll be in the green room, OK? Next to Amelia's. I hope it'll be comfortable for you.'

'I'm sure it will be,' I soothed her. Surprisingly, she sounded anxious, although I was pretty sure she was used, far more used than I'd ever been, to having overnight guests in her home – and she certainly didn't have to try to impress me, of all people. I was impressed enough just by her use of the palace-worthy title *the green room*!

'Amelia's still at Grace's house,' she said, looking at her watch, frowning, and I realised now why she was anxious. Amelia might be a pain in the neck, but she was Kirsty's daughter: she must worry about her, like all parents. 'She's supposed to be home by now; I'll give her a call. I don't want her walking home on her own any later than this – it's already dark now. Craig will have to go and pick her up.'

'Or I could?' I felt obliged to offer. 'If you and Craig are in a rush to get ready to go out.'

She'd told me the wedding celebration started at six o'clock but I wasn't sure how far they had to go.

'No, Craig can do it,' she insisted. 'It's not as if he does much else.'

I felt my eyebrows rising. I'd never heard her criticise Craig quite so blatantly before. Was the gloss wearing off their relationship? Living together would have brought reality sharply into focus, as it always does; sharing a home with someone would be totally different from the thrill of those secret assignations they must have had before Craig made his big confession to me – the secret assignations that I'd tried so hard not to think about.

She went off to talk to Craig, and presumably to call Amelia, while I duly made myself comfortable in the lounge. At one end of the room there were floor-to-ceiling bookshelves. I gazed at them in wonder: had Kirsty actually read all of these books? Where did she find the time? But of course, when her kids were at school, if she wasn't in a meeting, she had all the time in the world. I wondered how it must feel to be able to sit down and just read to pass the day. I scanned the shelves and chose a book – it looked like a good thriller – made myself comfortable on her sofa and decided to give it a try.

Ten minutes later, Craig poked his head around the lounge door.

'Kirsty said you offered to go and get Amelia from her friend's place for us,' he said, sounding a little chastened. 'She wanted me to go, but I really need to get myself showered and changed for this bloody party. I could do without it, frankly, but what can you do?' He shrugged helplessly and I felt a stab of complete dislike for him. What a pathetic specimen of a man he was actually showing himself to be now. 'Would you mind, Tash? I've got the postcode if you want to put it in your phone.'

I got to my feet. 'Of course I don't mind,' I said evenly. The irony was that I didn't mind doing it, for Kirsty's sake.

'Thanks. We'll have to wait for you to get back, obviously, before we can leave.'

'Obviously. Don't worry, I won't hang about.' I didn't want to be a single minute longer than I had to with Amelia in the car. 'Tell Daisy where I'm going, would you, in case she worries?'

He laughed. 'She won't. She's like part of the furniture here now; she wouldn't mind if you were here or not.' He saw the look on my face and added quickly, 'Well, she would, but – you know...' He tailed off then and looked at his feet. 'OK, I'll tell her.'

I put the postcode into Google Maps, put my coat on, grabbed my car keys and set off, cursing Craig out loud as I drove. Why did I used to think he was so wonderful? Had he changed completely since he'd been living with Kirsty? Why was she putting up with him? Let's face it, however you looked at it, she was far too good for him. Once you'd got over his – I was sorry to admit it – boyish good looks and the charm he could turn on when he actually wanted to, I could see now that there wasn't very much left. On his own admission he couldn't afford to contribute much to her lifestyle, and didn't need to, and it appeared he didn't do much to help in the home or with the kids, either. What good was he, what use was he to her, apart from the obvious? And in retrospect I didn't think that was ever anything special, either!

I was at Grace's house within a few minutes. I was surprised to see it was a fairly modest-looking place, semi-detached, not particularly smart, and probably similar in size to the home I'd had to leave behind in the village. I reminded myself that not every family who sent their kids to a private school was filthy rich like Kirsty. I rang the doorbell and a minute later the door was opened by a tall, good-looking man with wavy brown hair. For a moment I just stared at him – it was hard to quite take in who he actually was, away from the only place I'd ever seen him before, and he seemed to be having the same problem, because he blinked once or twice as he stared back.

'Tasha!' he said, finally breaking into a smile. 'Um, hello. What can I do for you? How did you know where I lived?'

'I didn't,' I said, still staring. What a strange coincidence. 'Hello, Lee. I've actually come to collect Amelia, for Kirsty. I, er, presume Grace is your sister?'

Quite an age gap, unless he was even younger than I thought.

But he was laughing now. 'No, she's my daughter! Come in for a sec – it's cold out there. I'll give Amelia another shout. You know how stone-deaf these girls can be when they want to carry on playing their Xbox games.'

I stepped into the hallway and waited as he went halfway up the stairs and hollered for Amelia. This was so strange; I felt almost disorientated by it. How had I not known, why had Kirsty not told me? But then, how could I have known, and why should she have done? He'd only been working with me for a short while, and not even every day yet. Kirsty would have no idea, neither would Amelia – not that she ever spoke to me – that her friend's dad worked in the same salon as me. And how was he even a father? Grace was thirteen, so he'd have to have been… well, OK, I supposed he'd only have to have been in his early twenties when she was born. It was entirely possible, after all. But he'd never even mentioned her. He never seemed to talk about his home life, his family, at all, come to think of it.

'Oh, it's you,' said a moody voice from halfway down the stairs, breaking into my thoughts as Amelia descended, reluctance in every step.

'Yes, it's me,' I confirmed, gritting my teeth and trying to hide my irritation. 'Your mum and Craig are getting ready to go to a party – remember? You were supposed to walk home a lot earlier.'

'Sorry,' Lee said at once. 'The girls didn't tell me that.'

I bit back the response that Amelia was old enough to remember her own instructions, and that her mum had just called her. I needed to try to make an effort with this girl, no matter how much I disliked her and how often I worried that she was being spiteful to my daughter.

'Not a problem. I'm staying at their house overnight to look after them. Well, to look after Freya, anyway – I realise you're capable of looking after yourself, Amelia.' I forced a smile, but she just glared back at me. 'Apparently your mum's already ordered us fish and chips; it's being delivered at six o'clock.'

'Can't wait,' she said sarcastically.

I ignored her. Rude little madam.

'Come on then,' I said as cheerily as I could manage. 'Let's get you home.'

'Bye, Grace,' she called behind her.

'Bye, Lee,' I said, looking at him again and shaking my head. 'What a coincidence, you being... you!'

'Yes. And you being you!' he agreed, smiling. 'Well, enjoy your evening with the girls. See you on Monday.'

'Yes.'

I opened the door and shepherded the reluctant Amelia out in front of me.

'Have a good time?' I asked as she settled into the front passenger seat, looking around her at the interior of my car with obvious disdain.

'All right.'

'Good.' I set off, sighing a few minutes later when I realised I'd taken a wrong turn because I hadn't set the app to direct me back again.

'It's left at the lights,' she said in the tone of someone speaking to a complete idiot. 'I thought you lived around here?'

'Not this part of town.' I had a feeling I was going to have serious problems keeping my patience with her this evening. But I was the adult here; I should be above snapping at a bit of pre-teen insolence. Besides, I owed it to Kirsty to be as tolerant and kind to her daughters as she was, endlessly, to mine. 'I know you didn't want to come home from your friend's yet,' I said, trying to keep my tone light. 'But your mum and Craig are going out, aren't they. Your mum probably wants to see you before they go – to say goodbye.'

She gave a snort. 'She couldn't care less whether she says goodbye to me. She doesn't care about me in the slightest. She'd be happier if I weren't there.'

I blinked in shock at the vehemence of her words, trying to remind myself that at her age, she was probably prone to drama and exaggeration.

'I'm sure that's not true,' I said, but she ignored me and we continued in silence until we were nearly back at Whitegate House, when she suddenly turned to me and demanded, 'Is he your boyfriend or something – Grace's dad?'

'What? No, of course not. He works with me, that's all.'

'Have you *got* a boyfriend?'

'No. Craig was my boyfriend.'

'I know. He should've stayed with you. I didn't want him living with my mum.'

'You make that fairly obvious, Amelia. Perhaps you should try being nice to him – that would make your mum happy, wouldn't it?'

'Huh. I've told you already, she doesn't care about me, and she doesn't care that my dad died. My dad was the only one who did care about me, and he's gone, and nobody cares.'

We were back at the big house. I pulled up the handbrake and switched off the engine, turning to look at her. She was scowling and kicking the bottom of the car door.

'Come on,' I said. 'It can't be that bad, can it? It's always tricky to get on with your mother at your age. I'm sure she did care about your dad, but she's tried to move on – perhaps you should be pleased for her.'

'Oh, you're just as bad,' she retorted impatiently. 'I don't know why I'm bothering to talk to you. I wish I'd stayed at Grace's for the night. I don't need a babysitter.'

'No, I don't suppose you do, but Freya does, so let's all just try to get on with it, shall we?'

She got out of the car, slamming the door, and strode up to the front door, still scowling.

'I've got my own key,' she snapped as I went to ring the doorbell. 'I'm not a baby.'

'Nobody's saying you are,' I returned as calmly as I could.

She let us both in, and immediately went straight upstairs, almost bumping into Kirsty, who was on her way down.

'Is she in one of her moods?' she asked me as Amelia's bedroom door slammed. 'Sorry, Tasha – how rude of her, after you kindly went to pick her up.'

I was planning to tell her about Grace's father being Lee

from work, but I could see that she and Craig were both already dressed and ready to leave, so I just smiled, wished them a good time and said how nice Kirsty looked.

*Nice* didn't really do her justice. She looked absolutely stunning, in a short silver dress that reflected the light as she turned to slip her feet into impossibly high-heeled silver shoes. Her hair was piled on top in a style that was probably supposed to look casual, and she wore just one stunning gold necklace, studded with a couple of stones that matched her earrings. Craig looked casually expensive too. If I'd still even so much as liked him, it would have hurt my heart to see how horribly handsome he looked, as he draped Kirsty's silver stole around her neck and helped her pull on a short fur jacket.

'Now, don't put up with any nonsense from these two,' she said, smiling at me. 'And help yourself to anything you want. There's wine or spirits in the bar in the lounge. Oh – that's our taxi, Craig, we'd better go.'

'Bye, Mummy! Bye, Craig,' Freya called out from the playroom, where she and Daisy were apparently watching a film on the TV.

'Bye, darling! Be good for Tasha, won't you?'

And they were gone. And I was left to spend my first ever night in Whitegate House.

## 15

After we'd all enjoyed our fish and chips – the two younger girls tucking in with gusto while Amelia ate hers in a surly silence – they all disappeared off to their rooms, so I settled down in the lounge to read the book I'd started. Max – who'd apparently been taken out for a long walk earlier to tire him out – lay at my feet, snoring gently, and an hour or so passed peacefully, with just the occasional giggle or shout of excitement echoing down the stairs from Freya or Daisy. I was just about to go and call up to ask them if they wanted something to drink before bed, when there was a sudden shriek, followed by a series of bumps coming from the stairs and the sound of Daisy crying. Max and I both jumped up and I ran out to the hall, where I found her at the bottom of the stairs and got a glimpse of the back view of Amelia disappearing round the corner at the top.

'What happened?' I asked Daisy, kneeling down to put my arms around her.

'I fell down the stairs,' she said, wiping her eyes and hiccupping as her tears subsided.

'How? What happened? Did you trip?'

'Yes. I tripped,' she said, not meeting my eyes. 'I'm all right, Mummy, my bottom only hurts a little bit, it just scared me when I fell down.'

'Are you sure that's what happened?' I said quietly, helping her to her feet.

'Amelia nudged her,' Freya chimed in. 'She was going up while Daisy was coming down, and she nudged her and made her slip. It might have been an accident, though.'

'It was,' Daisy insisted. 'It was an accident.'

Amelia, who'd obviously been listening from upstairs, immediately came halfway down, looking furious.

'I didn't nudge her,' she said. 'She's a little liar. She just wants to get me into trouble.'

'Did you see her fall?' I demanded. Daisy didn't seem to be badly hurt, but she was obviously shaken, and it could have been so much worse.

'Course I did. I was going upstairs and she pushed past me to come down. Must have overbalanced.'

'Didn't you try to grab her, to stop her falling?'

'Yes,' she said, sounding bored now. 'But she fell too fast.'

I didn't believe her. There had been too many incidents now, and I knew Daisy wasn't making them up. I've always tried to be a fair, rational person and I did realise it was – just, perhaps – possible that Amelia was telling the truth, that Daisy had stumbled rather than being pushed. But how many times were we going to let her off with the excuse of an accident?

'I'm going to have to tell Kirsty about this,' I said to Daisy. 'We can't have you keeping on having *accidents* like this whenever you're here.'

'No, don't tell her, Mummy,' Daisy said, sniffing back her

tears. 'I'm all right now. Please don't tell Kirsty. I don't want to be a tell-tale.'

'Well, come and sit quietly in the lounge for a little while before bedtime, OK?' I suggested. She didn't need to know that I was, definitely, going to tell Kirsty about the incident, whether Daisy liked it or not. Amelia stomped off back up the stairs, the two younger ones sat with me for a while to calm down, and when I suggested it might be time for bed, there were no arguments because they were so excited about sharing the bunk beds. When I went to kiss them goodnight, Amelia's bedroom door was closed and I didn't hear any more from her, although when I finally went to bed myself I could see from beneath the door that the light had been turned off.

I didn't hear Craig and Kirsty come home; the bed in their spare room was so warm and comfortable, I must have slept really deeply and woke up feeling guilty – what if one of the children had needed me during the night? Would my instincts have kicked in, like they always did with Daisy? There was no sound from Amelia's room but I could hear Daisy and Freya chatting in their room along the corridor. I had a quick shower, then went straight in to see them. They were both sprawled together on the top bunk, looking at a Julia Donaldson book, which Freya was reading to Daisy. They looked so sweet and so happy together, I suddenly felt a sharp burst of pain to my heart. Because I'd been planning, since what happened the previous evening, on telling Kirsty this morning that perhaps I needed to stop bringing Daisy here so often – even though I had no idea how I was going to manage without it. I had to put my daughter first, even if I lost my job, even if I starved.

**\* \* \***

'I need to talk to you seriously about Amelia,' I said to Kirsty, while I was helping her clear the breakfast things and the kids were all out of the way. Craig was still in bed; Kirsty had raised her eyes at me and said he was pretending to be tired but, of course, he'd had too much to drink at the party.

She turned away from the dishwasher to look at me, her face creased with concern. 'Oh no, what's she done now? Did she play up last night?'

'Not exactly.' There was no point discussing the girl's awful attitude and appalling manners; I knew Kirsty was already aware of this, and seemed to be clueless about how to deal with it. 'There was another *accident*,' I went on carefully. 'Or so Amelia claims. Daisy fell down the stairs. She says she doesn't want to tell tales, but Freya says Amelia nudged her out of the way and made her overbalance.'

'Oh no!' Kirsty said again. She shook her head. 'Was Daisy hurt?'

'Nothing serious, but of course she was shaken. She didn't want me to tell you about it – she actually looked scared when I said I was going to. I think she's frightened of Amelia, Kirsty. Look, I realise children tell fibs – I'm not saying categorically that I believe Daisy and that Amelia's a liar, but—'

'But she is,' Kirsty replied flatly. 'She does tell lies. I know she does.'

'Oh.' I blinked in surprise. I was fully expecting her to defend her own daughter, even if she promised to question her further about it.

She put down the cups she'd been about to put in the dishwasher and shook her head, sighing.

'I know I've tried to shrug off the previous incidents with Daisy as accidents. But there have been too many of them now.'

'Yes. Exactly.'

'I think she's jealous, Tasha. Jealous of Daisy being here, but jealous of Freya too. Because they're both only little and take up more of my attention.'

'That's what I've been wondering,' I admitted. 'So perhaps I shouldn't be letting Daisy come here so often. But...'

How could I put it? How could I come out and say, when she was being so fair and reasonable and understanding, that if Daisy couldn't come to Whitegate House, I had no other option and I was going to be, to put it crudely, in deep shit?

But before I'd even finished speaking she was grabbing my arm, lowering her voice but speaking so heatedly that I almost took a step back.

'No! That's not the answer. I'm not having poor little Daisy pushed out of our house by that vindictive little madam. She's got to learn to treat younger children – treat *everyone*, come to that – with kindness and respect. Leave it with me. Daisy doesn't have to know you've told me; she's so sweet for not wanting to tell tales, bless her. If Amelia can't learn to behave herself better, she's going to have to go and live elsewhere.'

I blinked again, taken aback by the vehemence of her speech. I'd already seen for myself how difficult Amelia was, but for her own mother to sound as though she'd actually like to be rid of her was quite staggering. Kirsty really must have had to put up with a lot from her, really must be at her wits' end, to feel like that. Ridiculously, I was almost feeling sorry for Amelia now.

'She does seem very unhappy,' I said. 'Losing her father—'

'Well, *I* lost her father too,' she retorted. 'I know what it's like to grieve, to feel unhappy and think you're never going to get over it. But that's no excuse for the way she behaves, the way she treats us all now. Poor Craig – she actually tells him she hates him.'

'Perhaps she needs help. Perhaps your doctor could refer her to someone,' I suggested gently, realising even as I said it that I'd been told the same, by Mr Frost, about Daisy, and had ignored the advice because I couldn't believe there was anything seriously wrong with her. I could hardly blame Kirsty if she felt the same way about her daughter. 'It must be so hard for you,' I added quietly, 'dealing with her moods all the time.'

She sighed, the tension seeming to evaporate slightly from her face.

'Yes, it is. It gets to me. I'm sorry for exploding like that, but you're right, she does need help. I've made appointments for her but she refuses to go, and at her age I can't exactly carry her kicking and screaming to the car. But the priority at the moment is poor little Daisy. I can't have her being scared to come here.'

'She's not,' I put in quickly. 'She loves coming here. I think she mostly tries to avoid Amelia, but—'

'But we can't have her getting hurt. Whether or not it's *accidents*,' she added. 'Leave it with me, I'm going to make sure in future that either Craig or I are always watching or listening out for Amelia when Daisy's here. If I can encourage her to go to Grace's house more often, that'll be even better. Apparently she behaves herself when she's there.'

Again I opened my mouth to tell her about the coincidence of Grace's father being my colleague, but then I stopped. Why would she be interested? She was frowning to herself now as she finished loading the dishwasher, probably worrying even more than usual about her wayward daughter because of what I'd told her. I couldn't help feeling guilty. She'd been so good to me, despite how much I resented her at first, and she had such a burden of anxiety because of Amelia's issues, but she seemed to genuinely care about Daisy, and even about me. To my own surprise, I found myself putting an arm around her, pulling her towards me.

'I'm sure it'll all be OK,' I said. 'Amelia's at a difficult age. She'll change again in another year or so. I'll keep impressing on Daisy that she should stay out of her way.'

'Thank you,' she said, hugging me back. 'I'm so glad we've become friends, Tasha. I... feel like I didn't deserve you being so nice to me. I thought at first you'd want to scratch my eyes out.'

'I did,' I admitted with a grin. 'But you've been *more* than nice to me – having my daughter here so often. And as for the thing with Craig... well, I'm beginning to realise perhaps it wasn't as good between us as I liked to believe.'

'Men, eh?' she said, smiling. 'We can't live with them—'

'—and can't live without them,' I finished for her, laughing. Actually laughing, joking about her stealing my boyfriend, the unfaithful boyfriend I'd loved enough to call a husband, but now looked at dispassionately and wondered what the hell I ever saw in him.

There was no contest any more. I preferred Kirsty to him. She was a much nicer person than that bastard who'd told me he was leaving me the morning after my big birthday, who'd told me so calmly that I'd actually vomited, who cared so little about me that he never even bothered to ask me now if I was coping OK, if I needed any help in my little shoebox of a house, or, God forbid, if I needed any more money. No doubt about it – Kirsty was too good for him. He didn't deserve her.

## 16

'That was so strange,' I said when I saw Lee at work, 'finding out you were Grace's dad. Is she your only child?'

'Yes,' he said, without elaborating any further.

'I suppose she's in the same class – same school – as Amelia.'

'Yep. For now, anyway. Until I finally run out of money.'

'I know. I mean – sorry, I don't know, but I can imagine.'

'What's your connection then, to Amelia?' he asked.

'Oh, well, she's the daughter of my ex's new partner.'

'You mean Kirsty's the one who looks after Daisy for you?'

'Yes. I was babysitting for them, returning the favour, while they went to a party on Saturday night. Daisy plays with Kirsty's younger daughter, Freya.'

'Nice that you've got a civilised relationship, for the kids' sake.'

I wanted to ask him about Amelia – how he'd found her behaviour, when she was with Grace, at his house – but I didn't really like to. I already privately thought of him as being too nosy, so I didn't want to give the impression of being exactly the same. And before I'd had the chance to say anything else, he smiled and added, 'She's a nice girl, Amelia. She and Grace are really good together.'

'Are they?' I couldn't hide my surprise.

'Yes. And I feel sorry for her, too. She took her dad's death really badly – it was so sudden.'

'So I hear. Does she get on OK with your... um, with Grace's mum? She seems to be having difficulties with her own mother.'

He was silent for a moment, concentrating on laying out his scissors and combs.

'Grace's mum passed away eighteen months ago,' he said quietly. 'I'm a single parent.'

'Oh! I'm so sorry.' I looked at his face; his expression was blank. I waited for him to say more, but he didn't, so I didn't feel able to pursue it. I turned away to prepare my own work station, but I couldn't help wondering whether this – the loss of a parent – had been what had drawn the two girls to each other. And he found Amelia to be a nice girl, so perhaps her problem was just a mother and daughter thing. Whatever, she was taking it out on Daisy, and the rest of her own household, come to that: I'd heard her being rude to Craig, and even Freya avoided her.

During the morning, I thought about Lee's situation a lot more, and I wondered if I'd got him wrong. He sometimes seemed so serious, but now I understood: he was probably still grieving, and perhaps money was a worry too, with those school fees for Grace. He was probably desperately trying to keep her at the school where she was presumably settled and happy, and with only his own income to cover everything. How on earth was he managing it? It must be a nightmare. It was hard enough for me, paying for everything myself, without the added burden of what must have been extortionate school fees. The more I thought about it, the more I realised I could have been nicer – more welcoming – to him since he joined the staff. He'd tried to give me advice about doing home or mobile hairdressing and I'd almost taken offence. I decided to try to be a bit kinder in future. After all, I knew what it was like to be worried about money, with the amount of debt I'd got myself into. I'd taken out another credit card – I had no idea how I managed to get through the credit checks for this one, as both my other two cards were maxed out – and I was steadily approaching the limit on the new one now. I knew I needed to stop what I'd been doing every night after Daisy was asleep – unable to resist the lure of the website where I'd been spending, and losing, money at such a ridiculous rate because I told myself it couldn't possibly go on like that, sooner or later I must get lucky. But I never did. I kept thinking, *Just once more, then I'll stop, then I'll be OK.* Christmas was only just over a month away and so far I hadn't bought any presents. Fortunately Daisy didn't yet seem to have started asking for all the latest must-have toys, and there was no way Craig would be getting anything from me this year, although I'd feel guilty if I couldn't afford to buy something small for Kirsty, and Freya. But right now, I'd be lucky if I could afford to give her much more than a packet of sweets.

My worries about Daisy were eclipsing even the worst of my financial concerns. She was becoming more and more withdrawn and moody at home, only brightening up when she was at Whitegate House, or about to go there, or even talking about what she'd been doing there. She endured school with a silent, sad stoicism, never wanting to talk to me about it, learning her weekly list of spellings and reading her daily pages from her reading books to me without complaint, but also without any visible sign of pleasure or enthusiasm.

I told myself repeatedly that I should do more about the school situation. Mr Frost was, of course, not only aware that she had issues, but was actually expecting me to take her to a doctor and get her diagnosed with something – something I was convinced was just a social difficulty that would eventually sort itself out. But if he mentioned it again, could I keep refusing to get her checked out? Was I just determined not to believe there was anything wrong with my baby girl? Did that make me a terrible mother? No, it simply didn't make sense to me, seeing how happy and excited and normal and *noisy* she was when she was with her other family at Whitegate House, to consider her having some kind of disorder that prevented her from speaking.

Then there were my worries about Amelia and her attitude to Daisy. Kirsty told me that she'd watched Amelia like a hawk every time she'd been near Daisy, and I was grateful for that, but uncomfortable with it at the same time. She was doing me enough of a favour already, without having to keep guard over her own daughter in case she did anything to hurt mine. It wasn't right. As Daisy's mother, shouldn't I be doing everything in my power to protect her myself? And didn't that now mean taking her away from Whitegate House before anything else *did* happen? Because if even Amelia's own mother didn't trust her, if even she now seemed to believe that the so-called accidents – the push into the road, the shove into the swimming pool, the fall down the stairs – *weren't* accidents at all, then what the hell was I doing, still sending my little girl there every day, putting her at risk of who-knew-what acts of spite or sadism that little madam might plot unless Kirsty watched her every move?

*But going to Whitegate House is the only thing that makes her happy*, one half of my brain argued fiercely. *How can you stop the only thing she seems to live for?*

*I have to!* I argued back. *I'm her mother, I'm supposed to protect her above all else.*

And then, the final argument that I couldn't find a way to counter:

*You'll lose your job if you lose that free childcare. You've already got no money. How do you propose to survive without it?*

It was this, this constant underlining of the most inescapable part of the argument, that eventually had me asking to talk to Kirsty again the next evening.

'What is it, love?' She looked at me with such concern that I actually felt like crying. 'You seem so worried. Come in here so we can talk properly.' She shepherded me down the hall towards the kitchen. 'Don't worry: Amelia's gone to Grace's house again. And honestly, I've been watching her constantly. She hasn't had a single moment alone with Daisy.'

'It's not that. Well,' I amended, 'yes, it is, partly. I know you're watching the situation, and I'm grateful, but you shouldn't have to, should you? It's not right.'

'Yes, it is. It's my problem, because it's Amelia who's apparently been behaving maliciously.'

'But you shouldn't have to be looking after Daisy all week like this anyway. That's the bottom line, isn't it?'

'It is right, because you're working, and you need to work, don't you? I completely understand. And here am I, with nothing much else to do.'

*Rub it in, why don't you?* I thought ruefully. 'But it's not fair,' I said. 'I mean, you've still got your own work.'

She waved a hand in the air. 'Oh, for heaven's sake, the company can manage without me. And I've told Craig, if I'm in a meeting, *he* needs to watch Amelia around Daisy. Now,' she added with a smile, 'you can't tell me Craig shouldn't be looking out for Daisy. She's his daughter – he should be stepping up to it a bit more.'

'Yes, you're right, he should,' I agreed. 'But, oh, look, I'm going to be completely honest with you, Kirsty. I'm only taking on the Saturdays at work because I'm... I'm...'

I swallowed. I couldn't. I just couldn't come out and say it, couldn't tell beautifully, expensively groomed, manicured and coiffured Kirsty, standing here in her perfect kitchen with its gleaming solid oak furniture and marble worktops – I couldn't tell her I was eating baked beans on toast for my dinners after Daisy was in bed, that the trousers and top I was wearing that day were from the charity shop and that I'd had to raid Daisy's piggy bank to pay her school dinner money for the week.

She looked back at me in silence for a moment, her forehead creased with concern. I turned away, feeling myself reddening under her gaze, but she reached out a hand and turned me back to face her.

'Is Craig giving you enough money, Tasha?' she asked quietly. 'Is he giving you enough to support Daisy, at the very least – if not a lot more, to help you with your bills?'

'It's what we agreed, when he left,' I said.

She tutted. 'I thought you were working so hard – all these hours – because you *wanted* to, because you were ambitious.'

'I am, yes, up to a point. But I do struggle, a little, sometimes,' I admitted.

Shame flooded me again. I knew it was mostly my own fault that I was struggling so badly. I knew I'd made things a hundred times worse, even though I'd only done it in trying to help myself, thinking I might win enough to make my life easier. How had I allowed things to get this bad? And why couldn't I even do the obvious thing, and just stop?

'Have you asked Craig for more?' Kirsty said. 'I'm sorry; I have no idea what he gives you, and I don't want to pry. It's his personal business – his and yours, I mean. But you should know, Tasha, that I pay him well, and frankly he doesn't have many outgoings. He had a lot to say, when we first got together, about wanting financial independence from me, and I admired that in him. But if it means he can't support you and Daisy properly, then—'

'Please don't tell him I've spoken to you,' I said miserably. 'I've tried to be independent myself, too. I don't want to ask him for more.'

'But the prices of everything have gone up. And I couldn't bear to think of you and poor little Daisy struggling through the winter because you're too proud to ask for help. It'll be Christmas soon: you'll need extra money for presents; Craig should be giving you more.'

'I can't ask him,' I said, staring at the floor now. 'He'd want to know why – why I can't manage, when—' I had to stop, a sob caught in my throat. 'When it's all my own fault!'

'Oh, Tasha, how on earth can any of this be your fault?' Kirsty exclaimed softly. 'You're the only one here who's done nothing wrong! Come here, don't cry, come and sit down, let me make you a cup of tea. Then you can tell me all about it – what's gone wrong, why you think you're to blame for anything – because you're not! If it's anyone's fault, it's mine, and Craig's, and you deserve for us to help you, you and Daisy, as much as we possibly can.'

I sank down onto the chair she'd pulled out for me and tried to get myself together.

'I'm sorry.' I blew my nose. 'It's just that everything's got on top of me. I've been spending too much. Buying things, running up too much on my credit cards.'

'Things for Daisy, probably,' she said, smiling. 'I know what it's like – the growth spurts they go through. All the clothes you buy them one year are useless the next year, aren't they, and as for the price of their shoes! I buy Clarks shoes for Freya, of course. They're so well made, aren't they, but so expensive.'

She'd turned her back to me now, to make the tea, so at least she couldn't see me raising my eyebrows. I'd bought Daisy's latest shoes from a cut-price store in town. I'd be considering the charity shop for those too, next time, if I hadn't managed to turn things around by then.

'Right,' she said decisively when she turned back to me, placing two cups of tea on the table. 'This is what we'll do. I won't say anything to Craig if you really don't want me to—'

'No, please don't.'

'But *you* should tell him. Seriously, love, you really should. In the meantime, just to get you over this little hiccup, I'd like to try to help you out a bit myself.'

'No,' I said again. 'Please, forget I said anything. I'll manage. I won't spend anything else until I've paid off the credit cards. I'll be OK.'

'I don't want you to be just *OK*. I can't see you struggling to pay off your credit cards while Craig and I are living like' – she waved her hand around the huge kitchen – 'like we are. Comfortably. No, it's not fair and it's certainly not what I want. So please let me do this – give you just a little, to help you out. Until you've had a talk to Craig. Think of it as a gift for Daisy.'

'I'd feel better thinking of it as a loan,' I said miserably.

What was I saying? How did I think I was ever going to pay her back whatever she was proposing to lend me? But how could I take money from her – my husband's *mistress*? It made me feel sick to even be considering it.

'OK,' she said calmly. 'For now, we'll call it a loan, to be reviewed once you get back on your feet, OK? Now, give me your bank details and I'll make a payment from my personal account, so there'll be no need for Craig to know about it. Not this time, anyway,' she added pointedly.

'Thank you,' I said in a tiny little voice. I felt terrible. I felt like I'd never be able to look her properly in the eye again. Not only was she looking after my child, almost every day, but she was paying me – or at least lending me – money, when it should have been the other way around. And how long would it take, anyway, for me to get back on my feet, as she put it? How soon would I get through the money she was so kindly lending me? I couldn't, was too embarrassed, to ask her how much it was going to be. Would I ever be able to repay her? Not only that, but she'd made it clear she'd expect me to talk to Craig, to ask him instead, if there were to be another time.

'Now, then,' she said after I'd given her my details and she'd apparently made the transaction – I wasn't going to look at my banking app until I got home – 'let's not mention this again. Let's forget we had to have this little talk, shall we? I don't like seeing you so upset, love.'

'Thank you,' I said again.

'And I haven't forgotten about Saturday. It's your evening out with your friends, isn't it? Daisy's coming here for a sleepover. Freya's so excited!'

'Oh.' For a moment I'd forgotten about Jackie's leaving do. Now I felt myself panicking all over again. 'Oh, I don't think I'll be going. I'll—'

'Yes, you are going,' she insisted. 'You mustn't think, just because I've tried to help you out a little bit, that you can't treat yourself occasionally. You've got some money behind you now, so please, Tasha, use it and enjoy yourself. I'll be very hurt if you don't.'

I got to my feet and gave her a hug. I felt like I was going to cry again.

'And don't say thank you again! It's my pleasure.'

I checked my bank account as soon as I got home. She'd given me more money than I earned in a month. I could pay more than the minimum amounts due on my credit cards, and still have some over to do what I wanted with. I could...

But no. I had to hold that thought. There was one thing I really mustn't do with Kirsty's money. I must *absolutely not* go online and do what had got me into this mess in the first place. Absolutely not. That would be unforgiveable.

## 17

'You've got your babysitter booked for Saturday night, haven't you, Tash?' Jackie asked me.

She was excited; she'd been talking all day about the restaurant she'd booked, the drinks we'd have in a nearby bar to start off with, the wine she'd pre-ordered and what was on the menu. I didn't blame her; she'd more than earned her retirement and I could understand her looking forward to her celebration. But I wasn't.

'Are you all right?' she added quietly when I didn't answer. 'You *did* say Kirsty was having Daisy for you, didn't you?'

'Yes. But I'm not sure, now, if I can—' I began, miserably.

'Oh, Tasha, come on! It'll be fun. You need an evening out. And, well, I'll be disappointed if you don't come. Please?'

I felt guilty. Well, to be honest, I felt like crying. I'd messed everything up, let everyone down, especially Jackie. I couldn't go to her celebration on Saturday because, despite everything I'd promised myself, despite sitting on my hands for half the evening to try to stop myself, I'd ended up going online again and I'd already spent most of the money Kirsty had given me.

The more I spent, the more I carried on, panicking, desperately trying to win some back. I hated myself. Why was I so weak? What was wrong with me? I'd been so determined not to give in to the temptation, so sure I could, for once, be strong, resist the urge, the itch that came over me every evening like a rash – a rash that just had to be scratched, but the scratching never brought any relief.

How could I possibly go out for the evening, spending more money that I didn't have? But how could I say that to Jackie, my best friend, who'd never look at me the same again if she found out what I was doing, how weak I was being? And how was I going to tell Kirsty I now didn't need her to look after Daisy for me? What excuse could I possibly give her for not going out, now that she'd specifically told me to use some of her money to enjoy myself on Saturday? I didn't answer Jackie – I just couldn't find the words. I felt so ashamed, so angry with myself, I just wanted to go home, shut the door on the world and curl up in bed. Perhaps take something to make me sleep, because I hadn't been able to do so since I'd blown so much money, the money I'd promised myself I wouldn't use.

I could feel Jackie's eyes on me as we finished tidying up for the night. I was last out of the salon, but as I locked the door I became conscious of her waiting behind me in the street.

'What's up, Tash?' she asked, linking arms with me. 'You've been so quiet all day. And what's all this, suddenly, about not coming on Saturday?'

'Sorry. I just don't feel very well.'

We walked together towards the car park just along the street. I could still feel Jackie looking at me, but I kept my eyes on the ground.

'I know you too well. You're making an excuse,' she said

eventually, and I could hear the hurt in her voice. 'You just don't want to come, do you? Why not? Tell me.'

I shook my head. I couldn't. The shame was engulfing me again. But it was true, Jackie knew me far too well to believe my excuses. She was leaving in a couple of days, and what if she felt upset enough with me to not bother keeping in touch? A friend who couldn't be bothered to go to her leaving do wasn't much of a friend, after all.

'Look,' I blurted out eventually, 'it's not that I don't want to come. Of course I do. But...'

'If it's a question of the cost,' she said quietly, 'forget that. I haven't told the others yet, but the meal's going to be my treat. It won't be overly expensive, it's a set menu. It's what I want to do, so please don't argue about it.'

'No! I can't let you do that, absolutely not. Kirsty's given me some money now.'

'But you've had to spend it already? Or you need it for next week's food, or the mortgage, or to pay off your credit card?' She stopped, pulling me to a halt beside her, and turned me to face her. 'I know how tough everything's been for you, love. I know you don't want to admit it, but this is me – nobody else needs to know. And it's the end of the month; I remember how slowly pay day used to come around at this time of year, when my own kids were little.' She smiled. 'Come on, I'm not stupid: however much Kirsty's given you – and I'm not asking – I can imagine how quickly it will have been eaten up, with the bills and everything. There's no shame in admitting it, is there? Not between friends. Not between *us*.'

I gave a little sob. 'Don't! Don't be nice to me, Jack. I don't deserve it. You're right, most of the money's gone already, but it's my own fault.'

'Of course it isn't,' she soothed me – making me feel even worse. 'It's Craig's fault. He should be giving you more; it makes me angry to think of you and Daisy struggling. If Kirsty's money's gone already, ask her for some more. Don't put up with it, Tash. I know she's looking after Daisy for you, I understand why you feel grateful for that, but by all accounts, they're rich, and they obviously don't realise how hard it's been for you.'

I just shook my head, miserably. If this conversation went on much longer, I'd end up blurting out the truth, and I couldn't bear for Jackie to know what I'd descended into – what I'd become. Fortunately, we'd reached the car park now and I was able to mutter something to the effect that I'd think about it, before we said goodbye and got into our cars to go our separate ways. I'd have to go on Saturday night, I realised. Hurting Jackie would be unforgiveable. And I couldn't go without buying her a little leaving present, either, even if it was just a bunch of flowers from the Co-op. I'd find a way, somehow.

\* \* \*

'How was school today?' I asked Daisy as I drove her home from Whitegate House. Since I'd made my decision to try harder to get to the bottom of Daisy's issues at school, I'd been pushing her a little more firmly every evening, hoping she'd open up more to me – but so far without any success.

'Same as usual,' she said, sounding, as always, like she simply didn't want to think about it, let alone talk about it. Then her voice suddenly brightened as she remembered. 'But we're going to see a play soon.'

'A play? Well, that'll be exciting, won't it?'

'What *is* a play, Mummy? Mr Frost said it would be fun but I don't know what it is.'

'Oh, well, it's when people dress up and act out a story for you. Like on the TV, but it's in real life. Did Mr Frost say what the play would be about?'

'No, but he said we'll have to go on a coach to a theatre. What's a theatre?'

I'd presumed this would be a dramatic group going into the school, perhaps as a pre-Christmas treat. But no, not at the school. I wondered, briefly, whether the school was funding this. Surely, if we had to pay, I'd have had a message about it?

'A theatre is a building where they act plays,' I explained. 'Remember when Daddy and I took you to the pantomime? Like that.'

'Oh, that's what he said the play would be: a pantomime. I forgot the word. And he said it would be before Christmas, and you'll get a message about it, Mummy, cos you have to send some money in.'

Oh dear.

'Well, that's exciting, isn't it?' I said as cheerfully as I could. 'Are you looking forward to it?'

'I don't know. If we don't go, we'll have to stay at school and do drawing and painting with a different teacher. So I do want to go, but...' She tailed off, and I heard her sigh. 'But I wish I had a friend, Mummy, like when I was at my old school, so that I could sit next to someone on the coach and when we watch the play. But I haven't got a friend.'

We'd pulled up at home, and I turned to look at her. Her little face was so downcast, my heart felt like it was going to break. I'd been hoping the new little girl might have started being friendly to Daisy by now, but Daisy had hardly even mentioned her yet.

'I thought Izzie was your friend now,' I said. 'You sit together, don't you?'

'Yes. And I do like her, but she still doesn't talk to me.'

'Does she play with the other children?'

'No. At dinner time she just sits in the playground on her own, so I sit on my own too.' She shrugged. 'She doesn't like me.'

'Daise, I'm sure that isn't true. She's probably just shy. I bet she tells her mummy she hasn't got any friends, as well, and perhaps she thinks you don't like *her*.'

'When we have to have a partner, Mr Frost always puts us together. But she still doesn't talk to me.'

I hesitated. It was one thing trying to take Daisy's issues seriously, but also Mr Frost had cautioned me against mentioning his fears to Daisy, and so far I hadn't. But now that I'd at least got Daisy talking about school again, I suddenly decided it was time to try to kill off this idea about my daughter having some kind of disease.

'So, when you say something to Izzie,' I said carefully, 'does she reply, at all? Or not?'

Daisy shrugged and looked away. 'Can we go indoors now, Mummy?'

'Yes, in a minute. I just wondered whether you've kept trying, Daise – if you've kept talking to Izzie, hoping she'll say something back? Because I think she probably would, eventually, if you're being really nice and friendly to her.'

'I'm cold, Mummy. Can we go indoors?'

'Daisy, listen, just for a moment. It's important. What I'm saying is, if Izzie still hasn't got any friends, I bet she'd really like to be your friend. You do talk to her, don't you, Daisy?' I added, finally giving up the struggle to find out without asking her outright.

She shrugged. 'I stopped trying cos she doesn't talk back.'

'But she might, now, if you keep chatting to her. She might just need some encouragement.'

'What's *couragement*?'

I smiled. 'Giving her courage. Making her brave. She really does sound very shy. She probably wants a friend even more than you do, but she's too scared to say anything in case you don't want her. I think maybe you have to make the first move. If you keep chatting to her—'

'She *doesn't want* to talk to me!' Daisy said angrily, trying to open the child-locked rear door. 'I keep telling you, Mummy, nobody likes me at this school, I want to go to Freya's school. Why won't you let me? Please, Mummy, I really want to go there, I really, really do.'

I got out of the car and opened rear door for her. If I felt bad before, I was now feeling even worse, because I knew she'd been trying to avoid answering my questions. I had a growing sense of unease that perhaps she really *wasn't* speaking – at all – in class. I'd promised myself to try to get to the bottom of Daisy's unhappiness, but had I been too ready to dismiss Mr Frost's concerns because it had sounded, frankly, exaggerated? I already knew Daisy wasn't happy at school, but obviously she must speak at times to the other children, even if only in the course of her lessons? It surely wouldn't be possible not to. But then, why was she so reluctant to answer me, to tell me if she'd been talking to Izzie, trying to be friendly to her? Why change the subject, why get cross and impatient, if she wasn't too nervous, or embarrassed, to tell me the answer? I didn't want my child to be too nervous to tell me the truth. I wanted to know, to hear it from her, if she really had a serious difficulty of some kind. I'd promised myself that if I hadn't got anywhere with Daisy, if things hadn't improved, I would make an appointment for her with the doctor in December – and we were nearly there now. I needed to get her to open up to me. But before we'd even got inside the house, she was continuing on her theme of Tudor Hall Academy.

'Why can't I go there, Mummy? *Please.* I know you said it costs a lot of money, but you can have what's in my piggy bank.'

I pulled her towards me for a hug, feeling guilty again now. If only the few coins still remaining in her piggy bank, after I'd unfortunately had to raid it, could help with anything. I managed to change the subject by telling her about the fish fingers I'd got for her dinner, but the mention of her piggy bank had sparked another idea in my mind, an idea I was ashamed to even think about, one that I was doing my absolute utmost to forget had ever popped into my head. The piggy bank wasn't the only place where Daisy had some money. There was a savings account that Craig and I had opened when she was a baby, which we used to put money into, every birthday and whenever we could afford to add a little. I hadn't, obviously, been able to add anything to it since we split up, and I'd forgotten about it. There wouldn't be a massive amount in it, but perhaps, with the interest that had been added over the years, it might be enough to—

But no! I was *not* letting my thoughts go down that route. It was Daisy's money, supposedly towards her future. We had hoped we'd be better off one day and would be adding more, making it a nice little nest egg for her when she was ready to go to uni, or get married, or whatever. Even if all it did was buy her a couple of driving lessons eventually, I would not touch it. It wasn't mine. Absolutely not. It was out of the question.

## 18

'Have another drink, Tash?'

It was the night of Jackie's leaving party, and she was leaning across the table in the bar, waving her glass of wine at me as if she thought I might have forgotten what a drink was.

'No thanks.' I indicated my half-empty glass of tonic. 'I'm driving.'

'Oh, Tash!' she complained, pulling a face. 'I thought you were going to get a taxi?' Then she brightened up. 'Oh, never mind, Dave'll take you home – he's picking me up later. You can collect your car tomorrow.'

'No, don't be silly. You live in the opposite direction, and anyway—'

'It's no problem. You're only a few minutes' drive away. I absolutely insist; don't argue with me at my own party!' she joked. 'Now, come on, what are you having? A gin, in that tonic? Or a glass of wine?'

'Honestly, I'm fine with just tonic. I've got to go and pick Daisy up in the morning.'

She shrugged. 'OK, if you insist. Camilla – another one for you?'

Camel was sitting next to me, drinking beer and talking mostly to Lee, who was opposite her. She seemed a lot chirpier than usual – I'd actually seen her smile twice – which made me wonder whether, away from the business, it might be possible that she could even be a quite normal person. I'd had time to ponder this, and plenty more, while I sipped my tonic, because although I was trying to make an effort for Jackie's sake, I really didn't feel much like socialising. I'd only turned up because I couldn't bear to hurt Jackie's feelings. I'd bought her a card and a bunch of flowers, as I'd planned, in addition to signing the official leaving card and contributing to the collection organised by Camel, with which she'd bought a lovely necklace and matching earrings. I was quite surprised that Camel had undertaken this, and that she had such good taste – or that she knew Jackie did. But I'd have liked to do more for Jackie myself, in a personal way, and felt miserable and guilty that I hadn't. I knew, too, she'd have liked me to have a few drinks and throw myself into the party, celebrating with her, but I couldn't.

Everyone else was in a happy mood, though, so I gave myself a little shake and, as we moved on to the restaurant, forced myself to join in the chat and laughter. At the table, I ended up sitting opposite Jackie, with Lee sitting next to me.

'Are you OK?' he asked as we studied the menu. 'You seem a bit quiet.'

'Oh, sorry, I didn't realise I had a reputation for being loud and amusing,' I said sarcastically.

He raised his eyebrows. 'Not at all. I was just expressing concern.'

'Oh. Well, thank you, but I'm fine. I won't be drinking this evening because of picking Daisy up in the morning. So I suppose I won't exactly be the life and soul of the party.'

'Me neither.' He smiled. 'I'm going to have alcohol-free Guinness. You should try it. It's as good as the other version.'

'If you like Guinness,' I said, pulling a face. 'But yes, I suppose I could have had an alco-free wine. I like tonic, though,' I added defensively.

'Fine, why not. Getting pissed is overrated,' he said lightly. Then he looked at me again, and added, more quietly, 'You're not worried about Daisy, are you? She'll be fine if she's with Kirsty. She's used to going there now, isn't she?'

'Yes. She really enjoys going round, actually. I think she'd rather be at Whitegate House than at home, to be honest.'

I didn't know why I'd told him that, even if it did seem to be true.

'Well, she would if it weren't for Amelia,' I added, half under my breath, before I could stop myself. What was the matter with me? My mouth suddenly seemed to be running away with me as if I *had* been on the hard stuff all evening.

I could feel Lee's eyes on me.

'She doesn't like Amelia?' he asked. 'Or you don't?'

'Well, it's not exactly that I don't like her.' I tried to back-track, fast. Lee's daughter was Amelia's best friend. I didn't want this getting back to her. 'It's just that she's a lot older than Daisy, and Daisy's not used to mixing with older kids.'

'Of course.' He was silent for a moment. Jackie was having a lively conversation with Paige, sitting next to her, so I turned to look at Lee again, to find him studying me thoughtfully. 'I've always liked Amelia,' he said. 'But she's apparently told Grace that she's not getting on with her mum any more, and she thinks her mum wants her out of the house. She's asked Grace if she can come and live with us.'

'Has she?' I pretended to sound surprised. 'Well, I must admit, ever since I've known Amelia she's seemed very unhappy. I worry that she resents Daisy coming into her house.'

'Perhaps she does, secretly. And she's been through a lot, losing her dad so suddenly. They were very close. He was a really nice guy. It was terrible, what happened to him.'

I guessed Lee was bound to sympathise with her; after all, his own daughter had been through something similar. So I just nodded.

'Would you want to have her living with you?' I asked him. I turned it into a joke, to lighten the mood. 'Two teenagers in the house – surely not!'

'Why not? She and Grace are no trouble when they're together. And Grace says Amelia is sure her mother would pay me for her keep, if it actually comes to it. But – really? Can you honestly see Kirsty, as a mother, giving up her own daughter just because she was being a typical teenager – a bit of a nuisance? I wonder if it might just be the two girls plotting together.'

'Maybe,' I said. But I suspected he was, in fact, taking it more seriously than that. He wouldn't have mentioned it to me otherwise. And I knew – I'd been told by Kirsty herself – that she actually seemed to be thinking seriously about Amelia's behaviour. I might have felt sad for Amelia if it weren't for the fact that Daisy was far more important to me. And anyone who might be hurting Daisy didn't deserve my sympathy. If she did go and live with Lee and Grace, quite honestly I'd be glad to see her gone.

\* \* \*

Our little group became livelier as the evening progressed and Jackie, Camel and Paige shared another bottle of wine. We lingered over coffee, talking about our various clients and some of their funny ways, about haircuts in the past that had gone wrong, colours that people had immediately regretted, and styles that had been popular but had now gone out of fashion.

'I'm going to miss you all,' Jackie said tearfully after she'd called for the bill – and was met with a chorus of, *Don't be silly, you can pop in all the time.* Even Camel was in a an uncharacteristically good mood, having insisted on buying the second bottle of wine, and telling Jackie she'd miss her. When the bill arrived, Lee got out his phone to use the calculator to divide the total between us, but Jackie immediately interrupted him.

'No, pass the bill to me, please, Lee. I've already decided to pay tonight. It's my party, I wanted you all here, and I want to treat you.'

Everyone protested, but she said we'd offend her if we didn't let her pay. During the uncertain pause which followed, Camel announced that she'd intended to pay for the evening herself, and suggested she share the cost with Jackie.

'This is on us, guys,' she said in a strangely jolly voice. 'Jackie and I will go halves. After all, she's the party girl, and I'm, well, I'm the boss!'

And she laughed – actually laughed out loud. I'd never heard her laugh before, and I think it shocked all of us into silence. It was a strange, harsh laugh, a bit like a donkey braying. No wonder she didn't do it often.

'Well, thank you both,' I managed eventually, as we all finally found our voices. 'That's very kind.'

I was aware my voice was sounding trembly, from sheer relief. I knew Jackie had already said she wanted to pay, but if everyone had insisted on paying their share, I'd been worried sick about the possibility of having my card rejected. I saw Jackie looking at me, and gave her shaky smile. Then I noticed Lee looking at me too, a puzzled expression on his face – and I immediately looked away. I didn't want him knowing I was broke. It was bad enough that Jackie knew. It was bad enough that I'd caused this situation, without anyone having to know about it.

As we all parted company, with promises to keep in touch with Jackie, I made yet another promise – to myself. I had to stop what I'd been doing. Like, *now*.

* * *

I found it hard to get to sleep, alone in the house, thinking about Daisy and wondering if she was OK. I told myself I should be used to it by now – after all, she'd been away to Center Parcs for a week at half term, and this wasn't the first sleepover she'd had at Whitegate House. Kirsty had said something about making the most of the chance to have a lie-in, but I knew I'd still wake up early, expecting to hear Daisy's little voice, singing to herself as she often did first thing in the morning, or talking to her dolls and teddies as she played with them in her bedroom. As I tossed and turned, I kept mulling over what Lee had said about Amelia. He seemed to genuinely like her. Perhaps she really was a nice girl who was simply going through a bad phase with her own mother – like a lot of girls of her age did. But she'd been surly and rude to me, too – and apparently to Craig. And more importantly, her dislike of

Daisy was quite clear; even Kirsty agreed she'd been caught being spiteful to her.

I'd only just, finally, gone off to sleep when I woke up again with a start. My phone was ringing and vibrating itself silly on my bedside table. Groggily, I reached out and grabbed it, rubbing my eyes, trying to read the caller display. As the name came into focus I sat bolt upright, immediately wide awake. I hit the respond button and asked, my voice coming out harsh and loud in the quietness of the night, 'Kirsty? What's wrong? Is Daisy all right?'

'Don't panic, Tasha. But I'm taking her to hospital. A&E. She'll be fine, it's just a precaution, but—'

'What? Wait!' I leapt out of bed, shivering with the cold and the shock of the call. I started, with my shaking free hand, to pull off my PJs, then gave up and picked up a jumper to throw on top of them. 'What's happened? Is she hurt? Is she ill? I'm coming! Tell her I'm coming.'

'We'll see you there, Tasha. Please don't panic, she'll be fine, I'm just getting her checked over, OK? I'm on the way there, we'll be there in ten minutes, so please don't rush and have an accident. Are you sure you're OK to drive?'

'What? Yes, of course I am – oh, I didn't have anything to drink.' I shook my head in exasperation. This was irrelevant, distracting from what was important. 'But what's happened?' I demanded, running out of the bedroom, down the stairs, grabbing my coat, looking frantically for my car keys.

'I'll tell you when you get here. I've got to go, Tasha. Drive carefully.'

My daughter was hurt. Ill, or injured, probably crying, wanting me. I'd left her there, with the woman who, let's face it, however much I might now have started to like her, was the bitch who stole my husband. I'd left Daisy with the girl she'd accused of trying to drown her, push her in the road, push her down the stairs – and what else that I didn't even know about?

If that girl had hurt my baby, I'd never forgive myself. She'd never be going to Whitegate House again.

## 19

Fortunately, for once, it was easy enough to park at A&E. I hadn't even checked to see what time it was, but it must have been the early hours of the morning, still pitch black and freezing cold. I'd had to waste time doing a hurried de-ice of the windscreen, probably not enough to drive legally, but enough to see vaguely what was in front of me. And now I was rushing across the frozen car park, through the automatic doors and into the sudden warmth of the A&E waiting room. I ran to the reception desk, shouting over the shoulder of the person already being dealt with.

'Daisy Fenton! My daughter! Where is she?'

The receptionist looked back at me calmly. 'If you wouldn't mind waiting for just a moment, until I've dealt with this gentleman—'

'Yes, I would mind waiting! It's my daughter, she's only six, she's hurt, I need to know—'

'It's fine,' the man in front of me said, giving me a sympathetic look and turning back to the receptionist. 'Deal with this lady first. I hope your little girl is OK,' he added to me.

'Thank you.'

My voice was shaking, and I was so close to tears that talking was actually hurting my throat. The receptionist directed me through a door and past a row of cubicles to another door, marked 'Paediatric Emergencies'. I had to press a buzzer to be admitted, and inside, the inappropriately jolly cheerfulness of the décor made me feel suddenly disorientated, as if I'd been transported to a nursery school in the middle of the night.

'Daisy Fenton!' I demanded again as a nurse approached me. I had to restrain myself from flinging open cubicle curtains to find her, instead having to follow the nurse as she, infuriatingly slowly, led me to the far end of the room and into a cubicle where, thank God, there was my Daisy, lying on a bed, holding out her arms to me and crying.

'Daisy! Sweetheart, what happened, how did you...?' I stared at the dressing on her forehead. 'How did this happen?' I finished, turning to Kirsty, who'd jumped up from her seat by the bed and was approaching me, a hand out ready to touch my arm, to try to calm me – as if I could possibly be calm!

'Tasha, it's not as bad as it looks,' she began, but I shoved her to one side, sitting down on the edge of the bed and pulling my daughter into my arms.

'All right, baby, it's all right, I'm here now, don't cry, I won't leave you again, I promise. Don't be frightened, I'm staying with you now, it'll all be OK.'

Daisy's sobs slowly subsided. She rubbed her eyes – she must have been tired, on top of the shock of whatever had happened. She lay back against the uncomfortable-looking NHS pillow, and I turned my attention to Kirsty.

'What happened?' I asked again, trying to keep the edge of censure from my tone, trying to remind myself that it might not have been her fault. It might not have even been her crazy daughter's fault, but I wasn't about to bet on it.

'Apparently Daisy got up to go to the bathroom in the night,' Kirsty said.

'I needed a wee,' Daisy interrupted tearfully. 'And Freya was asleep but I could see the bathroom, because of the light.'

'I left the landing light on for them,' Kirsty explained. 'So, bless her, she took herself to the toilet and then she must have somehow fallen—'

'I falled over and I falled down on the floor,' Daisy said. 'And I went to sleep, Mummy, and when I woke up I was frightened because Kirsty was there and Daddy was there and I didn't know where I was. And my head was bleeding all on the floor,' she added as an afterthought.

'She must have hit her head on the edge of the bath as she fell,' Kirsty said. 'We heard a bang and a cry – we both rushed to the bathroom, and poor little Daisy had fainted.'

'Fainted?' I repeated, sceptically. Or had she knocked herself unconscious... or been knocked unconscious by somebody?

'I felt all dizzy like when I was on the roundabout,' Daisy said, starting to cry again as she remembered it. 'It was horrible and I cried for you, Mummy, but Kirsty put a plaster on my head and said we had to come here, and I don't like it here, I want to go home.'

'We thought she ought to be checked, as it was a head injury.'

'Absolutely.' I lowered my voice, turning back to Kirsty again. 'It sounds like she's been slightly concussed, doesn't it?'

'She was lying right there next to the bath.' Kirsty had lowered her voice to a whisper now. 'And there was blood on the edge of the bath, as well as on the floor, so we guessed she must have either fainted and fallen, or—'

'She's never fainted before.'

'Or she somehow tripped, and passed out *after* hitting her head. Either way, she needed to be checked over.'

'Of course. Thank you for acting so quickly,' I conceded. 'Was there anything there that she could have tripped over?' I added in a whisper.

'No.' Kirsty met my eyes. 'There wasn't.' She got up, indicating to me to follow her to just outside of the cubicle curtain. 'Amelia was out of bed when we passed her room to get to Daisy in the bathroom,' she said very quietly. 'She said she'd just woken up because of Daisy crying out. But I don't know. She looked... kind of shifty. I have to be honest: I have my doubts.'

I felt tears coming to my eyes again – tears of fury, with myself as well as with Amelia. I *knew* I couldn't trust that nasty, vicious girl around Daisy. I knew I shouldn't still be sending her to Whitegate House, but I'd carried on, because I couldn't afford to do anything else. But that was my own fault anyway. And worse, last night hadn't even been important, I hadn't even been working. I'd put my darling child in danger, just for the sake of an evening out, an evening I didn't even really enjoy but felt obliged to go to, for Jackie's sake. I'd put my friend before Daisy's safety. Never again – never! I'd have to find another way to manage my work situation. I'd have to leave my job, if necessary, and go on the dole. Yes, voluntarily make myself jobless and claim benefits, like other people did – why not?

'I can't be sure, of course, that Amelia had anything to do with it,' Kirsty was going on. 'But—'

'But we both know she probably did,' I said. I could hear the anger in my own voice.

'Tasha, I'm so terribly sorry – I know I promised to watch her, around Daisy—'

'But it was the middle of the night, you were asleep, you weren't to know Daisy would get up. It's no good, Kirsty, I'll have to stop sending Daisy to you. I'll have to find another way; I don't care what, or how, I just can't risk anything like this happening again.'

'Of course you can't. Absolutely not. But there's no need to talk like that. You can't stop Daisy coming to us. I won't have you needing to fork out for childcare when we love having her at our place, and I think she loves coming, too. She's part of our family, now, I couldn't bear to think of her not coming any more.'

I shook my head, dismissing her, turning to go back into the cubicle, where I could now hear Daisy calling for me. But Kirsty stopped me, a hand on my arm, lowering her voice again.

'Please don't stop her coming to us,' she said again. 'I promise nothing like this will happen again. I'm sending Amelia to live with Grace. This settles it.'

I didn't really believe her. I found it too hard to believe she'd actually send her own daughter away in order to keep looking after mine. But to be honest, at that moment I didn't really care what happened to Amelia. Daisy needed me, she was my priority, and a doctor had just arrived to talk to us about her, so I needed to focus. He told us she should spend the rest of the day resting quietly but probably not watching TV. She should be given painkillers if her head continued to hurt, and I should take her to our GP if she still had headaches or trouble sleeping after a couple of weeks.

'She should be OK to go back to school tomorrow,' the doctor said, smiling at Daisy. 'But not to do PE or sports for another day or two. You should warn her teacher she's had a mild concussion so they'll know to give you a call if she starts to feel bad again.'

He checked her head wound again, declared that it wasn't deep, didn't need stitches and had only bled so much because 'head wounds always do'.

'It's stopped bleeding already,' he told Daisy cheerfully. 'You'll be as right as rain.'

'I didn't like the way he made light of it,' Kirsty said crossly as we walked back out to the car park, Daisy walking between us, holding our hands.

'I suppose he was just trying to be reassuring.' I'd calmed down a bit, now I'd seen for myself that the wound did look more superficial than I'd feared.

'Well, that doesn't change anything. I've made up my mind. Craig and I have had enough of' – she glanced down at Daisy – 'of you-know-who causing trouble in our home. I've tried my best, honestly, and it's obviously not an easy decision to make. But things are getting worse, Tasha. She's been in trouble at school a few times recently, I'm ashamed to say. Answering teachers back, not doing her homework, getting her phone out during lessons – all that kind of thing. I brought her up better than that – it's humiliating to hear how she's behaving.'

Despite myself, I couldn't help thinking that Kirsty seemed more upset about her own reputation – as a school governor, I supposed, as well as a mother – than being concerned about the reason for her daughter's bad behaviour.

'Anyway,' she went on, 'she keeps asking to go and live with Grace – it's obviously what she really wants. If she's going to be happier, and we don't all have to keep walking on eggshells, why not?'

*Because you'll just be confirming Amelia's suspicion that you don't love her,* I found myself thinking – but of course, I didn't say it. In fact, I shut the thought down quickly. I'd be glad to know that girl wasn't going to be at Whitegate House any more. Despite my knee-jerk reaction half an hour previously, I was already backtracking on my promise to myself. Kirsty seemed to love looking after Daisy. Daisy loved going there; I couldn't even imagine the meltdown she'd have if she couldn't see Freya regularly any more – she was her only real friend. And the bottom line was that I knew perfectly well I wouldn't go through with my bold ideas about making myself unemployed and looking after Daisy myself. I'd be too ashamed. Kirsty would be horrified, and insist on helping me out again. No, Whitegate House, and Kirsty, had become necessary to my survival, and Daisy's too. And it would be 100 per cent better without Amelia there.

## 20

Mr Frost looked concerned when I told him about the accident.

'The wound is healing already,' I said, 'but I've put a small plaster on it, just to keep it clean. Other than that, the doctor at the hospital said she mustn't do any PE for a couple of days. And of course,' I added, lowering my voice, 'if she seems unusually tired or... or anything out of the ordinary...'

'We would call you. Of course.' He smiled at Daisy. 'Well, you'll have something to write and draw a picture about for your news book today, won't you?'

She shook her head, looking worried.

'She didn't exactly enjoy the experience,' I said, smiling at her. 'And she didn't really know what happened – she passed out.'

'Ah well, maybe you can write about what you did before the accident, instead,' Mr Frost said tactfully, and Daisy nodded agreement before hugging me goodbye and walking off to her coat peg.

Mr Frost watched her and then turned back to me. 'She's

still completely silent in class. Have you – and her father – thought any more about what I suggested?'

'Yes,' I said, avoiding his eyes. 'Of course, I keep asking Daisy about school and whether she's talking to anyone, but it's been difficult to get a straight answer out of her. If I'm still getting nowhere in another week or two, I'll definitely take her to the doctor. She's obviously still not happy. She keeps asking to change schools.'

'Sorry to hear that,' he said. 'What is it – she still misses her old school?'

'No. She wants to go to Tudor Hall.'

'Oh dear.' Mr Frost gave me a sympathetic look. 'I hope you do the Lottery, then!'

Little did he know, but that wasn't even remotely funny.

\* \* \*

It felt strange at work, knowing that the set-up for Mondays, Wednesdays and Fridays – with Lee working alongside me – was now going to be the same for the whole week. No more looking forward to being able to chat with Jackie on the other days. And no more Saturdays off; I'd be working in future, and Daisy would be at Whitegate House all day. I wondered how she didn't get fed up with being there... but then I shook my head. Of course I knew why she didn't. As she'd already told me, it was 100 per cent more fun for her than the alternative – being at home with me, on our own, while I usually had housework or shopping to do. Compared with the fun she had with her best friend, her *sister,* there was no competition.

'You're quiet today,' Lee said as he passed me on his way to the reception desk to take his client's payment.

'I'm always quiet, aren't I?'

It had been OK talking to Lee at the restaurant on Saturday evening, but at work, I still didn't feel entirely at ease with him. I didn't like the fact that he asked so many personal questions; it made me feel uncomfortable. I regretted confiding in him as much as I already had; I didn't think, in retrospect, I should have let him know I'd had to take on the Saturday work for financial reasons. I should have pretended I was just doing it because I loved my work so much.

'Was Daisy OK with Kirsty, on Saturday night?' he asked when his client had left.

'No, she wasn't. I presumed you'd heard.'

'What?' He looked genuinely surprised. 'No, I haven't heard anything. What happened?'

I looked back at him suspiciously. Surely Kirsty must have told him. She'd said she was going to send Amelia to stay with him and Grace virtually straight away – I'd been feeling so relieved, thinking she wasn't going to be at Whitegate House when Daisy went there after school.

'Daisy ended up at A&E. A so-called fall in the bathroom in the middle of the night.'

'Oh God, Tasha, I'm sorry, I didn't know that at all. Is she OK?'

'She had concussion, and a cut on her head.'

'Oh, poor Daisy. Is that why...' He stopped, swallowed and looked away. 'Perhaps I shouldn't ask. But Amelia's definitely coming to stay with us; she's coming tomorrow after school, in fact. They wanted to bring her round straight away – today – but I'm out this evening, and obviously I want to be there to help move her stuff in and get her settled. It's supposed to be temporary, but Amelia insists she won't want to go back home. I wasn't aware there had been an incident at the weekend. Kirsty didn't mention it when she called me yesterday. She just said the decision had been made, and was I still OK with it.' He paused. 'Are you saying... do you think Daisy's accident was, well, not an accident? That Amelia was involved? Honestly, I find that hard to believe.'

'Perhaps you do,' I snapped. 'But I don't, and nor does her own mother, even if she doesn't want to admit it to you.'

'I'm sorry,' he said, looking surprised at my tone.

'My wet cut lady's here now,' I muttered, turning away from him and heading to the desk to greet my client.

Fortunately we didn't get much more of a chance to chat. The salon was busy and we both had a full schedule of appointments. When I went to Whitegate House to collect Daisy after work, Amelia had apparently gone straight to Grace's from school to do her homework and keep her company while Lee was out, but Kirsty and Craig were both eager to tell me what I already knew – that she'd be moving in there the next evening. I waited with Kirsty in the kitchen, with a cup of tea, as I often did now, because it took Daisy so long to part from Freya upstairs.

'You must feel weird – your daughter moving out,' I said, trying to be sympathetic. 'Even if things have been bad...'

'Yes – bad and getting worse, unfortunately,' she said. 'I've been told she's in trouble again at school now, too. Apparently she pushed a girl over during netball practice, after a tussle over the ball. Pushed her over deliberately! If she's not careful, she's going to end up being suspended, or even expelled. I'm surprised Grace still wants to be friends with her, to be honest.'

'Oh dear. Well, I'm glad she does. At least she has a friend to stand by her. I hope she'll start behaving better at school once she's moved in with Grace.'

'Me too. It'll still be me who gets the call, if she does misbehave, of course,' she added, sounding resentful about it – as if she thought her daughter's behaviour in school should now be Lee's responsibility!

'Well, of course,' I said gently, struggling to ignore my shock at her attitude. 'You're still her mum.'

'Yes,' she said. She sounded so unhappy about it that, once again, I felt a quick flash of sympathy for Amelia. I decided it would be best to change the subject, and we chatted for a while about mundane things.

'I'll just use your bathroom before I go, if that's OK,' I said when I finally heard the girls saying their goodbyes. I headed out into the hall, Max galloping ahead of me, wagging his tail. He ran into the lounge, yapping with excitement.

'What's so interesting in there, boy?' I asked, peering around the door, puzzled by his sudden burst of enthusiasm, and laughed when I saw he'd dived on one of his toys and was now tossing it around the room. I turned to leave him to his fun – but my eye briefly caught on a bright blue laptop lying open on one of the side tables, with a matching blue USB stick inserted in it. The laptop looked new, and expensive, and I wondered whose it was. I watched the puppy bounding around the room for another moment, then turned back to go to the bathroom – but something, some impolite moment of curiosity, or I should perhaps say downright nosiness, made me linger by the open laptop and idly tap the touchpad to bring the screen to life. I shouldn't have done it. I'd had no right to do it, and as soon as I saw the words flash up on the screen, I felt bad. It was Amelia's, and the page that came up was obviously private – it looked like a diary. I caught sight of Daisy's name near the top of the page, so I'd have liked to read on, except that Daisy had now appeared downstairs and was calling out to me that she was ready, so I had no choice but to double back and scoot into the downstairs bathroom.

I'd have very much liked to know what Amelia might have been writing in her diary about my daughter. But I'd probably never get another chance to see it, especially now she was moving out.

\* \* \*

'How has your head been today?' I asked Daisy when we were in the car on our way home.

'OK,' she said. 'I liked it when it was PE, because I had to just sit and watch, and Mr Frost was extra nice to me because he thought I'd be sad about it, but I wasn't.'

'What did he say to you?' I asked.

'He asked if my head was still sore, and he asked if I felt sad about missing PE.'

'And what did you say?' I went on, hoping she'd tell me she replied, even if it was only in a whisper. How could she possibly not reply?

'I said no. With my head I said it.'

'You just shook your head?'

'Yes, because it means no.'

'I know, sweetie. But... couldn't you say it out loud, to Mr Frost, if he was being nice to you?'

'No!' she said fiercely. 'I didn't want to, and he knows what it means anyway.'

My heart was thumping with anxiety now. I wanted to ask Daisy why she didn't want to talk to Mr Frost, but she'd gone into a grumpy silence and I knew I wasn't going to get any more out of her. Did I really need to book that doctor's appointment? I still couldn't believe there was anything seriously wrong with her. But I knew I needed to get to the bottom of this quickly now, one way or another, to find out for sure whether it was just shyness, or... something else.

\* \* \*

'It's going to be even nicer now at the big house,' Daisy said later, while she was settling into bed. 'Now Amelia's going.'

'Doesn't Freya mind, that her sister's moving out?'

'No. She's glad too. So are Daddy and Kirsty, I think.'

Despite everything, I felt a burst of sudden and unexpected sympathy for Amelia. However much I needed to protect my own daughter, Amelia was still really just a child herself, not turning thirteen until February, and she obviously had problems – issues – of some kind, or she surely wouldn't have been behaving the way she had been. It was obvious that she missed her father – she was still grieving, but whatever other issues she had, it was awful to think of her own mother being happy about her moving out. Again, I felt the burden of guilt, knowing that the main reason Kirsty had felt the need to send her daughter away was Daisy's welfare, even if she and Craig, and Freya too, did feel relief at her absence. But I had to put my sympathy for Amelia to the back of my mind. I couldn't afford to dwell on it. And after all, if she was going to be happier at Lee's house, and behave better there too, then surely we were all winners?

\* \* \*

The next evening when I arrived at Whitegate House there was a lot of bustling about going on. Craig was coming down the stairs carrying a bundle of pillows and sheets under one arm and a suitcase in the other hand, and Amelia was following with a stack of books and Nintendo games.

'Honestly, Tasha,' Kirsty said, ushering me into the kitchen, out of their way, 'I can't believe how much she's insisting on taking with her. All her bedclothes, for heaven's sake!'

'Perhaps she thinks it'll be helpful – to Lee,' I pointed out.

'What, do you think he might not have enough pillows and duvets in his house?' she asked, looking at me sceptically.

'I think that's very likely, actually,' I said, smiling at her naivety. Did she not realise that most people didn't have money to spend on extra bedding at a moment's notice? 'I take it you've checked that he *has* got a spare bed for her?'

'Of course. Amelia stays overnight there often enough.'

'Yes, but she'll need spare bedclothes, won't she? For when they go in the wash.'

'Oh, goodness, I should offer to bring all her washing home here, shouldn't I. Poor Lee shouldn't have to do it. He has to work so hard. I was hoping that giving him a bit of extra money – you know, to pay for Amelia's keep – would help him out. Perhaps enough for him to give up his second job.'

'Second job?' I repeated faintly. 'I didn't know he worked in the evenings.'

'Oh dear.' She put a hand to her mouth, looking guilty. I'd obviously mentioned by now that Lee and I were colleagues at work. 'Perhaps he doesn't want people at the hair salon to know about that. Could you possibly forget I said anything? I'd hate to get him into trouble, he's such a nice man. Maybe he's keeping it quiet for, I don't know, tax reasons or something.'

'Maybe,' I echoed faintly. But my mind was whirring. Lee was working evenings as well as full time at the salon? 'Does he work *every* evening?' I couldn't help asking.

'I don't think so, no. Because sometimes he's at home when I pick Amelia up from there, and sometimes he isn't.'

Presumably he didn't work on Saturday evenings, as he'd been able to come to Jackie's leaving do. I knew Kirsty wanted me to forget she'd mentioned it, but I couldn't help turning this information over and over in my mind, even after I'd collected Daisy and taken her home. Was he doing home hairdressing? No, because Kirsty had said he was at home some evenings, at work on others. Perhaps he was doing mobile hairdressing. That would explain why he'd seemed to know a lot about it, when he'd been suggesting I tried that myself. Or maybe he was working in a completely different field. Grace must have been left alone at home a lot in the evenings; no wonder she was looking forward to Amelia going to stay.

* * *

I couldn't resist asking him, the next day at work, how Amelia was settling in.

'Fine, thanks.' He smiled. 'She and Grace are so happy to be sharing a room. You'd think, at their age, they'd like their privacy, but no, they're loving it – chatting away together long after I've gone to bed. I'm hoping that'll wear off after a while, or they won't be fit to get up for school in the mornings.'

'I'm glad she's happier. I felt sad for her, having to move out. Hopefully, after a break from her family, she'll be able to move back and start again.'

'It's not your fault, Tasha. Not Daisy's, either. Whatever the truth is about her home life, she wasn't happy, that's for sure. Perhaps now, everyone can settle down. And I wouldn't count on her moving back after a while, whatever Kirsty says. I really don't think she wants to.'

'It's good of you,' I said, pausing on the way to the reception desk to look at the appointment diary. 'I mean, it must be more work for you, having an extra person in the house.'

'Not really.' He laughed. 'Kirsty's said she'll take all of Amelia's washing home, even her bedclothes, and bring it back clean and ironed – she's insisting. She says she's got more time than me, and, well – she's not wrong, of course!' He laughed again, looking completely at ease with the situation. 'Besides,' he went on, 'it has benefits for me, too – it's company for Grace when I'm out. She's had to spend a lot of time on her own, unfortunately, and that's made me feel guilty. So, it's a win all round, really.'

'I'm glad, then.'

I couldn't ask. I just couldn't come out with a random question about where he was when he went out. He obviously didn't want to tell anyone here at the salon that he had a second job and, to be honest, it didn't really matter to me what his reasons were. Perhaps he was just a workaholic.

## 21

Fortunately, Daisy had no further problems with her head, and today was her last swimming lesson before Christmas. The teacher made it fun, with games and races for the children. Daisy was by far the best swimmer now in her beginners' group, and at the end of the lesson I was told she would be moved up to the next group when lessons started again in January. I took the opportunity, while the teacher was talking to me and Daisy had gone ahead into the changing room, to ask whether Daisy talked to the other children at all.

'Well, I haven't really noticed, to be honest,' she said thoughtfully. 'They don't really get much chance to talk during the lesson. But she doesn't talk to me. I just assumed she was shy.'

'Yes,' I agreed. 'She is. But if you say anything to her, does she respond?'

'Not really. She just does whatever I'm asking her to do – swim across the pool when it's her turn, and so on. She's very well behaved,' she added with a smile. 'But if I ask the whole group something, she's never one of the ones who responds. It's fine. Don't worry, I'm used to shy children.'

I thanked her and went to help Daisy in the changing room, my heart sinking again. I'd already been pretty sure she didn't speak at the lessons: I always watched from the viewing area, but because of the thickness of the glass I could only hear them talking if they were shouting, as the teacher needed to do for all the children to hear her. She assumed, as I had done, that Daisy was just shy. But was that all it was? I wasn't sure any more and I was now pretty much resigned to taking her to see a doctor during the school holiday, just to put my own mind at rest, and to stop Mr Frost worrying.

'Isn't it great that you're moving up a class, Daisy?' I said as we walked back to the car. 'You've done so well with this teacher.'

She shrugged. 'It's because of the pool at the big house, that's why I've got good, because Kirsty helps me and Freya and I like going in there.'

It was true that, even now the weather was colder, the pool room at Whitegate House was kept lovely and warm. I wondered about Kirsty's heating bill, but I supposed it was just a drop in the ocean to her. I had enough trouble heating my little house, without a swimming pool to consider.

But Daisy was sighing. 'I *wish* I could live at the big house, Mummy, I would be so happy if I lived there all the time.'

'Even though you wouldn't be living with me?' I said, teasing, but inside screaming with insecurity.

'Well, you could come and live there too, couldn't you? There are lots of bedrooms, and Kirsty's so nice, she wouldn't mind. You could cook everyone's dinners and just... go to work.'

I shook my head, sadness engulfing me at this picture of myself as a modern-day Cinderella at the palace.

'Well, thanks, but no, Daisy. We've got our own home.'

'It's not as nice as Kirsty and Daddy's house.'

'Maybe not.' My patience was starting to feel a little strained. 'But it's ours.'

'But if I lived there, I could go to school with Freya.' She indicated the magnificent building of Tudor Hall Academy, which stood behind us now as we walked away. 'And that's what I really want, Mummy, more than anything in the whole world. More than anything on my Father Christmas list. More than *anything*. Freya wants me to go there more than anything, too. We talk about it all the time, and sometimes I cry because I want to go there so much, and Kirsty says she would pay for me to go there but she says you say no. Why do you say no? It's not fair, Mummy.'

I opened the car doors, waiting for her to get in, but she was now working herself up into a tantrum. Other people in the car park were looking at us, and I suppose I'd just had enough.

'Come on, get in the car,' I said, quietly but firmly.

'No! I want to go to school with Freya!' Her face was turning red; she was crying and shouting now. 'Why won't you let me?'

'You know why. Get in the car, Daisy. You're tired. You'll feel better in the morning.'

'I won't! I want to go to Freya's school and I want to live with Freya. I don't want to live in our silly house and I *don't* want to go to my horrible school. I hate everybody at my school and I hate you!'

'Daisy,' I said, choking back the misery her words were causing and trying to stay calm. 'If you don't get in the car right this minute, I'll have to lift you up and put you in.'

She hadn't behaved like this since she was about three. I tried to tell myself it was simply tiredness after the swimming lesson, but that didn't make it any easier.

'I'm counting to ten,' I warned her. 'One, two, three, four...'

'I don't care.' She stamped her foot as she shouted each word. 'I. Don't. Want. To—'

'...eight, nine, ten. Right.'

I lifted her under her arms, fighting off her hands as she struggled and tried to push away from me, screaming in fury. A mother who was helping her two perfectly behaved children into the car next to mine turned to look at me, shaking her head in disdain, and somehow I fought the urge to put Daisy back down and stomp over to pick a fight with her instead.

'Why is that mummy making that little girl scream?' I heard her own daughter asking.

'Well,' the cut-glass tone of the mother's response floated back to me, 'Some people just aren't very good at—'

She shut her car door just in time to prevent me hearing what exactly I wasn't very good at, but I could guess, and by the time I'd forced Daisy into her car seat, strapped her in and slammed her door, I was feeling too frazzled and too upset to care. I tried to pull myself together before starting the car, and as I drove us home, Daisy gradually sobbed herself into silence apart from the occasional sniff.

'Are you all right now?' I asked quietly when I opened her door again to let her out. 'I'm sorry I had to do that, Daisy, but you're a bit big to be having silly tantrums like that, aren't you?'

'I was upset, and you didn't care.'

'Oh, sweetheart, of course I care. But we can't go shouting and crying every time we're upset about something, can we? I'm upset too, that I can't afford for you to do some of the things you'd like to.'

'But you *can* afford for me to live at the big house, because Kirsty would—'

We were going indoors now, but I stopped halfway through the front door and looked down at her, shaking my head. How was I ever going to get through to her? I could feel my annoyance rising again. Had Kirsty been encouraging this? Had she actually been saying things to Daisy about how nice it might be if she lived at Whitegate House?

'Daisy,' I said firmly, 'I've told you over and over again, you are *not* going to live at the big house, and you are *not* going to go to Freya's school. And it doesn't matter how much you scream and shout, that's not going to change. Some poor children would be grateful just to live in a house at all and have their own bedroom. In fact, you're just making yourself sound like a horrible, spoilt little girl, and if I hear one more word about it—'

'I hate you!' she yelled in response. 'I'm going to live with Freya, so there!'

And she stomped off upstairs, crying loudly again, leaving me so close to tears that I had to sit down in the kitchen to recover before I could even start to cook dinner. It was a sad meal, punctuated by the occasional little self-pitying sob, but Daisy was probably too hungry by then to refuse to eat. When she went to bed, I sat with her for a while, trying to talk everything over more calmly, but she just turned over onto her pillow with her eyes closed, pretending to be asleep. Again, I felt like crying myself. I'd have to have yet another talk to Kirsty, and it had better be soon. The next day, in fact, before things got any worse – if that were even possible.

* * *

'I've had to make an urgent appointment... um, at the dentist,' I lied to Camel on the phone in the morning. 'They've fitted me in at nine o'clock. I don't think I've got a client until ten, so all being well, I should be there—'

'I suppose I'll have to take your client myself if you're too late,' she said, sounding put out about it. She rarely did anyone's hair herself these days.

'Sorry, Camilla, but I won't be able to concentrate if I don't get this tooth dealt with.'

I felt bad for lying; it brought back that awful day after my fortieth birthday when I'd had to make an excuse to stay home because I'd cried myself sick about Craig leaving me. But I didn't want to put this off: it was too important, and I wanted to do it while the girls were all at school.

I dropped Daisy at school a little earlier than usual and was at Whitegate House well before nine. I'd already messaged Kirsty to say I wanted to call in for a chat, but I noticed both cars were on their drive anyway; their girls started school early.

'Come in, Tasha,' Kirsty said when she opened the door. 'Are you OK? Aren't you at work today?'

'Yes, but I'm going in a bit late.' I brushed this aside. 'I haven't got long, but I need to talk to you. It's important.'

'Well, let me at least make you a cup of coffee.' She took me through to the kitchen. 'Sit down. What is it? You look upset.'

'I am, to be honest. It's Daisy. She's been having dreadful tantrums.'

She stopped in the middle of making the coffee, turning to look at me in amazement.

'Daisy's having tantrums?' she repeated. 'Really? I can't believe that, she's always so sweet and well behaved.'

'Well, I'm glad she is, when she's here. And I'm not

surprised; she's so happy here, and so unhappy,' I went on, feeling suddenly tearful again, 'at home.'

'Oh, Tasha!' Kirsty abandoned the coffee-making and came to sit next to me, putting an arm around me. 'Don't cry. What is it? What's happened? Is poor little Daisy upset about something?'

'Yes, she is!' I exclaimed. I was too used to the 'poor little Daisy' bit by now to react to it. 'She's upset because she wants to live here. She wants to live in this house, with you, and with Freya, the only friend she seems to have at the moment. And with the swimming pool, and the dog, and the Nintendo, and... and everything. And she wants to go to Freya's school – she never stops talking about it, and it's worse when she goes there for her swimming lessons. I lost my cool with her yesterday and told her she was acting like a horrible, spoilt child. I keep telling her it's never going to happen – she can't live here, and she can't go to Tudor Hall, but—'

'Well, she *could*, if you'd let us pay for her,' Kirsty said sadly.

'No!' I must have shouted it, because suddenly Max, who'd been lying on my feet under the table, jumped up and started barking, and then Craig was looking round the kitchen door, asking what had happened. 'No, please don't offer,' I went on more quietly after both had been calmed down. 'Please don't say that to Daisy; it would be undermining what I'm trying to get through to her. I have to try to manage, and I *can* manage, but she's got to understand that our lifestyle isn't the same as yours, and that's the end of it.'

'What's the matter?' Craig asked, having come back into the room to find out why I was upset. 'Is this about Daisy? Is she all right?'

'Yes, she's fine,' I snapped. 'Apart from the fact that she's behaving horribly.'

'Really?' His forehead creased in a frown. 'Well, she's perfectly behaved when she's here, isn't she, Kirsty?'

'Yes, and that's the whole point, Craig,' Kirsty said with exaggerated patience, turning to raise her eyebrows at me in exasperation. 'Honestly, Tasha, men can be so dense, can't they? Look, I'm really sorry to hear Daisy's giving you a hard time at home. Would you like me to talk to her? I can try to underline what you've been saying, so she doesn't keep thinking her daddy and I would take her side in any arguments like this, against you.' She paused and then added, with a hand on mine and with a sincere little smile, 'We wouldn't, you know. We'd never do that.'

'I know.' I took a deep breath to try to calm down. 'Thank you. Yes, that might be helpful. But I also think I need to cut out any... unnecessary time she spends here. It's getting so that she's here almost more than she's at home, so I suppose it's inevitable that she's starting to want to live here.' I swallowed again. It was awful, having to admit that my own child wanted to live apart from me.

'The school situation obviously doesn't help,' Kirsty said gently. 'It's such a shame she hasn't made any friends there yet.'

'Hasn't she?' Craig interjected.

I looked at him in amazement. He picked her up from school every day, and not only that, I'd already had a serious conversation with him about Mr Frost's concern regarding her lack of speech. Had he forgotten already?

'Men!' Kirsty said again, shaking her head and giving me a sympathetic look when I couldn't even bring myself to answer him. 'Well, look, of course you must do whatever you think best. But obviously, Daisy needs to come here while you're working and, well, it would be sad if we couldn't ever babysit for each other again, wouldn't it? Freya loves their sleepovers.

Look, we'll make it our... our mission, to impress upon poor little Daisy how lucky she is to have two homes to go to, but that her home with you is the most important one. We'll work on it, I promise – won't we, Craig?'

'Um, OK,' he said, scratching his head, obviously completely clueless about the whole thing. I really was beginning to wonder about him.

'Thank you,' I said. 'And, well, I'm sorry if I'm overreacting. You know how grateful I am to you. But it's just so hurtful, as well as being frustrating, to hear Daisy continually pleading to be anywhere else but with me.'

'Aw, I'm sure it must be, but don't take it too personally, love. She's only little; they can only think of their own needs at that age but she does love you, she'd be lost without you, you know that.'

Did I? I was grateful to Kirsty for being so nice, for saying all the right things, offering to help – doing, frankly, all the things Craig seemed totally incapable of doing. But still, I wasn't convinced Daisy would miss me, now, as long as she had her new family, and her much nicer home, and especially if she thought she could wheedle her way into going to Tudor Hall.

I thanked Kirsty and said I'd better get off to work, where I had to remember to talk as if I'd just had a tooth filled, and Lee, who obviously suspected something, gave me strange looks all day. When he asked if I was all right, I just said I was fine but it hurt to talk. I was pretty sure he didn't believe me, but I didn't really care.

## 22

'Tasha, Craig and I would like to ask you something,' Kirsty said a couple of weeks before Christmas.

'OK,' I said, a little hesitantly, wondering what on earth it was going to be. If it was a favour, whatever it was I'd have to try to do it, considering how much Kirsty was doing for me.

'We'd like you and Daisy to come to us for Christmas,' she went on, smiling. 'Well, we – and especially Freya – would like Daisy to come, and we'd like you to come, too, unless you'd rather have a quiet day on your own – peace and quiet for once, a chance to rest up a bit – I wouldn't blame you.'

'Oh! No, I wouldn't want a quiet day on my own.' It sounded awful – lonely and sad. 'I was expecting to spend it on my own with Daisy at home. Especially as we've just had that conversation, about cutting down on her spending extra time here. And I did think Daisy might like me to invite Craig for a little while on Boxing Day, if you were OK with that?'

'Well of course, if you'd prefer that, it's no problem, of course. And I understand – I know we agreed to cut down the extra occasions. But this is Christmas! I really don't like to think of you and dear little Daisy being on your own.' I was pleased that recently, 'poor little Daisy' seemed to have been replaced sometimes with 'dear little Daisy'. Even though, right then, 'poor' might have been more appropriate. 'You could both stay over, for both days if you like? We'd love to have you! And frankly, Freya would be intolerable if she couldn't see Daisy for Christmas – she's already talking about what we can buy her.'

'Oh, don't, please don't go buying her anything! Well, obviously, Craig will want to, or I hope so – he's always left the present-buying to me, so I was wondering whether he'd remember.'

'Don't worry, I'll be on his case about that. But seriously, love, we'd both like you to join us here. We'll be getting a turkey and all the other stuff anyway, so it honestly won't make the slightest little bit of difference – just a few extra potatoes and so on.'

'Well, you must let me contribute, at least. Let me buy the pudding and mince pies, or something.'

'No need, they're all on my Waitrose order already. I always start planning early; it makes it go so much more smoothly, doesn't it?'

'But surely you'll be inviting other people.' I'd never even heard her mention her family. She never seemed to go to visit parents, or siblings, aunts or cousins at the weekend. 'Relatives—'

'Relatives?' she said scathingly, raising her eyebrows. 'Haven't got any, well, none that I want to visit, or even talk to, unfortunately. And I understand from Craig that neither of you have parents still alive either, sadly. So it makes sense for us all to get together, doesn't it? Oh – I'll have Amelia home here on Christmas Day. It would be difficult not to have her here for Christmas, but I've invited Lee and Grace to join us too. So she's unlikely to take any notice of dear little Daisy, while she's got Grace here. Grace is a good influence.'

'Well, of course; Amelia's still your daughter, you wouldn't want to spend Christmas without her.' I hesitated. I felt as if I was going against what I'd been so determined to do. But I'd been dreading the quiet, sad Christmas Daisy and I would have had on our own, let alone her sulks about not being with Freya. 'OK, then, if you're absolutely sure it won't be too much. I'll help, obviously.'

'Oh, Craig's going to cook the dinner,' she said breezily.

'Is he?' I couldn't keep the shock from my voice. The only thing I could ever remember Craig cooking during the years that we were together was eggs on toast – and he managed to fry the eggs for so long that they were solid. The very idea of him left alone with a turkey and an Aga made me feel slightly weak.

'Well, I'll help him, then,' I said firmly. 'I don't want us all going down with salmonella.'

She laughed heartily at this, as if it was the funniest thing she'd ever heard.

'He's a better cook than me,' she retorted.

I stared at her in disbelief, shaking my head. She'd not only stolen my man, she'd changed him, too.

* * *

'Would you like to go to Whitegate House for Christmas Day?' I asked Daisy on the way home.

To my surprise, there was no response. Perhaps she was tired, perhaps she'd even dozed off in the back of the car. I waited until we were home, and we were sitting down for dinner, before asking her the same question – and again, she didn't reply, but looked down at her plate, playing with her food, an unhappy frown on her face.

'What is it, sweetie? Tell me. If you don't want to go, it's fine, it doesn't matter, nobody will mind. We can just have Christmas here at home, on our own, and maybe Daddy will come round on Boxing Day.'

She nodded, slowly, but to my horror, a single tear ran down her face and dripped into her dinner. I got to my feet and pulled her into my arms.

'What's the matter, sweetie? Don't cry. I thought you'd be happy and excited at the idea of going to the big house for Christmas, but it doesn't matter, really it doesn't. We can just—'

'I do want to go there, I really, really do,' she said, choking on a sob. 'But Mummy, I don't want you to be here on your own at Christmas. It would make me very, very sad.'

'Oh, Daisy, I'm sorry, I didn't explain properly. I'll be coming too. Kirsty's invited both of us, and Daddy's going to cook the dinner, and—'

'Daddy's going to cook?' she squealed, her expression a picture of comedy. 'Really?'

I laughed. 'That's what I said, too, but apparently he's suddenly learnt how to! Don't worry, Daisy, I'll help him, if we do go for Christmas. But only if you'd like to.'

'Yes! Yes, I do want to go!' she said, her tears suddenly forgotten, her face alight with excitement. 'We can both go? And I can be with Freya *and* you at Christmas? Can I, Mummy, really?'

'Yes, sweetie, you can – we both can. I wouldn't want to be without you on Christmas Day, either, of course I wouldn't. Isn't that kind of Kirsty, to invite us both? And she said we could stay over for Boxing Day, too, if we're both very good.' I paused, then went on more quietly, 'Amelia will be there, though. It is her Christmas too, so it's right that she should come home to her family, OK?'

'Yes. I'll just keep away from her like I always tried to do.'

'But Lee and Grace are coming with her, Daise, so she'll be more interested in being with Grace. I'm sure she'll leave you and Freya alone.'

'OK. Oh, I'm excited now, Mummy! I'm really pleased that we're both going to the big house for Christmas.'

'Good.' I smiled. It was lovely to see her so happy. But I still felt uneasy that I'd so quickly been talked out of my promise to myself, that I was going to restrict her visits to my working days in future. Well, it *was* the most special time of the year, and if accepting Kirsty's invitation meant that it would be a happier day for Daisy, I had to make an exception. Kirsty and I were almost friends now: it would be good to spend time with her, too. And Craig and I had promised all along that we'd be civilised with each other for Daisy's sake. It would be weird spending the festive occasion with a work colleague – but I'd have to try to tolerate Lee, for everyone's sake. He wasn't so bad, really, when he wasn't asking personal questions. I'd even started to feel a bit sorry for him since I found out about his wife. It'd be OK. I was going to look forward to it.

* * *

'It seems we're going to be spending Christmas together,' Lee said a couple of days later at work. He was smiling, looking really happy about it.

'Yes. Well, it'll make things more convenient. For all the kids, in particular. And it's good of Kirsty.'

'Not being funny, Tasha, but she's got all the time in the world to get everything organised, hasn't she? It's not a big deal for her. She says Craig's even going to cook the dinner, so she hasn't really got anything to do, has she, apart from being the gracious hostess.'

'That's a bit harsh,' I said.

'I didn't mean it to sound harsh. I like Kirsty, and I agree with you, it's good of her. All I'm saying is, if I tried to host Christmas for, what is it – eight of us? – I'd be really stressed about it, trying to find the time to do all the shopping, let alone the money to pay for it, and I'd have to borrow extra chairs, not that I've even got room round my table.'

'I know,' I conceded. 'Same here.'

'So you're right, it's good of her, but not as hard for her as it would be for most people. Anyway, I'm looking forward to it.'

'Me too.'

'Just got to buy the presents now,' he said. 'What would you like?'

'Me?' I said, alarmed. 'Oh, don't go buying me anything. Just, surely, get something for Kirsty and Craig.'

'Well of course, but it'd be much nicer if we're all opening our presents together, wouldn't it? I don't think children should have all the fun at Christmas.'

'Maybe not, but honestly, I don't want anything, there's nothing I need.'

I was panicking now. I was going to have trouble just finding the money for Daisy's present, and I'd thought perhaps I'd just take Kirsty and Craig a bottle of wine, or a box of chocolates. True, it didn't seem much when they were doing the whole of Christmas for us, but where the hell was I going to find the money for anything more? And if I was going to be buying presents for Freya, Amelia, and perhaps

Grace too – let alone Lee – I'd have to consider robbing a bank.

He was looking at me, a concerned expression on his face.

'Tasha,' he said quietly, 'Christmas presents don't have to be expensive. It's the thought that counts. A bar of chocolate, or a cheap pair of socks, or a little plant in a pot, anything like that, anything from the pound shop, frankly, is just as thoughtful as a big expensive gift. Isn't it? If it's chosen with the person in mind.'

I felt myself going red with embarrassment.

'I know that. I'm just saying, you don't have to bother with me, OK?'

'Dammit,' he said, laughing. 'I was going to give you a cheap pair of socks from the pound shop. Now I'll have to keep them for myself.'

I forced a smile. I felt annoyed – patronised. I didn't need him lecturing me about the spirit of Christmas. I *would* get him something from the pound shop, then, and if my tips this week were good, I'd do the same for all the kids. Luckily Daisy was still young enough to be pleased by pretty much any present. But she did still believe in Father Christmas, so I'd have to buy some little things – sweets, a colouring book, and so on – to go in her stocking. I'd have to manage it. I'd get the money. Somehow.

* * *

One evening later that week, I had a call from Jackie.

'If the mountain won't come to Mohammed...' she began cheerfully.

'Sorry, Jack. I've been meaning to call you, honestly. It's just been—'

'Busy. I know, I'm only teasing. So, are you all ready for Christmas?'

'Not really.' I sighed. 'I mean, I've put the tree up. Daisy wanted it up as soon as we got into December. And a few bits of decoration. But I haven't bought any presents yet.'

'You'd better hurry up; the shops will be emptied out! Are you and Daisy doing anything for Christmas Day? If not, Dave and I were wondering if you'd like to come to us.'

'Ah, that's so nice of you both. But we've actually been invited to Kirsty and Craig's for both Christmas Day and Boxing Day. Anyway, haven't you got your own family coming?'

'Dave's mum, yes, and my sister and brother-in-law. As well as our kids, obviously.' Jackie had a grown-up son and daughter, both of whom had partners.

'You've got enough of a houseful, then!' I laughed.

'I know, but we wouldn't have wanted you and Daisy to be on your own.'

'Thank you, love. But well, we won't, now. Actually, Lee's going to be there, too. Amelia's staying with him and his daughter, Grace, her best friend.'

'Lee from the salon?'

'Yes.'

'I didn't think you liked him much.'

'Well, I don't, not really. But it's not up to me who Kirsty invites, is it? Anyway, how's retirement going? Are you bored yet?'

'Not yet. I've been busy with Christmas stuff. I think I will be, though, after it's all over. I'll have to start knitting, or join a reading group or something.'

'Nothing wrong with that. You deserve some relaxation.'

'So do you, love. Have a good Christmas. Don't let Craig wind you up. Or Kirsty. Or Lee!'

'I won't,' I laughed.

I sat for a while after we both hung up, holding my phone, thinking about what she'd said. She was right: I wouldn't let any of them wind me up, as she put it. I'd be a gracious guest, grateful for Kirsty's hospitality, and hopefully even for Craig's cooking. And meanwhile, I'd get myself onto Poundland online tonight and buy Daisy's present, her stocking fillers, and all the presents for everyone else, and just hope against hope that I didn't go over my credit limit again. I was going to enjoy this Christmas, if it killed me.

## 23

Needless to say, I was being overly optimistic. I found out soon enough that I had, of course, again gone over my credit limit, and had a fee added to my next payment – which was already bigger than I could afford. My other credit cards were both already over the top, and I hadn't got any food shopping in yet for the week ahead. Most of my clients paid my tips in cash, which helped a little with day-to-day expenses, but I wouldn't get my December salary from Camel until after Christmas.

'Some employers pay their staff early this month,' Lee commented, raising his eyes at me.

'Yes, well, Camel isn't one of them, unfortunately.'

'Are you managing OK? With all the Christmas stuff?'

I stared at him. Hadn't he ever been taught that it was rude to ask people questions about money? I really wasn't in the mood to talk about how badly I was *not* managing. I'd actually gone to the bank and withdrawn most of the money from Daisy's savings account – the one thing I'd sworn to myself that I'd never, ever do. I felt sick just thinking about it, and even sicker thinking about how I'd spent most of it already.

'Sorry,' he said, seeing the look on my face. 'I wasn't prying. It's just that we were talking about it the other day, weren't we – about buying presents – and I could see you were worried.'

'Isn't everyone, at this time of year?' I shot back. Then the bell over the door jingled. 'Ah, hello, Mrs Watson, come in. Cut and blow-dry today, isn't it?'

I turned my back on Lee and tried to concentrate on my client, but I found it hard to listen to her rambling story about a present she'd bought for her husband that had to be sent back, without my thoughts turning again to my own problems. If I couldn't get a grip on things now, and quickly, and permanently, I was going to have no other option but to go back to Kirsty asking for more money. And this time, she'd insist on telling Craig he had to give me more. The humiliation would be even worse than all this worry. Or would it? Wasn't Kirsty right – why shouldn't he give me more? But a nagging little voice in my head was telling me that if he knew why I was in so much debt, he'd refuse to give me another penny. He'd be disgusted with me. Everybody would. And I couldn't blame them.

\* \* \*

Lee and I left work at the same time that evening, and he caught me up as I walked back to the car park.

'Got time to stop somewhere for a quick coffee before you go and collect Daisy?' he asked cheerfully.

'Not really,' I said, wondering why on earth he suddenly wanted to be so friendly.

'That's a shame.' He fell into step beside me, and we walked in silence for a moment before he sighed and started, hesitantly, 'Look, I don't know what I've said. I mean, sorry, I know you thought I was out of order, asking if you were managing financially. I didn't mean to be rude, I was just concerned for you. But, well, I'm aware there's, generally, a kind of, what you might call *frostiness* between us, isn't there?'

'Is there?' I retorted without turning to look at him.

'You know there is. And OK, I can ignore it at work – we don't get a lot of chance to talk, anyway. But I wouldn't like it to spoil the atmosphere at Kirsty's place on Christmas Day, and I'm sure you wouldn't want that, either. So whatever it is I've said or done to upset you, do you think we could try to get along together then, at least? For their sakes, and the kids' sakes?' There was a hint of a smile in his voice as he added, 'Well, for our own sakes too. It would be a shame not to enjoy Christmas, wouldn't it?'

For a minute I didn't know how to respond. He was right, of course – I knew that perfectly well. However much I resented his nosiness about my affairs, it would be the decent thing to do, to try to get on with him over Christmas.

'OK,' I agreed, still not looking at him. 'Point taken.'

'Good. Well, have a nice evening, Tasha.'

'You too,' I said between my teeth. And despite myself, I knew it wasn't his fault – wasn't anyone's fault except my own – that I wasn't going to have a nice evening at all. I was going to give Daisy the last couple of fish fingers from the freezer, with half the last tin of baked beans, the remainder of which I'd have on toast after she was in bed, so that she couldn't ask me why I wasn't having a *real dinner*. Then I'd have to sit on my hands to stop myself from going online and throwing away more money that I didn't even have. And probably end up crying again. How had it come to this?

\* \* \*

Daisy was going to the pantomime with her class the next day. I was hoping this would cheer her up, and stop her complaining that she wanted to go to Freya's school, but she didn't look particularly excited as she got ready for bed that evening.

'Are you looking forward to the show tomorrow?' I asked her, and she put her head on one side, as if she was trying to decide.

'I am, a bit,' she conceded. 'It's better than being the only one staying in school.'

It was because she'd told me everyone else in her class was going to the pantomime that I'd found the money for it, from my tips, before I could spend it on food.

I asked her whether she'd spoken to Izzie about sitting together in the theatre but she just shrugged and picked up her book, wanting me to read her a story. I felt a shiver of concern. Mr Frost had been hoping this new little girl would help Daisy to turn the corner, but it seemed it was making no difference.

'Daisy,' I said, suddenly deciding now that I had to take the plunge and ask her outright about this, 'are you frightened to talk to Izzie?'

She looked away and shrugged again.

'Why would you be frightened, Daisy?' I asked gently.

'I don't know,' she said, her bottom lip beginning to tremble.

I put my arms around her. I didn't want to make her cry, but I sensed I might be on the edge of a breakthrough here. I needed her to open up to me. I needed to find out if Mr Frost was right, and it would be helpful if I could find out before I called the surgery, as I'd promised myself, to make an appointment during the forthcoming school holiday. 'I just want to help you, sweetheart. I know this is upsetting you, and all I want to do is make you happier.'

Tears began to run down Daisy's pink little cheeks.

'Are you frightened to talk to *anyone* at school?' I went on more quietly, pulling her even closer and holding her tight, wanting her to feel safe enough to confide in me.

'I can't,' she whispered against my ear.

'You can't talk to them because you still feel shy? Or do some of the children frighten you?' I prompted her.

'No.'

It was like teasing the words out of her, one by one. I wanted to stop – I was obviously making her even more unhappy. I could feel the wetness of her cheeks against mine and it was breaking my heart. But I had to go on. I felt like we were so close to getting to the truth now.

'Daisy, if anyone's frightening you, I need to know,' I began. 'Because—'

'I'm not frightened!' she burst out, suddenly struggling to get out of my arms and trying to hide her face under her bedclothes. 'I just *can't*,' she went on, really quietly as if she was talking into her pillow. 'I can't.'

'You try to talk to them, but you can't?' I asked her gently, stroking her hair, my heart in my mouth. 'Why can't you, poppet? What happens when you try?'

'I just *can't* talk to them, Mummy, my voice won't come out, it just *won't*, even if I try really hard to push it out, it won't!'

'So you don't ever talk, at school, at all? Not to any of the children? Not even to Mr Frost? Why haven't you told me this before, baby?'

She threw the duvet off her face again and sat up, suddenly animated, as if all the words, all the anxiety and fear she'd been hiding from me, were coming rushing out in a torrent, along with the tears.

'I didn't want to tell you, because it's silly. Because I'm six, not a baby, I can talk at home, I can talk at the big house, why can't I talk at school? Everyone thinks I'm a baby, they must do, they must hate me—'

'No, they wouldn't do, Daisy, if they knew—'

'They would!' she shouted. All the emotion she'd been bottling up about this seemed to have burst out suddenly in a huge outpouring of grief and shame and fear. 'They think I'm weird, even Mr Frost must think it because I can't even talk to him, and I want to, I really try hard to talk to him but it comes out like this.' She whispered the last few words, starting to cry again.

'All right,' I soothed her. 'Don't cry. It's just being at the new school that's made you lose your voice there, OK? I just wish you'd told me this before, sweetie.'

'I didn't want to tell you. I thought you'd say I was being silly, cos I talk to *you,* don't I, and I talk to Freya and—'

'Of course I wouldn't have said you were silly. I'm so glad you've told me now.'

'Is that why nobody at school likes me,' she asked sadly, 'because I can't talk to them?'

'I'm sure they don't dislike you, they probably just think you're really, really shy so it's better to leave you alone,' I managed to say, holding her tight while I tried to keep my own tears back.

Why had it taken me so long to have this conversation? Despite Mr Frost telling me he thought there was a problem, I'd buried my head in the sand for too long, and even since I'd begun to suspect he was right, I hadn't sat her down and asked her enough questions to get to the truth. I'd been too afraid of upsetting her, but I hadn't been doing my daughter any favours by putting it off. I could have already started getting her the help she needed – whatever that was. Well, I just hoped it wasn't too late. I wasn't going to put it off any longer now.

'I want to have friends,' she said miserably. 'I want to talk to them but I just can't get the words out of my mouth.'

'It's all right, Daise, please don't cry, I'm going to see what we can do to help you, OK? It's not your fault – that's what you need to understand. It's just a little problem, but what are little problems to superheroes like us, eh? I'll find out how to help you, and before long you'll be chatting away at school just like you do here at home. And at the big house! You were quiet when you first went there, weren't you, but not now.'

'My words wouldn't come out when I went there, either, at first,' she admitted. 'But then Freya and Kirsty were nice to me and I managed to push my words out, and now I don't even have to try.'

'So that's how you'll be when you're at school, eventually.'

'But I want to talk to Izzie tomorrow. I want to ask her to sit next to me.'

'Well...' I looked down at her, thoughtfully. 'Why don't you just take hold of her hand when everyone lines up to get on the coach? And give her a smile.'

'She might not like me holding her hand.'

'But you won't know until you try. And if she doesn't, you won't have lost anything.'

'Then I'll still be the same. The person with no friends,' she said with an air of resignation. 'Apart from Freya.'

'But you'll still be going to a pantomime. As well as going to play with Freya after school. And I'm going to do whatever I can to help you to talk to Izzie soon. I promise.'

I wondered how I even dared to make that promise.

Because the truth was, I had no idea how I was going to help her. But I was going to find out. Because I was going to call the doctors' surgery the very next day and ask for an urgent appointment. No more putting it off. No more head in the sand. Daisy needed me to get this sorted out now.

* * *

As soon as Daisy was asleep, I messaged Mr Frost to tell him I'd had a breakthrough, that Daisy had finally confided in me and that I was going to book an appointment with my doctor. I also told him that I'd suggested Daisy could try to show Izzie, without words, that she wanted to be her friend. His reply was very encouraging. I then called Craig, and poured out the whole story, refusing to let him interrupt me with his protests that there was nothing wrong with Daisy. I'd made the mistake of listening to him before.

'I'm going to try for an urgent appointment with the GP,' I told him. 'I'll let you know when it is, and you can either come with me and support me, or you can keep your head in the sand. I did that for too long myself. This is real, Craig. Our daughter has a problem, and we need to help her.'

I felt better for spelling it out to him. I called the surgery as soon as they were open the next morning and got an appointment for the day after Boxing Day, which was apparently as urgent as they could give me. I then spent most of the day at work wondering how Daisy had got on with Izzie and whether she'd enjoyed the pantomime. She was in a happy mood, of course, when I went to collect her from Whitegate House, and when I asked her, on the way home, whether she'd sat next to Izzie for the outing, she said yes, they'd held hands to get on the coach and sat together at the pantomime.

'That's good, then!'

'Yes, so at least I've got one friend at school, even if I can't talk to her.' She was silent for a moment before going on, 'I still wish I was at Freya's school, though. Freya talks about it all the time, she says it's really good there, and she thinks I would love it too, and I'm going to save up all my piggy bank money until I've got enough to pay for going there.'

I felt myself go cold. Daisy didn't know there wasn't anything left in her piggy bank – I'd hidden it temporarily and luckily it was too difficult for her to open it on her own, anyway. I needed to put that money back, quickly, before she started looking for it. I'd managed to buy one of her favourite Lego sets for her Christmas present, and some token gifts for everyone else for Christmas Day, and by the time she broke up from school I had everything wrapped up ready. Kirsty had told me several times not to bring any contributions of food, saying she'd already ordered everything in advance, but I didn't feel right about going empty-handed, so I'd bought a cheap bottle of wine and some mince pies from Asda. The pies were on their best-before date and reduced, but I hoped she wouldn't notice that.

I couldn't remember ever feeling so low and depressed.

After Daisy was in bed on Christmas Eve, too excited to sleep because of Father Christmas coming, I sat on my own in my living room, looking at the shabby décor, which I'd originally hoped to change soon after moving in but couldn't afford to, and looked at what I was eating for my own dinner – eggs on toast – and wondered how the hell I'd managed to get myself into such a state. I glanced at my laptop. I shouldn't; I really shouldn't keep going online, kidding myself that I was just playing a little game to keep myself occupied, kidding myself that I was simply trying to put things right, but always

ending up making everything even worse by getting deeper
and deeper into debt. I knew I shouldn't, mustn't – knew in my
heart of hearts that I had to resist that urge. But on the other
hand, I'd feel so much happier, so much more ready to face
Christmas, if I could just get lucky this one time. I needed to
give this up, that was obvious, but perhaps I could make it my
New Year's resolution: to completely stop from the first of
January – to stop, and never start again.

## 24

'Look what Father Christmas brought me!' Daisy squealed as she burst into my bedroom at five o'clock in the morning. 'Look, Mummy! A new bobble hat!' She'd put it on, pulling it right down to her eyes, adding a festive touch to her old pyjamas which were really too small for her. 'And look!' She tipped her Christmas stocking out onto the middle of the bed as I struggled to sit up and open my eyes properly. 'Some sweets! And some pens and a colouring book, and some hair bands, and a game, and—'

'My goodness, Father Christmas *was* kind to you, wasn't he?' I said, feeling a flood of relief that she was still young enough to be thrilled with a bag full of bargains from Pound-land. 'Well, happy Christmas, sweetie. But it's still not even properly morning – look, it's still really dark outside. How about trying to go back to sleep for a little while?'

'Can't I go back in my room and play with my toys?'

'I don't want you to be tired halfway through the day. Why not just snuggle down with me until it's time for breakfast?'

She agreed, quite happily, but while I closed my eyes and

tried my best to get a few more minutes of peace, Daisy fidgeted about next to me, looking at her colouring book, and her new book, then opening the box of her new game and trying to put the hair bands in her hair, until eventually I gave up. I hadn't had much sleep at all; I'd gone to bed late, furious with myself for once again giving in to my urge to go online and waste even more money that I didn't have. I'd tossed and turned all night, sick with self-recrimination and sheer panic at the realisation that I'd given into the urge so easily, somehow managing to convince myself that this time it would be OK – not only OK, in fact, but that finally I'd win, finally be able to make everything all right again.

'Right,' I said eventually, when obviously neither of us were going back to sleep, 'let's get up, then. I've got a present for you somewhere!' I reached into my hiding place in my wardrobe. 'Here you are. I hope you like it, sweetheart.'

She ripped the wrapping paper off, squealing with excitement.

'Oh, it's Lego, it's the one Freya's got! Thank you, Mummy.' Then her face dropped for a moment. 'I haven't got you anything.'

In the past, of course, Craig used to buy something for her to give me.

'Don't worry about that. There might be presents for all of us at Daddy and Kirsty's house.'

We'd arranged to go there around midday, so it felt like a long morning from when we ate breakfast at six o'clock. I helped Daisy to start putting her Lego Treehouse set together, then we watched some TV and waited for the time to pass, while I tried my best to put my worries, and my guilty conscience, to the back of my mind and pretend to feel happy and festive.

'Hello Daisy!' squealed Freya at the top of her voice, literally jumping up and down on the spot as we walked into Kirsty's hallway and exchanged kisses. 'What did you get for Christmas? I got a *massive* doll's house, it's got real electric lights, and a TV and everything, and we can both play with it at the same time, come and have a look, it's upstairs in my room, and we can move the furniture around and—'

'All right, Freya, calm down and give everyone a chance to get inside and get their coats off!' Kirsty laughed. 'What time were you woken up this morning?' she added quietly to me.

'Five. How about you?'

'Same.'

We both laughed, and suddenly, listening to the two girls chatting eagerly together about their presents, I managed to start putting my issues to one side and feeling a bit more cheerful.

'Hi, Tash. Happy Christmas.' Craig came out into the hallway, wearing a garish Christmas jumper and holding out his hands as if he wasn't sure whether or not it would be appropriate to hug me.

'Happy Christmas.' I turned away from the possibility of a hug. It might have been the season of goodwill, but I didn't think we needed to go that far.

While Daisy ran upstairs with Freya to look at the new doll's house, I followed Kirsty into the kitchen, taking my pathetic contributions.

'I told you not to bring anything,' she chided me.

'That's hardly anything. I'm sorry it isn't more.'

'Stop it, Tasha,' she said firmly. 'I don't want to hear any more of that today, OK? I enjoy hosting Christmas, I enjoy treating my family and my guests to nice things – please let me have that pleasure and don't feel guilty about it.'

'OK. Well, thank you. I really appreciate it. The turkey smells delicious already,' I added.

'Craig's supposed to be looking after it. I'll remind him to check it again in a minute. Oh – there's the doorbell again. It must be Lee and the girls.'

Apparently Kirsty had offered to have Amelia back for Christmas Eve night but she refused to come, wanting to stay with Grace. And Kirsty went on to tell me that she'd had a talk with her about whether she might want to come back to live with the family again at some point – but only if she'd changed her attitude while she'd been away, and if Daisy and I were happy to give her another chance.

I was surprised to hear Kirsty had made this offer, and it made me reflect that she was, after all, a mother who loved her daughter but had just reached the end of her tether. But I couldn't help thinking that few girls of her age would react kindly to an invitation home being phrased quite like that. Then again, didn't I hope, more than anyone, that Amelia could change her attitude?

She looked a little less surly than usual when she walked in, but immediately went to sit with Grace in the lounge without talking to any of us. I felt a shiver of unease. I really hoped she wasn't going to spoil Christmas for Kirsty, or for any of us. I still felt like I'd need to watch her if she went anywhere near Daisy.

'Happy Christmas, Tasha.' Lee leant in and gave me a peck on the cheek before I could avoid it. 'This is for you,' he added, handing me a brightly wrapped package. 'It's not much,' he added quietly.

'Thank you. Here's yours. It isn't much either!'

We both laughed, and I felt the ice was broken a little. I remembered my promise to make an effort today, and when I unwrapped my gift to find a box of my favourite chocolates, I thanked him quite genuinely.

'You've mentioned a couple of times that you like those,' he said with a smile. He held up the cheap pair of socks I'd bought him and added, 'And I know I mentioned that I needed some of these! Thanks.'

When we'd all finished unwrapping our presents, Kirsty got to her feet and tapped a spoon against her wine glass.

'Sorry to interrupt all the jollity,' she said, beaming. 'But Craig and I have an announcement to make.'

The room fell silent; all eyes turned to the host and hostess.

'We wanted you all to hear the news first,' she went on. 'We're going to need you to save a date for us. We're getting married.'

There was a hush. I felt my head spin. I looked at Craig, but he wouldn't meet my eyes. The silence lasted for just a moment longer than would have been polite, before finally Lee raised his glass and called out, 'Well, congratulations to you both.'

'Yes,' I croaked. I cleared my throat. It was hurting me even to say it. 'Um, congratulations.'

There was a crash, as Amelia got to her feet, stomped out of the room with a face like thunder, and slammed the door. Grace, looking around guiltily and saying a faint, 'Er, congratulations,' got up and ran after her.

'What's happened, Mummy?' Daisy asked anxiously, shifting closer to me on the sofa and leaning against me, obviously picking up on the sudden tension in the room.

'Are you getting *married*, Mummy?' Freya squawked to Kirsty, sounding horrified. 'Aren't you too old?'

Fortunately, this did at least lighten the mood a little. Kirsty laughed, a false-sounding high-pitched giggle, and told Freya that no, nobody ever got too old to get married, anybody who was in love could get married – and then probably regretted her words as Freya proceeded to make a great show of asking Daisy to marry her, because she was her best friend and she loved her. Throughout all this, Craig sat with a fixed grin on his face, thanking us for our proffered congratulations and still avoiding eye contact with me.

The bastard. All those years we were together, he'd professed that marriage was unnecessary, a waste of time and money, and furthermore, it was merely society's trick to keep people together who should have been free to leave.

'You should know I'll never leave you,' he used to say, which seemed so ironic now. 'You shouldn't need a ceremony and a piece of paper to convince you. I'm your husband, you're my wife, we've decided for ourselves, we don't need anyone's blessing.'

I drained my glass of wine, put the glass down with a little too much of a thud, and stared at him across the room. It wasn't as if I still wanted to marry him – I couldn't think of anything I wanted less. To be honest, I was surprised Kirsty wanted to marry him, now that she'd had time to find out what he was really like.

Lee was looking at me across the room.

'Are you all right?' he mouthed, and I nodded. I was fine. Absolutely fine. Nothing to see here.

'We're hoping to have the wedding as soon as possible, and I've got a venue in mind that could do it in the middle of January,' Kirsty was going on, smiling happily and seemingly blissfully unaware of any tension. 'We'd like you to be there. And we'd like to have two very special little bridesmaids. We'd like Amelia too, of course, but we'll have to work on that one!' She gave a little laugh before turning her beatific smile to

Freya and Daisy. 'Would you do that for us, girls? Would you like to be bridesmaids when Craig and I get married?'

'YEEEES!' shouted Freya, jumping to her feet and pulling Daisy up beside her. 'I'll be a bridesmaid, so will Daisy, won't you, Daisy? I've never been a bridesmaid; *all* my friends at school have been bridesmaids apart from me. Can I carry flowers? Can I wear a pink dress? Can I have flowers in my hair too? Can I—'

'All right, Freya, calm down,' Kirsty said, laughing. 'We'll work out all the details together, OK?'

The two girls went into a huddle, talking about dresses and flowers and new shoes, and my heart sank again at the thought of the expense.

'I'll be paying for everything, of course,' Kirsty said, looking across the room at me. 'That goes without saying.'

Of course it did. The ever-magnanimous, ever-loaded Kirsty would insist on paying for everything. Why had I ever thought I liked her? Suddenly, I was going off her again, rapidly. As for Craig, he looked as if the whole topic was beginning to bore him. He got up and gathered the empty glasses, asking who wanted a refill, and when he carried them out to the kitchen, I followed him.

'You could have warned me,' I said.

'I didn't realise she was going to do it like that,' he said, finally turning to look at me. 'I thought we'd tell you quietly, on our own.'

'You should have done. You, not Kirsty. It would have been...' I sighed. 'Oh, why am I even bothering to talk to you? You've got no idea, have you? But well done, I suppose you've done what you set out to do, now.'

'What's that supposed to mean?'

'You've netted the prize fish, haven't you? Money, lifestyle, big house, never really have to work hard again or worry about anything.'

'It isn't like that.'

'Isn't it?' I shot back, giving him a sharp look. 'Well, if you say so. I'll have another glass of wine if you're pouring.'

I carried my wine and my resentment back into the lounge and sat, brooding angrily to myself, while Lee tried to talk to me – gently, as if I were an invalid – about Christmases he'd known and loved, sounding very much like someone who was just talking for the sake of it, in the desperate hope of trying to keep things normal.

'Aren't you drinking?' I asked him, finally noticing as I finished my second glass off, a little too fast, that his glass contained orange juice.

'I was a bit too thirsty for a wine,' he said with a shrug. 'And anyway, I'll be driving home tonight. The girls and I aren't staying over. I think it goes without saying that Amelia's coming back with us.'

I was beginning to wish I wasn't staying over either, now. But I was relieved to hear Amelia wouldn't be around overnight. I'd planned to tell Daisy to wake me up if she needed to go to the bathroom so that I could make sure she wasn't attacked.

We didn't actually see Amelia or Grace again until they were called to come downstairs for dinner. Amelia sat at the table with a face like thunder, and halfway through eating her turkey, suddenly put down her fork and announced that there was *no fucking way* she'd go to this *ridiculous fucking wedding* – at which Kirsty got to her feet and told her in deadly tones to get out of the room and not to dare, ever again, use such language in their home and especially not in front of the little ones.

There was an uncomfortable silence after she'd stormed out again, with Grace looking awkwardly at her plate, probably unsure whether to go after her friend or finish her dinner, Kirsty apologising to us all profusely, Craig just looking uncomfortable, and Freya, for once, shocked into silence. Daisy nudged me.

'Mummy,' she said, sounding puzzled.

'Ssh. Eat your dinner up.'

'But...' She raised her voice to be heard above the inappropriately jolly Christmas song playing from Kirsty's music system. 'But Mummy, what does *focking* mean?'

\* \* \*

'You didn't have to laugh,' I told Lee ruefully, after we'd all finished eating and gone back to collapse with coffee in the lounge.

'I think it was the best thing I could have done,' he retorted with a grin. 'It lightened the mood, didn't it?'

'I suppose so. Poor Amelia,' I added quietly. 'For once, I found myself in agreement with her.'

'Ah, I can understand how you feel, Tasha, but life's too short. Let them get on with it. Live your own life.'

'Easy for you to say,' I began, then stopped and corrected myself. 'Sorry. It can't have been easy for you, at all.'

'No. It hasn't been. But we survive. We have to.' He nodded at Daisy, who lay stretched out on the floor at the other end of the lounge with Freya, playing a game of Connect Four. 'If we have kids, we have to.'

'Yes.' I was surprised how relaxed I felt in his company for once. I found myself thinking I'd probably quite like him if only I didn't feel like he was interrogating me in every conversation.

I spent a while in the kitchen helping Kirsty to load the dishwasher and tidy everything away. I felt awkward with her now, and when she suddenly turned to say she was sorry, she probably should have told me quietly about the wedding at a more appropriate time, I just shook my head and said it was fine. I really didn't want to talk about it any more.

Lee and the two older girls left straight after we'd all somehow found room for sandwiches and Christmas cake, early in the evening, and both Daisy and Freya were rubbing their eyes and yawning, so I offered to take them up to bed and settle down for the night myself.

'Father Christmas's reindeer must have woken me up early this morning,' I joked – but nobody laughed.

It was a relief to lay my head on the pillow and close my eyes. And so what if a few tears escaped through my eyelids before I fell asleep? They must have been tears of exhaustion.

## 25

I felt better on Boxing Day. To be honest, it hadn't helped that I'd been so tired when it had all kicked off the previous day. I lay in bed for a while after I woke up, thinking things through. Did I *really* care if Kirsty and Craig got married? It wasn't as if I was ever going to want him back. No, it was just the insensitive way she'd announced it, and at least she'd realised – at least she'd apologised. Perhaps Lee was right: we had enough to worry about in our own lives, without giving a fig what Kirsty and Craig did. Besides, Daisy was obviously excited about the whole bridesmaid thing, and I wouldn't want to spoil that for her. No, I'd just have to accept it and try not to care that my so-anti-marriage boyfriend had somehow changed his mind when there was a fortune to be shared. If anything, it just made me look down on him even more.

It was a fairly quiet day, if anything could ever be quiet while Freya was around. We all went out for a walk with the dog, which gave us an appetite for a light buffet lunch of cold turkey, ham and salad.

'I think Daisy and I should probably head off now,' I said as I helped Kirsty clear up afterwards.

'Oh, you don't have to! Stay for supper! We can play some games.'

'No, honestly, it's fine. I've got work tomorrow. Thank you so much for your hospitality.'

'You're both very welcome. And look, I'll say it again: I'm sorry if I misjudged things yesterday. I really wouldn't have wanted to hurt you, Tasha. You're my friend now, I'd never want to do that. Do you believe me?'

She looked at me with those wide, innocent blue eyes, pleading with me to say that we were still friends, and I just didn't have it in me to say anything other than yes, of course, everything was fine.

'And as for the incident with Amelia, I can't apologise enough. Her language! I don't know where she learnt that from, but it can't possibly have been from Tudor Hall.'

I laughed. Was she really so naïve? 'Oh, I think that word is very common with kids these days. I doubt the pupils at Tudor Hall are any less capable of swearing than those at state schools.'

'Really? You think so? Well, I feel inclined to have a word with the head teacher about it. It's not acceptable, not when you consider the fees we're paying – to say nothing of all the work I do on the board of governors.'

I just shook my head, smiling. She really *was* naïve if she thought her money would make any difference to the way her daughter spoke when she was angry. And I could understand her anger. She was still grieving the loss of her father. She didn't like Craig – that was obvious – and of course she was going to resent her mother marrying him. But that was as far as I was prepared to go with my sympathy. I hoped for everyone's sake that in the end, she'd give in and go to the wedding, even if she didn't want to be a bridesmaid.

I warned Daisy that we were getting ready to go home, and went back upstairs to pack my things. As I walked along the corridor to the guest bedroom, passing Amelia's room, something made me decide to have a look inside. I'd never seen the inside of her room, as she always kept it closed whether she was in there or not. I don't know what I was looking for; I told myself I was just curious about how she'd left it: tidy, empty and deserted, never to be returned to? Or still essentially Amelia's special space? My first thought was right: the room was stripped bare of everything but the furniture, giving it a sad, unloved appearance. I was just about to quietly close the door again when something caught my eye – something small and bright blue, lying on the dressing table as if it had been overlooked. I recognised it straight away as the memory stick I'd found before, stuck in Amelia's laptop. The memory stick that might have her diary on it – her diary, where she'd mentioned Daisy. Without even giving it a second thought, I went in, picked it up and took it into the guest room to put in my bag. I didn't feel the slightest twinge of guilt. If somebody was writing stuff about my daughter, I felt entitled to read it. I'd bring it back and leave it lying where I'd found it, when I'd finished. Amelia wouldn't be coming here to look for it, anyway.

Needless to say, Daisy didn't want to say goodbye to Freya, but I reminded her that she'd be coming back the next day, and every day of her school holiday while I was working.

'Freya will get fed up with you if you stay much longer,' I teased her.

'I wouldn't, not ever!' Freya replied. 'We need to plan our wedding, don't we, Daisy?'

* * *

'I do love Freya,' Daisy said solemnly on the way home. 'But I don't know if I really want to marry her. Do you think I should say so?'

'I wouldn't worry,' I said. 'She'll probably change her mind by the time you're both grown up.'

'Like Daddy changed his mind? Did he want to marry you and now he wants to marry Kirsty?'

'Oh, he was never going to marry me,' I said, keeping my tone as light as I could. 'Daddy and I just wanted to have a lovely little girl together, that's all.'

'And after you had me, he wanted to marry Kirsty?'

'Something like that.'

'So who are *you* going to marry, Mummy?' She thought for a moment, and then went on, excitedly. 'I know! You could marry Lee, because he hasn't got anyone to marry either.'

I laughed. 'I don't think so. I'm quite OK without being married, thank you.'

* * *

After Daisy was in bed that night, I put the memory stick into my laptop and found the file titled 'My Diary'. I started reading, but the entries seemed to be from some years earlier, as Amelia was mentioning her father, describing days out they used to have together and funny things he used to say. I intended to skip forward to find the more recent entries, but it was actually quite fascinating, reading her schoolgirl thoughts and dreams from more innocent times. Perhaps she really had only become so difficult since her father had died. I wished, again, that I could be more sympathetic to the unpleasant girl she seemed to be now – but I couldn't afford that sympathy, not when she'd been putting my own daughter at risk. I closed the laptop with a sigh, deciding to look at some more recent entries the next evening. I didn't really know what I was hoping to find. Some evidence, I supposed, that Daisy hadn't been fabricating or exaggerating her claims against Amelia. I wanted to ease my conscience about the girl being sent away from her home.

\* \* \*

It was unusually quiet at work the next day. I had one regular lady to do a blow-dry for, and Lee had just one mother who'd brought her two little boys in for haircuts. Camel was in a strangely magnanimous mood, telling us at lunchtime that we might as well all finish early as it was unlikely we'd get any more walk-ins during the afternoon.

'That's a first!' I commented to Lee as we left the salon together.

'Well, she was probably bored. Are you going straight back for Daisy?'

'I suppose so, although I doubt she'll be happy about being brought home early from Freya.'

He smiled. 'How about a cup of tea and a toastie?'

'No, I don't think—'

'My treat,' he went on. 'Come on, we should be celebrating getting off work early – it'll probably never happen again.'

'That's true.' I had to admit, at the mention of a toastie, my stomach had rumbled. I hadn't had time at home that morning to make myself a sandwich to bring in as usual. 'OK, then, why not? But I'll pay for my own.' I was sure even I could rake up the money for a toasted sandwich.

We were sitting for a while with our hot toasties and tea, making small talk about the salon, and about Christmas Day at Whitegate House, before the subject changed to our working hours and I was suddenly overcome with curiosity again about his evening work. I decided that, as he seemed to have no boundaries himself when asking questions about my own life, I might as well do the same and just ask him about it.

'Kirsty happened to mention you had another job – in the evenings,' I said casually.

'Yes. Although I'm hoping I might not need it for much longer.'

'Oh. Why's that?' I asked. Perhaps Kirsty was giving him so much money for having Amelia staying with him that he was in a better financial position.

'I'm expecting to be a bit better off, in the near future,' he said, smiling. 'The restaurant work was only ever meant to be a short-term thing. Just kind of bridging the gap.'

So it wasn't even hairdressing he was doing in the evenings.

'Has Camel promised us all a pay rise, or something?' I asked. It was a joke, of course, but if only it could be true!

'What? No, of course not – I'd have told you!' He laughed. 'No, I'm expecting an insurance payout. It's taken far too long to come through, but finally, finally, my solicitor says it's imminent. It should be a fair amount. Not that it makes up for what happened.'

'What happened?' I repeated.

'To my wife. She died in a road accident, Tasha. It was a drunk driver. There's—'

'Oh, Lee.' I felt terrible now for persisting with my questions. He probably didn't really want to talk about this at all. 'I'm so sorry. I didn't know.'

'Why would you? I tend to avoid talking about it. But it's

fine, no, don't apologise. The thing is, you see, there's a bereavement settlement; it's obviously never going to be enough to compensate for what happened, but I'm entitled to it, so I wanted my solicitor to fight for it. And there was a fight: the driver's insurers were trying all manner of loopholes to get out of paying up. But it's apparently going into my bank account next week – at last.'

'I'm glad.'

'It'll help. It means I can afford the school fees for the rest of this school year. After that, I may have to think again. Grace might have to accept that she'll end her education at the local high school. But she's a sensible girl – not spoilt. She knows that's on the cards.'

'Amelia would miss her at Tudor Hall,' I commented.

'Yes. Well, I don't have Kirsty's kind of wealth. Kate – my wife – was the one with the better-paid career, and she didn't take out life insurance, unfortunately. Nobody ever thinks they might die in their early thirties.'

'Of course not, no.'

'So I had to downsize from our four-bed detached house after she died. Still,' he went on, putting on a cheerful face. 'I'll be OK for a while now, with the insurance money, together with what Kirsty's giving me for her daughter's keep. I thought that was only going to be temporary, but it looks like it might be ongoing, now, for a while at least.'

'Well, you'll be earning that, having Amelia living with you.'

He shrugged. 'She's no trouble to me at all.'

'I must admit, I did feel a bit sorry for Amelia on Christmas Day. The wedding announcement was pretty tactless.'

'Yes – for you as well as for Amelia. She was never likely to take well to her mother marrying again, let alone announcing it so soon after she's kind of thrown Amelia out.'

'I know,' I said. 'I feel bad about the situation, but—'

'But you just have to protect Daisy, don't you,' he said firmly. 'I still don't understand that situation. I can't see why Amelia would find Daisy a threat – she's so much younger, and I'd have thought she'd be glad Daisy keeps Freya quiet? Well, not quiet, exactly—'

We both laughed. I looked at him, smiling as he ate the last mouthful of his toastie, and I understood that I'd had him wrong all along. He wasn't being rude or intrusive when he tried to talk to me about personal things – he was just trying to be friendly. He had his own issues, his own tragedy to come to terms with, his own daughter to look after as best he could. He was a nice guy. We could be friends.

'I enjoyed that,' I said as I finished my own toastie. 'I'm glad you suggested it.'

'Good.' He looked at me thoughtfully for a moment before adding, 'Look, as we seem to be having a bit of a heart-to-heart here today, I hope you won't be offended if I ask you something?'

'Go ahead,' I said, suddenly wary despite what I'd just been thinking.

'Well, it's a bit personal. But I've kind of got the impression you're in some sort of trouble.' He paused and gave me a very direct look. 'Financial trouble.'

'Aren't we all?' I replied, as a pathetic attempt at a joke. But my heart was racing and I could feel my face burning. He'd guessed. My humiliation was complete.

'Tasha, you don't have to tell me if you don't want to – of course not. But, well, I think it sometimes helps to confide in somebody.'

'There's nothing. I don't know why you think...' I muttered desperately. He was right, of course. I'd wanted to tell someone for longer than I could say. I'd considered telling Jackie, but she'd have been too nice to me. She'd have been shocked, but would have hidden it. Perhaps Lee would give me what I knew I needed: some sharp words of disapproval. Perhaps he'd tell me to stop – just stop. Why *couldn't* I stop?

'OK, forget I asked,' he said gently, pushing his plate to one side and turning round to get his coat.

'I keep losing money!' I said it in a rush, looking down at my empty plate.

He turned back to me, his face calm and sympathetic. 'Gambling?'

'No! No, it isn't gambling. It's just... really silly. It's just bingo, online bingo, but—'

'That's gambling, Tasha,' he said softly. 'Give it its name. It's nothing to be ashamed of.'

'I *am* ashamed! It's ridiculous, I can't seem to stop myself. I've lost so much money, and I can't afford to. I'm letting my daughter down – letting everyone down. I can't ask Craig to give me more money – I know he should – but how can I, when I'm just spending it on bingo? I keep saying I won't do it any more, but then I get a little win, and I think, OK, one more time, but then I keep going, I can't stop, I just keep on until I've lost loads. I empty my bank account and have to transfer money from my credit card and now I'm in terrible trouble, I've got nothing left. I've taken money from Daisy's savings account, emptied her piggy bank – what kind of parent does that?'

I realised, to my further embarrassment, that I now had tears streaming down my face. I wiped them away, crossly. Why was I telling him all this? Why Lee, when I couldn't even bring myself to tell Jackie, my closest friend?

'What kind of parent? A desperate one,' he answered me quietly. 'And sorry, but also – an addicted one.'

'I'm *not* an addict!' I retorted. 'It's just *bingo*, for God's sake!'

'If you can't stop yourself from doing it, even though you want to, even though you know you should and it's getting you into trouble, you're addicted. Trust me, I know. I'm an addict myself.'

I looked up at him, shocked. 'You? You're a gambler? Is that why you needed to work another job?'

'No!' He smiled ruefully. 'No, that's all the fault of the school fees. I'm not a gambler, Tasha. I'm an alcoholic.'

'An alco—' I stared back at him, remembering the alcohol-free drinks at Jackie's leaving do, the fruit juice on Christmas Day. He'd been driving, so it hadn't seemed odd. But...

'I've been sober for eighteen months.'

'Since... your wife died?'

'Exactly.' He sighed. 'She'd been telling me for years that I had a problem, but I wouldn't listen, couldn't admit it. After the accident – the fact that it was a drunk driver who killed her...' He shook his head. 'I knew I needed to get help. I didn't drink and drive, well, I hadn't ever done, anyway, up till then, but I knew it was a risk I might have taken one day, if the temptation had arisen. I couldn't have lived with myself, knowing that that driver, the driver I hated with all my heart for taking Kate's life, might have been me one day – that I might actually kill someone too. I went to AA, and I've never looked back.'

'You must be proud of yourself. You should be.'

'Yes, I am. And that's why I'm saying you should do the same. I imagine Gamblers Anonymous works the same way as AA. Everyone there will sympathise – they're all in the same boat, they'll all support you. Trust me, it's the only way.'

'I don't think I'm really at that stage yet, honestly. I'll make myself stop. I'll have to.'

'The longer you keep up the self-denial, the harder it'll be. Once you join GA, you won't be on your own.'

'But I feel so silly. It's just *bingo*.'

'That's probably half the problem. It sounds so innocuous, doesn't it?' he said sadly. 'Let's find the GA website. Right now, come on. Before you have time to talk yourself out of it.'

'I haven't talked myself into it yet,' I protested miserably. But as I watched him searching on his phone, as he sent me the postcode of the nearest branch of GA, and told me I was in luck, there was a meeting the next evening, I felt something totally unexpected. It was like I'd seen a light at the end of the tunnel. I'd told someone. I'd admitted it. I was being helped. By the very person I'd been grumbling to myself about because of what I considered his nosiness. He'd guessed I was in trouble, that was why he was asking questions. He wanted to help. I could have felt guilty, but there was no room in my head for that. All I could feel was relief.

## 26

'I don't suppose you'll want to ask Kirsty to babysit for you tomorrow evening,' Lee said casually as we walked to the car park.

'Oh, I hadn't thought about that.' But now I had, the very idea of telling Kirsty where I was going – assuming I even plucked up the courage to actually go – made me feel quite nauseous. 'Perhaps Jackie would—'

'Let me,' he said. 'Seriously, Tasha, I'd be happy to. Then you'll only need to have one person who knows about it.'

'What about Grace, and Amelia? Can you leave them on their own?'

He laughed. 'Of course. Grace has already turned thirteen, and Amelia's not far behind. Fortunately they're fine at home on their own for a few hours. Grace is used to it, from me doing the evening shift at the restaurant three days every week.'

'OK, then. Thank you, I really appreciate that. Daisy will be asleep, she's not normally any trouble.'

'And you won't be able to duck out of it at the last minute, if I'm there,' he added, giving me a grin.

'I'll still feel like it.' My heart was racing just at the thought of walking into a room full of strangers and admitting I had a problem. I didn't know how I was going to do it.

'I know,' he said sympathetically. And I felt some comfort from knowing he'd been through something similar – and seemed to have come out the other side unscathed.

'You do realise we've got another problem coming up, don't you?' I said. 'We're both invited to this wedding. It's bound to be on a Saturday. How are we both going to get the day off?'

'I did actually broach it casually with Camel today,' he said, to my surprise, 'as she was in a good mood. I said that if she could only let one of us have the time off, she should give it to you. It's more important for you to be there with Daisy.'

'Oh!' I was surprised, and grateful. 'What did she say?'

'That as soon as we knew the date, she'd book herself to do some of our clients, and give Jackie a call to see if she'd like one day's work, to take on the others.'

'Really? Wow, she *was* in a good mood!'

'That's why I decided to strike while the iron was hot,' he laughed. 'So hopefully we can both go.'

'That was nice of you, Lee. Thank you.'

* * *

I was glad to have finished work early, as I had the doctor's appointment that evening, about Daisy. I'd already arranged to leave her with Kirsty for a little longer than usual, and Craig had agreed to meet me at the surgery.

'You wanted to talk to me about your daughter?' Dr Salter said. 'I presume it's something you didn't want her to hear us discussing.'

'That's right. Plus, I doubt she'd have spoken to you if I'd brought her.'

'She's shy,' Craig put in.

'It's more than shyness,' I insisted. 'Her teacher's worried too. She doesn't speak at all, in class. She's told me she tries her hardest to talk to the other children, but her voice won't come out. She can only manage to answer the teacher in a whisper. He's taken the pressure off her now by not asking her questions directly. She's very unhappy about it, and I'm worried, too, that it'll affect her education.'

I went on to explain that Daisy had started at a new school in September, that we'd moved house and there'd been quite a lot of changes for her to face.

'Her father and I split up,' I said, indicating Craig, and the doctor nodded in understanding.

'But she's not shy at my house,' Craig said. 'In fact she's very vocal and lively.'

'She was quiet to begin with, though, wasn't she?' I reminded him. 'She says she found her voice because your partner's little girl was nice to her.'

'I see.' The doctor nodded again. 'Well, I think this sounds like what we call selective mutism. It's—'

'Daisy doesn't *select* it,' I retorted. 'She's very upset about it. She wants to be able to make friends – she certainly doesn't choose to be like this.'

'That's not what the term implies. It just means that she's not mute all the time; only in certain stressful situations. It sounds as if she's had to go through a lot, recently, and children react in different ways to stress and anxiety. You're quite right, she doesn't choose it, she can't help it.'

'So what can we do about it?' Craig demanded.

'I'm going to refer you to the speech and language therapy

clinic. The therapist will probably want to speak to you first, then they'll try to interact with Daisy—'

'But she probably won't be able to speak.'

'They're used to it,' Dr Salter said with a smile. 'They have ways and means of communicating.'

'OK.' I couldn't help feeling less than confident about how this was going to work.

'I'm sending the referral as urgent,' she went on. 'As this has already been going on for a few months, the sooner we get some help for Daisy, the better.'

'Agreed. Thank you.'

'Her teacher was right to alert you to the problem.'

Yes. And we were wrong to dismiss his concerns to begin with. But I could only hope we hadn't left it too late.

* * *

I'd planned to carry on reading Amelia's diary that evening, but as soon as I opened my laptop, the lure of the bingo site was stronger. By the time I went to bed, I'd lost even more money and was crying with self-disgust. Even now, now I'd accepted I had a problem, now I'd agreed I needed help, I couldn't stop myself, not even for a single evening. If nothing else, at least it made me determined to go to the GA meeting the next night. I'd told Daisy I was going out with a friend and that Lee would be downstairs if she woke up and needed anything, and she'd looked at me in surprise.

'Why can't I stay over with Freya, then?'

'Because I won't be out for long. So this is easier,' I said firmly. 'Kirsty doesn't want you there every time.'

'Yes she does! Freya does!'

'Well, sorry, but you'll be asleep the whole time I'm gone, so it would have been a waste of a visit to Freya's house.'

She'd shrugged moodily, and got ready for bed in a sulk, but I wasn't about to give in. Lee was right. I was happier if only one person knew about my problem – and he was the most appropriate. He understood.

The meeting was held in a church hall on the outskirts of town. I parked in the street nearby and felt my legs shaking as I walked up to the door. Hesitating even as I held the door handle, I dropped my hand again and wondered, even now, if I could walk away and try to cure myself instead.

'Hello,' said a friendly voice from behind me. I turned to see a young man, probably only in his twenties, smiling as he reached past me and opened the door wide, leaving me no real option other than to walk inside ahead of him. 'You're new here, aren't you?' he went on. 'I'm Dan. Don't look so scared. I know exactly how you feel, trust me, but we're all very friendly here. It's the one place where you can be sure nobody's going to judge you.'

He was right, I realised, taking a deep breath. As Lee had said, everyone here must be in the same boat. They would all know the desperation and the shame I was feeling, how much I wished, even now, that I was back at home, logging on, trying my luck.

The meeting was chaired by an older man called Hugh. I introduced myself shakily to the others, admitting that I was a gambler and needed help. Saying it out loud myself for the first time made me feel sick.

'Hello, Tasha,' everyone in the circle said together.

Hugh assured me that we were all the same, all there purely to help ourselves and each other to get well, that only our first names were required and anything we confided in the group would go no further.

'We never win,' said an elderly lady called Claire who told me she was going to be my sponsor. 'Other people who gamble can quit when they're winning, but we can't. We always end up losing.'

I realised she'd just put into words exactly what my problem was. It was a revelation to me, hearing it put like that, having to recognise the truth of her words. I never won, because I always kept going until I'd lost my winnings and lost even more. Every day, I lost more. I might as well have been standing outside my house giving my money away.

'How did I get myself into this situation?' I asked myself aloud, and Claire smiled at me.

'There are lots of reasons we start. Some like the risk, the excitement. Some are just desperate for money and won't give up... and then can't. Some just start because they're bored. It's the little wins that keep us going back for more. We get deceived into thinking it'll be worth it in the end.' She gave me a very direct look. 'It won't, not for us. Because we can't stop – that part of it is an illness, and we can only get better if we really want to.'

'I definitely do,' I assured her, then added, 'Have you got better? Stopped?'

'I hope so. But, well, you've heard about AA, and we're the same. We take one day at a time. If you manage not to gamble tonight, that'll be your first success. If you slip up another day, you'll remember that you *can* do it, and you'll try again.'

'Thanks so much,' I said when we said goodnight at the end of the meeting. 'I really should have come to a meeting months ago.'

'Nobody can help you till you're ready, love. But I can tell you are, now. I've got your number, and I'll call you in a couple of days to see how you're getting on.'

\* \* \*

Lee stayed for a coffee after I arrived home. He seemed to sense that I didn't want to talk too much about the meeting, but he lingered, and I knew why. He wanted to be with me for as long as possible, to prevent me going online.

'It's OK,' I said eventually. 'You don't need to keep guard any longer. I'll be going straight to bed.'

'Maybe leave your laptop and phone down here?' he suggested.

'Thanks. I really want to do it, Lee. But I need a distraction. Something else to do. My sponsor said a lot of people start through boredom, and I'm wondering if that was part of my problem: being on my own, after Daisy was in bed.'

'Good point. Maybe read a book?'

What I really wanted to do was start reading Amelia's diary – but I knew that once I'd turned on my laptop, it'd be too easy to make the same mistake as the previous evening. I had a couple of paperbacks upstairs that I hadn't started; perhaps I'd take Lee's advice and read until I fell asleep.

I was proud to tell Claire, when she called me a couple of days later, that that evening was my first success. I'd slipped up the following day, and I'd felt so cross with myself, but I actually managed to log off before I'd lost very much. I felt like I might be getting somewhere, already. The thought of replenishing Daisy's savings account was what was keeping me going.

\* \* \*

It was another week before I felt brave enough to turn on my laptop and read some more of Amelia's diary, without giving into temptation to slip over to the online bingo site. We were into January now, Daisy was back at school, and the appointment for the speech and language therapist had come through – it was in two weeks' time. I was pinning all my hopes on getting some help for her there.

This time when I opened up Amelia's document, I skipped forward a little. I read a few entries from when her father died – a horrible accident in their own garden – and once again I couldn't avoid a shiver of heartfelt sympathy for Amelia as I thought about her sudden loss.

> I can't believe my daddy's gone. Why did it have to happen? I can't stop crying, it's the worst thing that's ever happened, the worst thing in the world. Mum says it will get easier but it won't, I feel like I'm going to cry forever. I just want him back.

I felt guilty – worse than on the previous occasion, when I'd only read her happy childhood thoughts and could kid myself that I'd picked up the memory stick by mistake and was simply looking to see whose it was. Now I was deliberately opening up something that should have been so private, a secret place where an unhappy young girl had begun to pour out her heart. But I reminded myself that Amelia wasn't just unhappy now; she'd also, almost certainly, been spiteful to my little girl, and I justified my intrusion into her privacy by reminding myself of that.

There was a long gap in time after the entry about her father's death, with nothing else until after Craig had moved in. The tone of her writing had now completely changed; anger and resentment leaked out of every line.

> As if it's not bad enough that my dad's dead, and my mum doesn't even seem to care, now she's brought ANOTHER MAN into our house already, like it doesn't even matter that Dad's dead, she just went straight out and found someone else. And she's sleeping with him in my dad's bed which is so GROSS, it makes me SICK. And all they do is get on my case about my 'behaviour' although all I do anyway is stay out of their way, stay in my room or go out cos I just want to get away from here cos they make me feel sick the way they call each other 'hon' and 'babe' and kiss in front of me, like Dad didn't even MATTER.

And then I came to the first entry about Daisy. The tone of this entry was completely different – not just unhappy, not just angry but now beginning to sound completely vicious. I almost froze in horror as I read on.

> Now I've got to be 'nice', Mum says, to this little kid called Daisy who's, like, scared to even look at me, let alone say a single word to me. Or to anyone. And she's only coming here cos she's HIS daughter and her mum's got to go to work and leave her with us. If he cares about his stupid daughter why didn't he stay living with her and her mum? I hate him, I hate my mum for letting him come and live here, and I hate his stupid kid and I don't see why I should be nice to her if I don't want to. Mum keeps asking why I stay in my room. What else does she expect me to do? I wish I could have my dad back, he was the only one who cared about me around here.

The more I read, the worse it got.

I wish I could get rid of Daisy. I keep trying to think up ways to stop her coming here. If I say something horrible to her or give her a shove, it doesn't work cos she's such a stupid pathetic little mouse, she just looks at me with big frightened eyes and runs away from me. But if she was to have an accident, like, fall down the stairs or something, she might not want to come any more, or her mum might not want her to come cos she'll say my mum should have looked after her better. The stupid baby thinks she's so clever cos she can swim with one armband but if she fell in the pool without wearing it – like, with all her clothes on – she wouldn't be able to swim then, would she? I'll think of something. Something to really put her off coming any more. It'll have to be something bad. I don't care if I hurt her, I just need to get rid of her.

I heard myself gasping out loud as I read on, reading Amelia's own callous accounts of how she'd shoved Daisy into the road, pushed her into the pool at Center Parcs, nudged her so that she fell down the stairs and finally caused her head injury in the bathroom. She'd admitted it – all of it – in this diary. Not only was she saying really nasty things about Daisy, but the pushes, the shoves, the trips, all the attempts to hurt my little girl were described exactly as Daisy had claimed. I felt weak with shock, however much I'd suspected it. Seeing Amelia's spiteful intentions actually written down in black and white made me feel sick – with anger, and absolute horror that such a young girl could harbour those unbelievably terrible feelings and intentions about my poor, innocent little Daisy. Well, there definitely couldn't be any doubt about it now, so in one way it was almost a relief – a relief to have proof, to have actual evidence that Daisy wasn't exaggerating or fabricating the occasions when Amelia had hurt her, or tried to do her harm. I needed to tell Kirsty and Craig, before there was any more talk about whether to allow Amelia back again. As far as I was concerned, Kirsty was right; whatever the reason for that girl's unhappiness and spitefulness, she needed to stay away from the people she resented – most of all my daughter.

## 27

When I arrived at Whitegate House the next evening, Kirsty told me Craig was supervising Daisy and Freya in the swimming pool.

'They've been having a lovely time, it's so nice and warm in there for them and now Daisy's such a good swimmer they're wanting to swim together nearly every afternoon. Sorry they're a bit late – shall I go and chase Daisy up for you?'

'No, it's fine. I wanted to talk to you, anyway.' I took the memory stick out of my bag and showed it to her. 'Do you recognise this?'

'Let me see.' She held out her hand for it. 'Where did it come from? It's not mine, and I don't think Craig uses these. Oh, it could be Amelia's. She does use them, and she likes blue ones, to match her laptop. Thank you, Tasha – I'll get it back to her, she might have homework on it or something. Where did you find it?'

'I'm sorry, I must have picked it up by mistake when I was here at Christmas,' I lied. 'I thought it was one of mine, and I didn't realise until I'd put it in my laptop, and Amelia's personal diary came up.'

'Oh dear.' She gave a little laugh. 'I hope you didn't see anything too shocking. After that language at Christmas...'

'It's not the language I'm worried about. It's the things she says about Daisy. The things she admits to – everything we suspected. I think you should read it, Kirsty.'

She sat down as if the wind had been taken out of her.

'Really? She's actually admitted to all those incidents? Oh my God, Tasha, I'm so sorry. Despite everything, I still kept hoping against hope that we might be making unfair assumptions. But it seems I did the right thing by removing her from the house to keep Daisy safe – however difficult the decision's been.'

'I feel bad for you, Kirsty. After all, she's your daughter, you must be devastated to think that she really was capable of such spiteful behaviour. I wonder if she needs some help – counselling, maybe – to get over the loss of her father? That must be where her resentment stems from, I suppose.'

'You don't know her,' she retorted. 'She's always been an unpleasant little madam.'

'Oh!'

I was so taken aback by this, I hardly knew what else to say. It was so sudden – such an abrupt change from the way Kirsty usually spoke about Amelia. She'd always sounded anxious and sorry about her before, but never spoken in such an overtly hostile manner. I could understand her being upset at hearing that her daughter had been writing threats and plans to hurt Daisy, but as a mum myself, I couldn't imagine, whatever Daisy did now or in the future, talking about her with quite such unbridled aggression. And having read a couple of

Amelia's diary entries from before this all started – when her father had just died and she was so lost and upset – I still saw her as a hurt and unhappy child with problems, rather than somebody inherently wicked. 'Unpleasant little madam' was an odd phrase, to put it mildly, for a mother to use about her own child. Perhaps she hadn't liked me voicing an opinion on the matter. I supposed that was fair enough – she must know more about what made her daughter tick than I could do. But if anything, I'd have expected her to try to defend Amelia, even if she was now forced to accept that our fears about her behaviour were correct. It was odd that she was so protective of Daisy, who she'd only known for a comparatively short time, but couldn't seem to find it in her heart to look for any mitigating factors in Amelia's case.

As it happened, at that moment the door from the swimming pool annexe was flung open and in crashed the two little swimmers, already dried off and dressed, and rushing to tell us how they could both now do a *huge* running jump into the water and that Freya was going to show Daisy how to do a sitting-down dive next.

'That's great!' I enthused, holding out my arms for Daisy and putting my shock and discomfort to one side. 'Thanks, as always,' I said to Kirsty, nodding at Craig too.

'Well, thanks for telling me about this,' Kirsty responded, indicating the memory stick.

'And guess what, Mummy?' Daisy went on, excitedly. 'We're trying on our bridesmaid dresses on Saturday!'

'Yes, they're all ready,' Kirsty said, smiling, and I wondered how the hell, even with all her money, she was able to get things done at such speed, whenever the hell she wanted, regardless of how many other people's wishes might get trampled on in the process. 'And the venue's booked, caterers booked, no problem with the date – January must be an unpopular month. Two weeks this Saturday.'

'Well, you must let me know if I can help with anything,' I felt obliged, if pretty sickened, to say.

'Oh, no, of course not, what's the point of having plenty of people in your employ if you can't get them to do a few little personal extras for you?' she laughed.

She must have been unbearable to work for.

'Well,' I said, to change the subject, 'I'll leave... that other thing... with you, then, to look at for yourself when you get a chance. Come on, Daisy, time to go home for dinner.'

'See you tomorrow, Freya,' she said, putting her coat on.

'See you, Daise! Only two more sleeps till Saturday: Bridesmaid Dress Day!' Freya was doing a little dance of excitement.

'Yes. Bridesmaid Dress Day,' I muttered to myself as we went out to the car.

I supposed I'd have to sort myself out something suitable to wear for the wedding. No way was I forking out for a new outfit to go and watch my ex marrying his new flame. I was only agreeing to go at all, frankly, for Daisy's sake. But even I had to admit, Daisy and Freya looked sweet in their pink-and-white bridesmaid dresses, which they modelled for me, both squealing with excitement, when I went to collect Daisy that Saturday after work. So I felt pleased for them – if not particularly for anyone else involved. And I couldn't help wondering whether Amelia had given in and agreed to be a bridesmaid too. Nobody had mentioned it, there was no sign of another, bigger, dress hanging up and, frankly, after what Kirsty had said about her, I decided I didn't even want to raise the subject.

\* \* \*

The following week passed quickly. Kirsty told me she'd read all the diary entries on Amelia's memory stick and was waiting until after the wedding to confront her with the evidence.

'I don't want any more unpleasantness before the wedding,' she said. 'But I don't think it's right for her to keep living with Lee, either. Lee's a nice man, and Grace is a nice girl. It isn't right to risk her being influenced by Amelia. Not now I know how *evil* that girl is.'

I couldn't think of a single word to say in response to this. *Evil*? She was talking about her own daughter! However much I disliked and distrusted Amelia myself, I couldn't imagine ever speaking in those terms about my own child. Kirsty must have seen the look on my face, because she went on, quickly, 'Besides, she obviously needs help. She needs to be in... an institution of some sort.'

Poor Amelia. I couldn't imagine anything but unhappiness and trouble ahead of her in her life. To be written off and so obviously disliked by your own mother must be the worst feeling in the world for any child. If it weren't for her treatment and obvious dislike of Daisy, I'd have been begging Kirsty to be kinder to her.

Meanwhile, I was going to bed early every night, and had never read so many books in my life, downloading them from Amazon and reading them on my Kindle, where I had no access to the bingo websites. So far, since joining GA, I'd only slipped up twice and on both occasions my disappointment in myself was so extreme that even Claire had to tell me not to be so hard on myself.

'You're doing really well, honestly,' she assured me. And the fact that I'd been able to put all of Daisy's money back in her piggy bank, and was now starting to save enough, gradually, to pay back the larger amount I'd taken from her savings account, did make me feel proud. I knew I'd then have to concentrate on getting my *own* finances back in order – which would take time, but at least now I had some hope that I'd get there eventually.

Lee came to babysit each time I went to the GA meeting, and stayed afterwards for coffee and a chat. I was beginning to enjoy his company. We didn't get much chance to talk properly at work, and now that we understood and knew more about each other, we were getting on well together. He liked to read thrillers, like me, and always had some titles to recommend for my night-time reading.

'You need really gripping plots,' he suggested, 'to hold your attention and stop you thinking about other things.'

'Yes, you're right. And to keep me reading well into the night, so I'm tired enough to go straight to sleep when I put my Kindle down.'

'But not so scary that you can't sleep!' he added, laughing.

I appreciated his help and support, and the wisdom that came from his own struggle with alcoholism. I still hadn't told anyone else about my own issues, and didn't think I'd ever want to... until Jackie called me one evening and I admitted I was already in bed, and ended up blurting out the whole story.

'I wondered if it might be something like that,' she admitted.

'Did you?' I asked, shocked. 'How?'

'The way you were so worried about money. I mean, obviously we all are, but you seemed too embarrassed to talk to Craig about giving you more – as if it was your fault you needed it.'

'Well, it was. Kirsty gave me more, and I blew all of that,

too.' I sighed. 'It was awful. I couldn't stop. I still can't trust myself not to do it again. Lee's been a lifesaver.'

I explained how he'd persuaded me to go to GA, and Jackie gave a little chuckle.

'And you didn't even like him!'

'I didn't think I did, but I've got to know him now, and, well, I understand what he's been through, losing his wife, and his own addiction.'

'I'm glad you get on OK with him now. And how are things with Craig and Kirsty?'

I told her about the forthcoming wedding.

'Ah,' she said. 'So that's why Camel's offered me a Saturday.'

'Is that OK?' I asked anxiously, but she reassured me that she'd said, on retiring, that she'd always be happy to do an odd day's cover 'to top up the pension'.

I told her about the scene with Amelia at Christmas and the fact that Kirsty was now talking about sending her to an institution.

'Poor kid,' Jackie said. 'She's obviously terribly unhappy.'

'I know. If she hadn't been so spiteful to Daisy, I'd be more sympathetic, but—'

'But you have to put Daisy first; you shouldn't apologise for that.'

I knew I shouldn't. But how could I not feel sorry for an unhappy twelve-year-old whose mother seemed to hate her?

\* \* \*

Craig came with me for Daisy's appointment with the speech and language therapist. We told Daisy she was going to see someone who would know how to help her get her words out at school, and with anyone else she wanted to speak to.

'But I might not be able to talk to the person,' she said, looking alarmed.

'They'll understand that. They meet lots of children who have the same problem, who can't talk to people,' I explained.

'Oh!' She looked surprised. 'Are there other children the same?'

'Yes.' I smiled at her. She seemed pleased to think she wasn't alone with her problem.

'Do the other children learn how to get their words out?'

'I'm sure they do, with help. It might not happen straight away, though,' I warned her.

The therapist was called Esme; she was young and very charming, and quickly managed to put Daisy at ease. She made it clear straight away that she wasn't expecting Daisy to speak to her. Instead she gave her some paper and asked her to write down the people she managed to talk to easily, and then list those she'd like to be able to talk to, but couldn't.

'Mummy can help you with the writing,' she said, but Daisy was already managing to spell Freya's name correctly, adding Mummy, Daddy and Kirsty to the first list. She then asked me to help her spell Izzie for the second list, added Mr Frost and a couple of other girls in her class. Below these, she wrote *you*, pointing shyly at Esme, who smiled and said that was nice. I felt so sad, seeing Daisy literally unable to speak out loud to someone. Although I'd accepted that she had this problem now, it still felt such a huge barrier to her happiness and I couldn't help wondering how on earth Esme would get her past it.

'OK, well let's see if we can make a plan to gradually tick

those names off, shall we, Daisy? Who on that second list would you like to be able to speak to the most?'

Daisy pointed at Izzie's name.

'Right. Well, I know you find it impossible to get your voice to work at school, but do you think you'd be able to talk to Izzie if she came to your house?'

Daisy looked surprised. She looked up at me, a question in her eyes.

'You haven't wanted to have anyone home from the new school yet, have you, Daisy?' I said. 'But of course we can invite Izzie, if you'd like to?'

She nodded slowly.

'If she does come to your house,' Esme went on, 'don't worry if you still can't speak to her, OK? But if you can – even if it's just one word! – that would be amazing. If not, why don't you try writing things down for her. Is she good at reading and writing, like you obviously are?'

Daisy nodded again.

'That's great. So she might enjoy it if you write things to each other. It'd be like a game, wouldn't it? Can you think of other ways to "talk" to people, Daisy, without actually speaking?'

She thought for a moment, then picked up the pencil again and drew a picture of a house.

'Brilliant idea, Daisy!' Esme encouraged her. 'Drawing pictures can be a really good way of talking to people. And here are some more.'

She gave a little wave, then a smile, then put on a sad face, then held out her hands and shrugged a gesture of 'don't know', and finally blew a kiss.

'Did you know what I was saying there?' she asked.

Daisy nodded enthusiastically.

'Try some of those out with Izzie,' she suggested. 'It could be fun. Meanwhile, I'm going to contact Mr Frost and ask if he'd be happy for you to write down things in a notebook – or draw a picture if the words you need are too hard – so that you can ask him things, if you need to. OK?' She turned to me and Craig and added quietly, 'That'll take the pressure off, a little, for now.'

'Thank you. That all sounds really helpful, doesn't it, Daisy?' I said.

She nodded again.

'I'm also going to suggest some exercises,' Esme said. 'Only a couple of easy ones for now – I want the emphasis this time to be on helping Daisy to relax and cope with social situations even without speaking.'

She went on to describe a couple of breathing exercises and, when Daisy immediately started trying them, without any difficulty, and seemed eager to continue, she added another, where she had to take a deep breath and then slowly *blow* out an 'f' or 'v' sound.

'We'll see how things go with Izzie,' she told me quietly as we got our coats on, 'and if the friendship seems to be doing well, we'll get Daisy to practise that when she's with her – at home, where she's more relaxed.' She smiled, and added, 'Try not to worry. We'll get her voice back, I'm quite confident of that.'

'She's got a good voice on her when she's at my house,' Craig put in.

I wished he wouldn't always be so desperate to shrug off any responsibility for Daisy's problem.

'She does at *both* of our homes,' I said quietly. 'Because she's relaxed there.'

'That's exactly right,' Esme said calmly. 'And pretty soon, she'll be relaxed at school too. We'll get there.'

I looked at the smile on Daisy's face as we walked out to the car park, and felt myself smiling in response. Daisy trusted Esme. She believed she was going to help her; she was eager to follow her advice. I had a feeling the battle might already be half won.

## 28

On the morning of the wedding, Daisy was awake early, wanting to get into her bridesmaid's dress straight away. I reminded her that Kirsty had kept her dress hanging up at Whitegate House, with Freya's, and that they'd get dressed together there and go in a wedding car with Kirsty to the venue. I'd found out now that Amelia definitely wasn't going to be a bridesmaid – she'd been asked, but had refused point-blank. Kirsty had told me that she'd still been saying she didn't even want to go to the wedding, but had given in when she was told Grace could come with her. 'To be honest, I'd have been happier without her there,' Kirsty had added. 'She's bound to cause trouble of some sort.'

Again it had shocked me profoundly, to think that she could even consider not having her elder daughter at her own wedding. I was beginning to wonder why I'd begun to think of Kirsty as a friend. This side of her wasn't at all like the woman I'd started to like.

'Will you come in the wedding car with me, Mummy?' Daisy asked as we got ready to head off to Whitegate House.

'No. I'll go in my own car.'

'With Daddy?'

I smiled. 'No. I think Daddy will go in his own car. The bride and the bridesmaids always go together, and have photos taken of them arriving.'

She looked puzzled. 'Why doesn't Daddy have bridesmaids?'

She'd never been to a wedding, of course, and had no understanding of the terminology. I explained that it was all because of old traditions, and that the bridegroom usually used to turn up with a best man. Then I realised I shouldn't have said this, because Daisy was now worried about her daddy not having one.

'Couldn't Lee be his best man?' she asked anxiously.

'Lee isn't really a friend of Daddy's.' It struck me then, suddenly and with a kind of sadness, that Craig didn't seem to have kept up with any of his old friends since being with Kirsty. I wondered if perhaps they didn't think much of the decisions he'd made. 'Lee only knows the family because of being Amelia's friend's dad,' I explained to Daisy.

'And he's your friend, isn't he, Mummy?'

'Well, yes. We work together.'

She continued to worry about Craig having to go to the wedding on his own, until I pacified her by saying he and Kirsty would go home together afterwards, so I was sure he didn't mind.

There were already a lot of cars parked at the upmarket wedding venue on the outskirts of town by the time I arrived. I wondered who all the wedding guests were, as Kirsty had made it clear to me that she had no family to invite, and I'd never even heard her talk about friends. I realised later that they were all members of staff from her company, of course, probably feeling obliged to accept the invitation for fear of being overlooked for promotion. Apart from our two little bridesmaids, there were no children, and I was relieved that Amelia was coming with Grace, as she was unlikely to be difficult or cause a scene while they were together. I saw Lee as soon as I entered the wedding room.

'Shall we sit near the back?' he asked me. 'I've sent Grace and Amelia to sit at the front as instructed and warned them to be quiet. Did you notice whether the groom's here yet?'

'Yes,' I said. 'He's having photos taken on his own outside.'

I'd felt a bit sorry for him, to be honest. He'd looked awkward and a little uncomfortable in his new suit and buttonhole.

We chose a row near the back, and I grabbed a seat next to the aisle so I could have a good view of Daisy when she came in, and he sat beside me, giving me a sympathetic smile.

'Are you OK?' he asked quietly. 'This must be pretty painful for you.'

'It isn't, actually. I've got past caring,' I said. 'I only wanted to be here for Daisy's sake.'

'Of course. She looks lovely. And so excited!'

Craig came in as we spoke, and there was a hush as he walked to the front of the hall, where he stood alone, facing the celebrant. Then the opening notes of the 'Wedding March' sounded, and heads turned to watch the bride entering the room. She was dressed in a chic but massively expensive-looking short white satin dress with a matching jacket. For just a split second, I imagined how I'd have felt if this had been my marriage, if it had been me walking down the aisle now, with Craig waiting at the front for me, and I took an involuntary gulp of air – but the tears that came to my eyes weren't sad ones, but ones of tenderness for my beautiful little daughter, so perfect and lovely in her pink and white dress and white shoes, her blonde hair brushed until it shone and held in a garland of white flowers. Beside her, Freya nudged her and pointed to me and they both gave me huge grins of excitement. I gave another little gasp and wiped away a tear, and suddenly realised Lee had taken hold of my other hand.

'OK?' he whispered as the bride and bridesmaids reached the front of the room and the groom turned to smile at them.

I nodded. 'Fine, thanks.'

But I didn't turn to look at him. Because he still had hold of my hand. And to my complete confusion, I found I... actually didn't mind it, at all. I quite liked it.

\* \* \*

There were no speeches, thankfully, at the reception, which was an informal, but very lavish, buffet, so Lee and I sat together for this too – we seemed to be the only guests who didn't work for Kirsty's company. Daisy was in a state of huge excitement now that her important role had been successfully discharged. She'd sat with Freya to eat, probably, far too much sugary food and drink too many additive-laden drinks, and the two of them were now chasing each other around the room, squealing, and I'd needed, twice, to stop her from tripping people up and warn her to calm down.

'I think I'm going to be taking her home soon,' I said as the afternoon wore on and I noticed her rubbing her eyes. 'I did warn Kirsty that I didn't think we'd stay for the evening party.'

'I gave my excuses for that, too,' Lee admitted. 'It's not much fun when you're not part of the crowd who all know each other, is it? And I should take Grace and Amelia home soon, anyway. They're both looking so bored that it's almost verging on rudeness.'

Frankly, I was just relieved that Amelia had got through the wedding without doing or saying anything controversial, and without so much as glancing at Daisy, let alone interacting with her in any way.

I headed for Craig and Kirsty to thank them and make my own excuses.

'Daisy looks like she's heading for a meltdown,' I said apologetically.

'Yes, we were just saying that Freya probably won't last the evening, either,' Kirsty agreed.

'Would you like me to take her home with Daisy? They're both exhausted – they can sleep together in Daisy's bed, just this once, and I'll bring her home in the morning. You've put the dog in kennels for the day, haven't you?'

'Yes. Oh, are you sure you don't mind? She can sleep in her undies for tonight; she won't care, as long as she's with Daisy. Thanks, Tasha. We should have thought to arrange this before-hand, but there were so many other things to sort out.'

'And it's all gone perfectly. Congratulations to you both,' I said, hoping it sounded at least halfway sincere.

Craig was giving me a strange look.

'You and Lee looked very cosy together, today.'

I gave him a cold stare in response, and Kirsty, noticing, nudged him and told him not to make insinuations.

'Tasha and Lee are colleagues,' she said sharply. 'And they didn't know anyone else here. Make yourself useful, Craig: go and get Freya's booster seat out of our car and put it in Tasha's, please.'

'I can do that, if you—'

'No, let him do it, Tasha, he's done little enough,' she

retorted, in a tone that I didn't think boded particularly well for a wedding day.

I made a point of saying goodbye to Lee as quickly as possible, while Kirsty went to find the two little girls and tell them – to a response of much squealing – that they were going to come home with me and sleep together.

'Thanks again for today,' I said as Craig handed me the booster seat, out in the car park.

'Thanks for coming,' he responded gruffly. 'And sorry if I spoke out of turn, about Lee. Truth is, Tash, I'd be happy for you if—'

'We're just friends,' I snapped, turning away. 'Come on, girls, my car's over here. You both look shattered.'

We left Craig standing by his own car, watching us go, looking strangely out of place in his best suit and shiny shoes. As if he couldn't quite remember why he was there.

## 29

I felt awkward about Lee after Craig's comments at the wedding – remembering how nice it had felt, his hand holding mine. Over the rest of the weekend at home, I kept thinking about how kind he was being, how much I appreciated his support with my personal struggle, how grateful I felt to him. But had I been giving him the wrong idea? I decided to be a bit more careful how I talked to him in future, just in case. Much as I liked him now, as a friend, there was no way I wanted to consider getting myself into another relationship. Not that he'd be interested in me in that respect, obviously – I was older than him and he was... well, he was fit. He could have his pick of younger, beautiful women with no ties.

He had something else on his mind, anyway, when we went back to work that Monday.

'Kirsty called me about Amelia,' he said quietly while we were getting ready for our first clients. 'She's saying now that she thinks she should send her away – like, *right* away. That there's something wrong with her and she shouldn't expect me to have her living in my home.'

'I know.' I filled him in about the diary entries. 'To be fair, Amelia does come across as pretty disturbed. But honestly, I just think she needs some counselling. And to be shown some love, not sent away. I think it'd make her worse – she'd never forgive her mother, and who could blame her?'

'I agree. I tried to tell Kirsty that I'm happy to keep Amelia with me. Honestly, she's absolutely fine with me – polite, sensible, calm – like a different girl. But Kirsty seems determined. She says she's looking for somewhere to send her. Grace is going to be devastated, too.'

I found myself thinking about Amelia a lot during the next few days, wishing there was something I could do to help, but on the other hand, being aware of how much better the situation at Whitegate House was for Daisy without the constant threat of violence from the older girl.

On the Wednesday morning, I managed to catch Izzie's mother as she was leaving the school gate. She was an older mum, quietly spoken, and like me, didn't seem to know any of the other parents yet, but when I explained who I was, she gave me a smile and said Izzie had told her all about Daisy.

'I gather she's having trouble speaking,' she said gently.

'Yes. Since we moved here. It's all been a lot of upheaval for her – her daddy moving out, then a new house, a new school, and I've had to work longer hours.'

'You can never tell how anxiety is going to come out in children,' she said sympathetically. 'Izzie says she really likes Daisy and she's trying to help her, by reading her notes, and guessing what she wants to say. I do hope she'll soon find her voice again.'

'Thank you. I wondered if you'd let Izzie come to our house to play with Daisy? Perhaps on Sunday afternoon? The therapist thinks Daisy might eventually be able to speak to her, in a more relaxed environment.'

'I'm sure Izzie would love that. Thank you.'

The arrangement was made, and I went to work feeling a lot happier and more hopeful. I was pleased, too, when I collected Daisy from Whitegate House that evening, that she was excited by the news herself.

'I'm going to try really, really hard to make my voice say something when she comes,' she said.

'Well, don't get too disappointed if it takes a bit longer,' I warned. 'She can come again – as often as you like.'

She did a little hop and a skip out to the car. 'Freya's still my best friend,' she said. 'But Freya's got other friends at her school, hasn't she – so I want to have other friends as well.'

'It's always a good idea to have more than one friend,' I agreed, smiling. 'We all need lots of friends.'

Then I stopped, wondering why I'd really only got one, myself – Jackie. I'd begun to think of Lee as a friend, but now I was nervous about giving him the wrong impression, I'd tried to cool that down a little. I supposed that, like Craig, I'd lost touch with our mutual friends from before we split up.

'Kirsty's your friend, isn't she, Mummy?' Daisy said, as if she'd been reading my mind.

I raised my eyebrows. I'd thought so, too, but perhaps I'd been too quick to warm to her. I really wasn't sure how I felt about her now. If she could hate her own daughter as much as she seemed to, did I really know her at all?

\* \* \*

The play date with Izzie that Sunday went well. She was a nice little girl – quiet, especially compared with Freya! – with sweet manners and an easy, amiable smile. Daisy looked at her anxiously as she came into the house, then smiled and pointed up the stairs.

'Your room, Daisy?' Izzie said. 'Yes, OK.'

When I checked on them after a little while, they were sitting on the rug in Daisy's room, playing with one of her Lego creations. Daisy was communicating with gestures and had her notebook beside her on the floor, and Izzie seemed to be doing a good job of working out what she was trying to say, so I left them to it. When they came downstairs a little later for a drink and biscuit, Izzie told me excitedly that Daisy had been showing her the exercises the therapist had set her.

'She puffed, like this,' she said, demonstrating, 'and then she made an *F* sound and it was quite loud! So I asked her if she could say *foo, foo, food* and she did! Out loud!'

Daisy nodded, her little face pink with pleasure, and Izzie put an arm around her.

'You spoke to me, Daisy!' she said encouragingly, and I was so touched by the little girl's kindness, I had to look away and wipe my eyes.

'You're going to get there,' I told Daisy after Izzie's mum had come to take her home. 'If you keep practising like that, I bet you'll be able to talk to Izzie, really soon, even at school.'

'I really like Izzie,' Daisy said, nodding. 'I don't even think I want to go to Tudor Hall school any more, Mummy, because even if I did, Freya wouldn't be in my class, and Izzie wouldn't be there, so I'd still have to make more new friends, wouldn't I? And I don't really like their brown uniforms.'

I laughed. 'Well, that's good, then. You can save your piggy bank money for something else.'

'Yes,' she said, seriously. 'I might use it for when I want to buy a car.'

* * *

I was beginning to feel more optimistic. My life was slowly settling and improving. Thanks to Lee, and Claire at the GA, I felt like I'd finally regained some control of my addiction, and was slowly getting my finances back under control too. Jackie had visited me a couple of times, calling on me unexpectedly during the evening and keeping me company, chatting over a cup of tea, so I didn't feel the need to hide myself away in my bedroom to keep from going online, onto the gambling websites. The fact that I didn't know when she might turn up was another way to keep me from slipping up; I'd have felt embarrassed if she'd caught me out, breaking my promise to myself. Although I still missed the little thrill of it, the excitement of getting close to a win, even just the fact that it had helped pass the time when I was alone after Daisy was asleep, I was proud of myself for now being able to resist it, *nearly* every night. And the relief at not losing money at such a terrible rate was worth all the struggle. I felt like other things were improving, too. Daisy was happier, I was happier, Kirsty and Craig were married, whether happily or not was up to them, and before long, spring would be here; the evenings were already getting lighter.

And then, in the middle of that week after Izzie came to play, as I walked away from the school gate after dropping Daisy in the morning, I saw someone leaning against my car, waiting for me. It was Amelia, and as I approached, I saw she looked terrible. She was in her brown school uniform, but with her hair loose, possibly unbrushed, and her coat unbuttoned, as if she'd dressed in a hurry.

'Can I talk to you?' she asked. Her voice sounded croaky, like she'd been crying. 'Please, Tasha?'

'What is it?' I asked. 'Why aren't you at school?'

'I couldn't. Look at me. I'm a mess.' She shrugged. 'Grace is making an excuse for me. I need to talk to you. Please,' she said again, sounding desperate.

'You'd better get in the car – it's raining.' I looked at my watch as I opened the passenger door for her. 'I haven't got long. I'll be late for work.'

'I know. Sorry. I didn't know how else to find you. I knew you dropped Daisy off here. I couldn't turn up at your work, could I?'

'OK. So what is it? I don't know if I can help,' I added, wondering if she was going to talk to me about her mother's plan to send her away.

'It's my mum.' So I was right. 'She's gone completely mad. She's saying I've got something wrong with me and she wants to get me locked up – but it's *her* who's not right in the head! Honestly, Tasha, I didn't do all that stuff—'

'What stuff?' I challenged her.

'The stuff she says I wrote in my diary, you know, about Daisy, about hating her and trying to hurt her. Look, I admit I was jealous at first, all right? I mean, the thing is, Mum never loved me, she only loved Freya, and then when Craig came along, and then you, and Daisy, well she even loves Daisy more than she ever loved me. I was the only one she didn't love, she hated me – how do you think that made me feel?'

She was crying now. I couldn't help but feel some sympathy for her. But on the other hand...

'Amelia, I'm sorry but I read those diary entries myself. I know perhaps that was wrong of me, but you've got to understand, Daisy is my child, my responsibility, and if I think she's in danger, being hurt—'

'I didn't write them!' she insisted hoarsely. 'I swear I didn't!

I haven't used that memory stick for *ages*. I used to write a diary on it, like, ages ago – but after my dad died, I didn't write it for much longer. I haven't written anything that's been put on there since then. Someone else has been writing it.'

I stared back at her. Did she really expect me to believe her? I didn't, I couldn't. Of course she was going to try to shrug off the blame, but it didn't make sense for anyone else to have written what I'd read on those pages – on her own memory stick, on the very document where she'd admitted keeping a diary.

'Why would anyone do that?' I said. 'What would be the point?'

'To get me into trouble, obviously. Mum won't let me go back home now, so I thought you might talk to Craig for me. I didn't think he hated me enough to want to get rid of me, but he did start bossing me around like he thought he was my father or something – and I suppose I was a bit rude to him. Perhaps he's written all that stuff because he wanted me out of the way?'

'*Craig*? Sorry, Amelia, but I don't think that makes any sense. You might have tried his patience a bit, but no!' I stared at her. 'You're surely not accusing him of writing those diary entries, pretending to be you?' I shook my head. 'You'd better get out of the car – I'm running late. This is between you and your mum, sorry.'

'Please listen, Tasha!' she wailed, beginning to sob. It was a sound of such utter despair that despite myself, I felt a wave of pure sympathy. Whatever her problem, Amelia was still only a child – an unhappy child, whose own mother seemed to want to get her locked up. I imagined Daisy, one day, being in trouble, pleading for someone to listen to her, to take her seriously – and suddenly I knew that despite all my misgivings about this girl, she deserved at least one adult to be prepared to hear her out, and if nobody else was doing it, I'd have to step up and at least give her a hearing.

'OK,' I said. 'Let me just call the salon and make an excuse. Then you've got ten minutes to tell me what you need to.'

I spoke to Lee, who promised to cover for me with Camel and take my first client if I wasn't back in time. Then I turned back to Amelia, who was sniffing into a hanky and rubbing her sore eyes.

'OK,' I said. 'Explain. From the beginning.'

'Well,' she said, looking up, straight into my eyes. 'It all started when my dad died. Because the thing is, you see, I think my mum killed him.'

## 30

It was ridiculous, obviously. A ridiculous, desperate attempt by an unhappy girl who was being threatened with something more drastic than she perhaps deserved, to wriggle out of any blame now that she'd realised she was going to face the consequences. I tried my best to be sympathetic – because her distress was all too real, and yes, I was sure she regretted her behaviour now, and would do or say anything to get someone's sympathy and turn the situation around.

A more mature person would have probably just made a heartfelt, genuine apology for her behaviour and promised to change her ways. But I knew it would be a rare twelve-year-old who had that level of maturity, even if she was close to turning thirteen now. The truth had hit her; her actions and intentions – as spelt out in that diary – had come home to roost, and she hadn't quite got away with it by moving in with her friend, as she'd hoped. Her mother wanted to take it further – not that I agreed with her, but fortunately, it wasn't my decision to make. To try to imply that Craig had falsified those diary entries was laughable enough to be easily dismissed. Craig – I now recognised – hadn't the wit or intelligence to dream up anything of that complexity or level of cunning.

I waited until she'd poured out her whole story, beginning with the ludicrous suggestion that Kirsty had murdered her first husband, and continuing through the theme of never having been loved by Kirsty, being hated by her younger sister and resented by Craig, and going on to say she now regretted her jealousy of Daisy, regretted *occasionally snapping at her or calling her a baby*, and she finished by saying that she'd ended up admiring her.

'Even though she's so little, she's gutsy,' she admitted sadly. 'Cos if I was nasty to her, she wouldn't tell on me. She didn't like telling tales, she said.'

'So you regret hurting Daisy, now?' I said.

'I keep telling you, I never hurt her, not on purpose. I called her names, I admit that. But all those other things, what Mum said I put in the diary – what *someone else* put in the diary – they were accidents. OK, I might have, like, tried to tug the dog's lead off her, but I didn't mean for her to fall in the road. I didn't *push* her. And at the pool, at Center Parcs, Daisy and Freya were being stupid, pretending to push *me* in the water, and she overbalanced and fell in. I scarpered because I knew I'd get the blame. All right, I admit, that time on the stairs I pushed past her, cos she was in my way and being a nuisance. But I didn't mean for her to fall. I'm not some sort of psychopath, whatever my mum thinks.'

'What about the fall in the bathroom – the concussion?' I challenged her.

'That wasn't me! I just got out of bed because I heard Mum calling for Craig, saying there'd been an accident. I hadn't even been in the bathroom, honest! I don't know why I got the blame. I didn't do anything, I was asleep, Daisy must have tripped or something.'

I looked at her doubtfully. It all seemed very convenient – an excuse, a get-out clause for everything, whereas the confessions were there in black and white in that diary document.

'I never wrote the stuff on that memory stick,' she said again, as if she was reading my mind. 'Honest. I never.'

'Well, I'm sorry, Amelia, I don't know what to say. I'm sorry your mother seems to want to send you away, but—'

'Why can't I just stay with Grace? Lee can tell her, I haven't been any trouble there, I help him cook, Grace and I help with the housework, it's better than being at home, I'm even doing better at school now because I'm not getting upset all the time. *Please*, Tasha, please talk to Mum for me? You know I'm right – even if you don't believe me, you know Daisy hasn't got anything to get upset about now. I know you've got to look after her but she's OK now; nobody can blame me for anything if I stay at Grace's, can they? Why do they have to talk about sending me away?'

She burst into tears again. I looked at my watch. I really had to go.

'Look, I can try to talk to her for you, OK? I'm not saying I believe you. Frankly, I think it all sounds a bit ridiculous, claiming you didn't do anything, and that you didn't even write your own diary entries – OK, OK, no need to keep on saying it – and as for the ridiculous idea of your mother killing your father, if you *really* thought that, Amelia, perhaps you should have spoken to the police long before now! I'm sorry, but I recognise hysterical storytelling when I hear it. Don't try to interrupt; I've got to go now – you'd better take yourself back to school, or back to Grace's house and tidy yourself up. I'll try to persuade your mum to give you another chance, and let you stay with Grace and see how it goes. That's all I'm promising. OK?'

'Thanks, Tasha,' she muttered. She opened the car door, then looked back at me and added, 'I'm sorry I've made you late for work. You're OK, really. I'm sorry I was mean to Daisy, but honest, I never hurt her, not on purpose.'

I watched her go, running a hand over my face, feeling exhausted.

\* \* \*

'Is everything all right?' Lee asked me anxiously. My first client, a cut and colour lady, was already in the chair and he'd just been mixing the colour ready for her. I was relieved to be able to take over before his own client arrived, and before Camel could become even more suspicious about my excuse of a traffic problem.

I shook my head. 'I'll tell you later.'

Not that I intended to go into too much detail with him about Amelia's far-fetched stories. He didn't need to be any more involved than he already was; he was getting on OK with her, she was apparently behaving well at his house and it wouldn't be fair to rock that particular boat. I was hoping I might still be able to persuade Kirsty to give Amelia a stay of execution, to let her stay with Grace, as she wanted, and if Lee was happy with the arrangement too, I couldn't see why that shouldn't be allowed. All I told him, when we eventually both had a gap between clients around midday, was that Amelia had turned up on her way to school, begging me to try intervening on her behalf.

'I've promised to speak to Kirsty again,' I said.

'That's good of you. I'd feel sad for Amelia – and for Grace too – if Kirsty carries out her threat. I've already spoken to her myself, assured her how well Amelia's been behaving since she's been with us – but Kirsty seems to have made up her mind, unfortunately.'

'Yes. Well, I did warn her I couldn't promise any miracles.'

\* \* \*

Unfortunately, that evening was Daisy's next appointment with Esme, the therapist, so I didn't have time to talk to Kirsty – we had to rush straight off to the clinic when I picked her up. I'd agreed with Craig that he didn't need to come to every future appointment; in fact, I preferred taking Daisy on my own. His insistence on continually mentioning that Daisy had no problems speaking when she was at Whitegate House was irritating to say the least – as if to imply that any blame for her difficulties must by default lie with me. Fortunately, I sensed that Esme was perfectly capable of understanding where her difficulties came from. She was thrilled to hear about Daisy's progress with Izzie.

'That's *great*, Daisy,' she enthused. 'That's happened much sooner than I'd dared to hope. And you're keeping up with your exercises? Well done. I'll add a few more this time: I want to get you practising making a *sssss* noise, like a snake, and perhaps Izzie will help you with that, too. Have you tried making your *f* sound with Izzie at school? No, not in class, I realise it's a bit soon for that – but perhaps in a quiet corner of the playground?'

She went on to ask Daisy if she could repeat the word she'd managed to say to Izzie in her bedroom – and after taking a deep breath, Daisy said *food*, so clearly that Esme beamed with delight and clapped her hands.

'Well *done*, Daisy! You're speaking to me, already, aren't you?'

'Yes,' Daisy whispered, turning pink with pleasure.

'I'm very, very pleased,' Esme told me as we said goodbye at the end of the session. 'I've got every hope that she'll soon be talking at school. If you're happy to invite Izzie to play at your house again, as often as possible, that's going to make a huge difference. When she manages to talk to Izzie at school – even just a word or two – I think we'll be well on the way to complete recovery. But don't be tempted to rush her. Just give her lots of confidence that she'll get there, in her own time. I'll see you again next week.'

'Thank you,' I said, my relief almost overwhelming me. 'Thank you so much, and of course, I won't rush her – I know you're right.'

\* \* \*

But that evening, despite my excitement about Daisy's progress, all I could think about was Amelia and the intervention with her mother that I'd promised her. There was only one thing I wanted to do to take my mind off the situation: go online and try my luck at a game – just one game. Surely just one wouldn't hurt? I'd proved I could give up, do without it when I wanted to, so perhaps now I wasn't even an addict any more? I opened my laptop. It would cheer me up to get just one little win, then I'd stop, I promised myself. It would stop me dwelling on the situation with Amelia. If I didn't win, I'd stop anyway – I knew I could do that, now. I wasn't going to go back down that slippery slope; I was better than that, now. I'd learnt my lesson, I was—

My phone rang, and it was Claire, from GA. I hesitated. I'd

better not take the call; I had the bingo site open ready on my screen, and she didn't need to know. But if I didn't take her call, she'd try again, and in the end I'd have to admit...

I covered my face with my hands. How had I let myself get so tempted – get so close, again, to throwing my recovery away? I slammed the lid of the laptop shut, and answered Claire's call at the same time.

'How did you know?' I muttered, my voice actually shaking. 'You've just... well, I suppose I should say you've just rescued me. I hated you there, for a minute.'

She laughed. 'I didn't know, obviously, but I'm glad I rescued you. Tell me what's made you nearly slip up. Talk about it, love. It helps.'

'Oh, it's kind of a family thing. I need to confront someone, try to persuade her to go easy on her daughter. It's not going to be easy; part of me feels like I should stay out of it, but on the other hand, the child involved... well, I don't even really like her, but I feel sorry for her.'

'That sounds like it's going to be difficult,' she said sympathetically. 'But I admire you for deciding to get involved. I won't ask what it's all about, but kids deserve someone to speak up for them, don't they? You can only do your best, Tasha. And trying to distract yourself by doing what you were just about to – well, you know that's not going to help anyone. Especially not your own daughter, seeing as you've been telling me how you're hoping to be able to take her on holiday this year.'

'Thanks for reminding me about that,' I said. 'You're right, obviously.'

'So distract yourself some other way, right? Go and read your latest book. Or put the laptop in another room and turn the TV on – a film, something really gripping, a thriller.'

'Yes. And well, I'm glad you called right at that moment.' I took a deep breath. 'You're a lifesaver, Claire.'

'I've had my own life saved a few times. That's how I know to call if I haven't heard from you. You hadn't checked in for a couple of days. It's when something happens – something upsets us or worries us – that we need help the most. Don't forget to call me if you feel like that again, OK?'

I promised I would, and did exactly what she'd suggested – put the laptop away, turned off my phone and went to bed with my book. And it was all I could do, the next day at work, to concentrate hard on my clients and listen avidly to their stories, to keep my mind from the conversation I'd promised to have with Kirsty. I needed to do it that evening, and I had no idea how my intervention was going to be received. If Kirsty took offence, would it be the end of the reasonable relationship we'd managed to build up together? Would she no longer be so happy to look after Daisy as much as she'd been doing? And how would it affect my tentatively polite relationship with Craig?

Well, there was only one way to find out. I'd promised to try, now, even if I was beginning to wish I hadn't.

## 31

'Come in for a minute, Tasha,' Kirsty said cheerily when I arrived at Whitegate House. 'The girls are just getting dried and dressed again – they've had another swim. Honestly, I think Daisy's an even stronger swimmer than Freya these days.'

'She really enjoys it. It's all thanks to you – having the pool here.' If I offended Kirsty now, would Daisy ever have access to the pool again? 'Actually,' I went on quickly before I could chicken out, 'I need to speak to you, anyway.'

'OK, I'll put the kettle on. Go through and sit in the lounge – the kitchen table's covered in Freya's stuff – her homework and the cakes she made in food science at school. Would you like one? They're not bad.'

'Not at the moment, thanks.' She was being so chirpy, chatting away about Freya and her homework, while I was feeling awkward and nervous and just wanted her to be quiet, come and sit down and let me say my piece. I headed off obediently to wait in the lounge, but as I passed Kirsty's study I paused, surprised. Unusually, the door was open – I'd never seen it open before and had never been inside; I must have disturbed her while she was working.

Checking that she was safely in the kitchen waiting for the kettle to boil, I couldn't resist having a quick peek inside. Her polished mahogany desk was massive, her leather captain's-style chair luxurious and comfortable-looking. On the desk were three huge screens, presumably for when she hosted her important Teams meetings with her minions. I idly tapped the touch pad of the laptop, directly in front of the main screen, and it lit up immediately, showing a page of type in an unusual font, like handwriting. I knew I'd seen this font somewhere before, but it wasn't until I noticed the bright blue memory stick in the side of the laptop that I remembered where: Amelia's diary. Restraining a gasp of surprise, I skimmed the few lines of type showing on the page.

They're married – Mum and stupid Craig, they've been married for just over a week now. I suppose he's happy now, he's got what he obviously wanted all along: half of OUR HOUSE and half of Mum's money. Well, see if I care, I'm not living there any more, I like it better at Grace's place. Still, I'm going to get back at Daisy, the spoilt little brat. I'll make her sorry her stupid father ever got involved with my mum. I'll make her sorry she wormed her way into MY place in MY house, even if I have to sneak into the house to do it. If she thinks I hurt her before when I pushed her down the stairs, or when I shoved her onto the bathroom floor, that was nothing to what I'll do to her next time. I'll get hold of her and—

There was a clink of teacups and I jumped away from the desk, physically trembling as I tiptoed quickly out of the room, reaching the lounge just in time before Kirsty arrived behind me with the tea tray.

'Why aren't you sitting down, relaxing, love?' she trilled. 'Here you are, a nice cup of tea, and help yourself to short-bread. Craig can keep the girls out of the way for a little while, so that we can have a chat. What is it that's worrying you?'

I swallowed. I could hardly even think straight. Had I really just seen what I thought I'd seen? A half-written entry in 'Amelia's diary' – half-written on Kirsty's laptop, with Amelia's memory stick inserted? Did that really mean what I thought it did?

'Has Amelia come back here at all?' I asked. My voice came out croaky, as if I'd been smoking.

'What? No!' Kirsty chuckled. 'She won't come back. She wants to stay at Grace's place, but as you know, I'm looking into getting her sent somewhere more secure. Somewhere where she can be properly looked after, and given treatment for her... problems.'

'Did she leave her memory stick here? The blue one, the one I found with her diary entries on it? I thought you'd given it back to her?'

She looked startled for a moment. Her eyes met mine, and I saw the recognition in them, the realisation. She knew I'd seen the stick in her laptop. Did she realise I'd looked? That I'd read what was on her screen?

'Oh, yes, you're right, she did,' she said quickly, looking away again, fumbling with a cup and saucer on the silver tray. 'In fact, I was just reading her latest entry; I thought it was only right that I should check whether she was still spouting that awful hatred about poor little Daisy. And of course, she was – so that's made me even more determined to—'

'Kirsty,' I said, quietly, trying to keep my voice from shaking, 'That diary entry wasn't on the memory stick when I handed it back to you. I read the last entry myself. If Amelia hasn't been back at all and the memory stick's still here, somebody in this house must have written what's currently on that screen. It's stopped halfway through a sentence—'

'I was just reading it before you arrived. You must have missed Amelia's last entry. She must have been disturbed while she was writing it – abandoned it, forgot about it and left the memory stick—'

'It's only been written very recently. It refers to the wedding being just over a week ago. If she hasn't been in the house within the last couple of days, then it definitely wasn't Amelia who wrote it.'

'She must have sneaked in. I'll remind Lee to get her key back from her. She keeps claiming she's lost it – the crafty little minx.'

I took a deep breath. My heart was beating so fast, I felt like I might faint. But what was I afraid of? I'd made a promise to Amelia – and that was before I'd even discovered this... this diary entry, which I was sure, now, Amelia hadn't been lying about. She didn't write the recent diary entries. Kirsty was writing them herself, and saving them on Amelia's memory stick.

'The reason I wanted to speak to you tonight,' I said, trying to sound bolder than I felt, 'was that Amelia came to see me yesterday. She came to plead with me to intervene with you.'

'Oh, I bet she did,' she said, scowling. 'Surely you didn't get taken in by her lies?'

'She's desperate to stay with Grace. She begged me, in tears, to ask you not to send her away. And honestly, Kirsty, Lee's been telling me he'd really like her to stay on there.'

'Yes, well, he would do!' she retorted. Her face had become

ugly, screwed up with anger. I felt suddenly nervous of her. Where was Craig? I'd feel happier if he were in the room with us at that moment. 'Of course Lee wants her to stay with him – he's being paid.'

'No, that's not the reason. It's because he likes Amelia, he says she's well behaved at his house, she and Grace are company for each other and he feels sorry for her.'

'Sorry for her? Why the hell does she need anyone to feel sorry for her?' she spat back.

'She feels unloved. She still misses her dad, and she thinks – rightly or wrongly – that you've always loved Freya more than her, and that now you even love Daisy more.'

'Can you blame me? She's completely unlovable! She's a miserable, rude, sulky, spiteful brat! Of course I don't love her, why would I? She isn't even my bloody child!'

I sat back in my chair, gasping with shock. *Not her child?* What...? But even as I struggled to make sense of it, there was an echoing gasp from behind me, and I swung around to see Craig standing in the doorway, his mouth open in obvious surprise.

'What do you mean?' he stuttered, staring at Kirsty as if she'd suddenly grown horns.

'Oh, for fuck's sake, Craig,' she muttered crossly, 'don't stand there looking so bloody gormless. What the hell difference does it make to you? You've got what you wanted, haven't you – shares in the business, half the house? What do you care whether Amelia's my daughter, someone else's daughter or was dropped here out of a fucking spaceship?'

I stared at her, completely nonplussed. I'd never heard her swear before, never seen her so ugly with anger. Her perfect, polite, clipped, posh tones had vanished in an instant.

'Where are the children?' I asked Craig quickly.

'Upstairs. Freya's bedroom. I didn't realise you were here,' he said, still gaping in shock at his wife.

'Good. Don't let them come down.' I turned back to Kirsty. 'Did you adopt her? Is that it? And then had your own child – Freya—'

'I didn't adopt her. I had her forced on me. She's my late husband's; he had an affair, fathered her with his mistress – a little slut who used to work for us – and the dirty little cow gave birth to the brat and promptly buggered off – disappeared. John was an idiot, he agreed to keep the baby – well, he lumbered *me* with her, frankly. I never wanted her.'

'Does Amelia know all this – that you're not her real mother?' I asked her, thinking of the tearful girl pouring out her heart to me in my car the previous day.

'Of course she does! Oh, she always called me Mum.' She gave a short little laugh. 'Sometimes she'd get herself in one of her moods – crying and showing off – and she'd say I was the only mother she'd ever known. Expecting me to feel sorry for her, I suppose. She was all right while she had her dad—'

'She told me,' I said slowly, remembering how ridiculous it had sounded when Amelia had said this, how I'd dismissed it and told her it was *hysterical storytelling*, 'that she thought you murdered him. Her father. She's always been suspicious.'

'Oh, for God's sake!' She laughed. 'Now do you see what I mean? She's a born liar, a fantasist. She's been like it all her life. And you must be a complete idiot if she's taken you in. Murder him? Why the hell would I want to murder him?'

'Wasn't he the owner of the business? Didn't he leave it all to you?' I said, my voice coming out in a whisper. 'And from what you've said, it sounds like you hated him for having the affair.'

'Mummy,' Freya called from upstairs, 'why are you shouting? There's a ring at the doorbell.'

'I'll get it, Freya,' Craig called back, turning to leave the room. 'Stay upstairs with Daisy, OK? We're just having... a discussion.' He looked back at me as he went, wide eyed, shaking his head as if he was completely perplexed. For a moment I actually felt sorry for him.

Kirsty sat down in the armchair, raising her eyes at me, trying to look unruffled.

'I want you to admit it,' I said. 'I want you to say it was you who wrote those diary entries.'

But before she could reply, Craig was back in the room.

'Amelia's here,' he said, his voice sounding hoarse, as if he was having trouble controlling it. 'And... so are... these officers.'

'I did what you said I should have, Tasha,' Amelia said quietly, standing back to let the two police officers enter the lounge. 'I went to the police. They want to talk to you, Mum.'

'We understand your late husband was using a lawnmower when he died,' one of the officers said to Kirsty, who had now closed her eyes as if in resignation. 'We'd like to have a look at it, if you don't mind. We'll take it away with us. Together with any wires, plugs, and safety devices he would have been using.'

'They've all been dumped. Years ago,' she said with a dismissive wave of her hand.

'No they haven't, Mum!' Amelia shot back. She turned to the police officer. 'I can tell you exactly where they are. Mum hid the lawnmower at the back of the garden, behind the sheds, and buried the safety thing there. She planted prickly bushes all round and wouldn't let anyone go near there. You'll have to chop the bushes back.'

'We'll call for back-up,' said one of the officers. 'Meanwhile, ma'am' – he turned back to Kirsty – 'I'm arresting you on suspicion of murder. You don't have to say anything, but—'

Kirsty had got to her feet again now, her face red, her eyes almost popping out of her head as she glared at Amelia.

'You little cow! You vindictive, nasty, spiteful little—'

'I'm not the spiteful one,' Amelia said, sadly. 'I didn't kill anyone. I didn't push Daisy, either, or do anything deliberately to hurt her, even if it did make me sad that you loved her, like you loved Freya. Like you never loved me.'

'Love you? Why would I love you? I never wanted you, you weren't mine, you were that dirty little scrubber's, hers and your filthy cheating father's.'

'You tried to blame me for everything!' Amelia cried. 'You actually wrote things in my diary, pretending to be me. What sort of mother would do that? What's *wrong* with you?'

'I'm not your mother, you stupid child,' Kirsty retorted, so coldly that even I flinched. I put my arms around Amelia as she began to cry.

'Tash,' Craig said softly, 'would you like to take all the girls home to your place while we sort things out with these officers?'

'Yes,' I agreed, leading Amelia out into the hallway. I called Daisy and Freya to come downstairs, trying my best to smile and reassure them when both their little faces appeared over the banister, pinched with anxiety.

'Why are there policemen here?' Daisy asked.

'Why's Mummy shouting?' added Freya. 'Why are you crying, Amelia?'

'I'll explain everything when we get home, OK?' I said gently – wondering, even as I did, how the hell I was going to explain any of this, especially to Freya. 'Come on, let's go and buy something nice for tea, shall we? Perhaps you can all stay the night.'

It was going to be the most difficult night of my life.

## 32

### THREE MONTHS LATER

'Apparently a murder case can take a year or longer to come to trial,' Craig said, shaking his head and sighing. 'I don't think I'll be able to sleep until it's over.'

'Didn't the solicitor say it could be quicker because she's pleading guilty?'

'Possibly. But she might decide to change her plea, change her whole story, at any moment. I'm still hoping it might all be a mistake, to be honest.'

It was true – even though it seemed ridiculous to me – that even now, he was having trouble actually believing Kirsty was really guilty. She'd manipulated him so thoroughly that he couldn't come to terms with the facts, even though she'd admitted them to him herself. I'd never have thought I'd end up feeling sorry for Craig, but now I did. He couldn't get over how easily he was taken in by Kirsty, and the thing was, I could understand it, because I'd been taken in, too. She was kind to me, she helped me – both practically and financially. I'd thought of her as a friend for a while. But Craig – he actually fell in love with her. I didn't think, any longer, that he was just being avaricious when he started the affair. Perhaps that was part of the attraction – and after all, she was beautiful and accomplished as well as being filthy rich – but no, I thought now, that he was just plain gullible. Although I hated to say it, maybe even a bit dim. Perhaps he always was, and I'd never realised it, because yes, I used to love him.

I didn't any more. I pitied him, and I was doing what I could to support him, because he was like a lost man, like someone who was on the winning team and suddenly got cheated out of the prize. He'd actually said to me, a couple of weeks after Kirsty was arrested, 'I think she *used* me, Tash. I'm not sure she ever really loved me. I was... just a useful idiot to her, wasn't I?'

It was hard not to agree – to tell him yes, he'd been a bloody idiot, why did he think somebody like Kirsty would choose to marry someone like him, a lowly employee, some-body with nothing really to offer her apart from, I suppose, his boyish good looks? Even they were suddenly beginning to fade now, probably from pure shock. She'd admitted everything; she'd seemed to take great pleasure in telling him, to his face, that she was guilty as charged. I guessed she knew there was no chance now of her getting away with murder.

My suspicion, which I felt too sorry for him now to actually spell out, was that Kirsty only decided to take him as a lover, with a view to marrying him, because she'd already begun to fear that Amelia was suspicious about her role in her father's death. She was afraid she'd be found out, knew she'd probably be convicted, and basically wanted someone, while she was inside, to be a caretaker for her home, a father figure to the only child she really cared about – Freya – and a puppet figure-head for her company.

Why she hadn't disposed of the lawnmower, and more

importantly the RCD device, both of which she'd tampered with, I would never be able to understand. Amelia suggested that she was simply so arrogant, so convinced of her own superiority, that she seriously believed nobody would bother looking for it once she'd buried it under a lethal covering of rose bushes and other thorny plants.

'She knew I was on to her,' Amelia said tearfully, a few days after the arrest. 'That's why she went to such trouble to try to get me locked away.'

I was sure that was true. And the fact that Kirsty was so confident she'd succeed in doing that was presumably another reason she didn't have to rush to dispose of the evidence. Poor Amelia. And poor little Freya. If I felt sorry for Craig, it was nothing compared with my sympathy for these two children. Amelia might have been thirteen now – I had to do my best to make sure her birthday wasn't overlooked, with all this going on – but underneath all the bravado, she was just a hurt little girl. Despite her own feelings, she'd been kindness personified to her bewildered little sister.

'I've always known Mum didn't love me,' she said to me one day, with a shrug of pretended nonchalance. 'But poor Freya's been devastated by all this. How could Mum do it to her? Not just depriving her of our dad, but walking away from her, herself, too – when she claims she loved her? I'll never forgive her for that, never.'

'She knew Craig would take her on,' I reminded her.

'I know. And don't get me wrong, I like Craig, he's a decent guy and I feel sorry for him now – Mum's hurt him, too. But he's not Freya's dad, and he's not mine, either.'

'He knows that. He won't try to pretend he is. But at least he can be a father figure, of sorts. And you know Lee's promised to do the same, for you. And for what it's worth, I'll try my best to be some kind of mum substitute, too, if you'll let me.'

She gave me a hug. 'You're a hundred times better than the last one I had,' she said, and I was glad she was managing to joke about it – even though she wasn't actually laughing.

Daisy and I had moved into Whitegate House, temporarily. Craig needed me – he was too traumatised, at the beginning, to cope with everything. Perhaps I should have turned my back, left him to get on with it, told him he'd made his bed and had better lie in it now, even if it had turned out to be a hard and lumpy one. But I cared too much about the children, and even about Max, their little dog, to just abandon them all at such a dreadful time. It was hard to explain the situation to Daisy, but so far, it had been enough, for her, to be told that Kirsty had had to go away, and Daddy needed some help because he was so busy taking care of the business.

That part of the story was, of course, frankly a joke. Craig was no more capable of running the business than he was of flying in the air. But Kirsty had left him a document, telling him who to appoint as an interim CEO, while he himself remained in charge in name only. He admitted, now, that he was already out of his depth even in his own role and could never quite understand why Kirsty had given him as much authority as she had. I suspected she quietly oversaw all his work. He'd hit the nail on the head by admitting that he must have been her useful idiot. He even wondered if the reason she taught him to cook was so that Freya would still be fed while she was inside. She'd presumed, too, that he was going to visit her in prison and take Freya to see her. That was up to him, of course, but when Freya was old enough to understand exactly why her mum had been arrested, I wondered if she'd even want to go. Whether she'd ever forgive her. I knew Amelia wouldn't, and nor, despite the difficulty he'd had in accepting what she'd done, would Craig. Nor would I, for what she'd done to them all.

I'd had a lot of support, myself. At the salon, Camel had been surprisingly good to me, giving me a couple of weeks of compassionate leave, which Jackie was happy to come out of retirement temporarily to cover for me. Lee had continued to have Amelia living at his house; she needed the continuity of her new routine, her friendship with Grace, and her school life at Tudor Hall, which Craig was still paying for.

'Can you afford to pay for Grace too, if Lee can't manage it next year?' I asked him during one of our conversations.

'I'll add that to the list of things to talk to the accountant about,' he said.

I was pleased he was beginning to sound a little more like someone in control – both of his emotions and of the practical things he needed to take care of. If nothing else, I felt proud of him for stepping up to the mark now, taking good care of Freya with my help, and keeping a fatherly eye on Amelia, not forgetting to include our own darling Daisy, who – from the day she'd spoken that first word – *food* – to her little friend Izzie, had come on in leaps and bounds, and now, according to Mr Frost, chatted away to all the other children in her class and was one of the first to raise her hand to answer questions in her lessons.

As for me, I couldn't say I was completely out of the woods with my gambling addiction, but I was still going faithfully to my GA meetings and it had now been four and a half weeks since my last slip-up. Both Claire and Lee had been the most amazing support to me in this, and since I'd finally decided to tell Craig about it, he'd also helped by keeping an eye on me during the evenings, making sure I was either glued to the TV or a book, or busy doing something in the house.

'So you're back together, now,' Lee said when we had a quiet moment at work one beautiful spring day when I was humming to myself, finally beginning to think that perhaps life could settle down and become something close to normal and happy again before too long.

'Sorry?' I frowned. 'Who's back together?'

'You and Craig. I haven't liked to ask, but I suppose, as you've moved in, and you're, like, co-parenting the girls, and—'

'What? No, Lee! I mean, yes I've moved in, temporarily, but we're not *together*.' I felt myself blushing. 'We've got separate rooms. We're not... we'll never be a couple again.'

'I presumed that was what he would want.'

'Really? Well, I certainly didn't think that, or I wouldn't have moved in!' I joked. 'No, that's over, dead and buried. I felt sorry for him. I'm just helping him get on top of things, get used to what he's had to take on. And to be fair, it's convenient. It's nice for Freya and Daisy – they've both had their worlds turned upside down; they're benefiting from each other's company. You know how close they are.'

'Of course.' He gave me an apologetic smile. 'Sorry. It's none of my business, really. Except that...' He hesitated, looking awkward, then shrugged and went on in a rush, 'Except that I was planning to ask you out. Before all that stuff kicked off, with Kirsty. I thought, as we seem to be getting on well together, perhaps you might...' He paused and shrugged again. 'But probably not. Forget I spoke. I'm probably being an idiot. I don't suppose you—'

I was laughing now. 'Oh! Well, no, you're not being an idiot at all.' I hesitated. I'd told myself I didn't want another relationship, but where was the harm in going out on a date or two –

and seeing where it went from there? 'I wasn't expecting that – but you're right, we do get on well, so why not? Yes, I'd like that, Lee. And at least I don't have to worry about a babysitter at the moment.'

'True. Perhaps moving in with Craig has its benefits,' he said with a chuckle.

I was smiling to myself as I went home – home to White-gate House, which of course wasn't my home really, and never would be. But I knew I was going to be welcome now, as long as Craig was living there. Who knew what might happen when, eventually, after however many years she served, however long *life* meant in her case, Kirsty was finally released? That would be for her and Craig to decide. I couldn't see him ever wanting to live with her again. Perhaps he'd actually divorce her, so presumably she'd have to buy him out of his share of the house. In the meantime he'd promised to give me more money for Daisy's maintenance when I moved back into my own place. We'd talked, at length, about the struggle I'd been having – not *all* of it because of my own stupidity with the gambling.

'I never liked the idea of giving you Kirsty's money,' he admitted. 'I felt like I should be supporting Daisy out of my own pocket.'

'She helped me out with some extra cash herself, once, when I was broke,' I told him, smiling at his surprise. 'I think she really felt sorry for me. I blew it all on bingo, though.'

He actually laughed at this.

'I'm sorry,' he said. 'I didn't treat you well. I was so flattered, I guess. You know, the classic stupid male – someone wealthy, powerful, beautiful...'

'Wicked, murderous, spiteful, cruel,' I reminded him, and he nodded, looking shamefaced, and I felt another rush of sympathy for him. 'Oh, come on, we were all taken in – I liked her too.' I grinned, and decided I might as well tell him now – he'd find out soon enough. 'It seems you're not the only man to be attracted to an older woman, either. I seem to have attracted a younger man myself, actually.'

'Have you?' For a moment I saw a flash of something like – surely not jealousy? – in his eyes, before he rearranged his face and asked, calmly, 'Anyone I know?'

'Yes: Lee. I know you dropped hints about us before – at your wedding – but I wasn't being disingenuous: we've only ever just been friends. But he's asked me out on a date tomorrow night.'

He raised his eyebrows. 'Well, what can I say?' He swallowed, took a deep breath, and managed a smile. 'I hope he has the sense to appreciate you more than I did.'

And that was enough for me, to be honest. He knew he'd made a mistake. He knew he couldn't un-make it. He hadn't lost his daughter: Daisy would always love him, he'd always be her daddy, and I was determined that both she and Freya – and Amelia too – would have a good relationship with him, hopefully for the rest of their lives. But he lost *me*, the day after my fortieth birthday when he told me he was leaving me for Kirsty, and now he'd lost her too. We both needed to rebuild our lives, separate lives that would only converge in support of those precious children.

Because a relationship between a man and a woman can be fraught with problems – it can be long term or it can be transient – but a relationship with a child is the greatest gift we can be given, and one that only a psychopath like Kirsty could ever neglect or turn their back on. Neither of us would ever do that to any of those beautiful girls. And my own precious daughter came first, always first, before any man, any job, any money in the world. It was the greatest love I'd ever know, and I'd never forget that or put it at risk. Daisy and I had been through too much, but now we were going to be fine. Kirsty could rot in prison for as long as it took. She'd never come near me, or my daughter, again.

* * *

## MORE FROM SHEILA NORTON

Another book from Sheila Norton, *If I Lost You*, is available to order now here:

https://mybook.to/IfILostYouBackAd

# AUTHOR'S NOTE

While I'm grateful to say I have no personal experience of gambling addiction, I thought it might be helpful for anyone reading this book who might be worried about their own gambling, to share details of the websites that I found helpful while doing the necessary research for this story.

- For information about problem gambling and how to tell if your gambling is getting out of control: https://www.nhs.uk/live-well/addiction-support/gambling-addiction/
- For advice and support with stopping gambling, by phone, email, WhatsApp, online community or local support: https://www.gamcare.org.uk/
- To join a fellowship of people who meet in local areas to help themselves and each other once they have recognised their gambling addiction and want to stop: https://gamblersanonymous.org.uk/

# ACKNOWLEDGEMENTS

As always, I want to thank my wonderful editor, Emily Yau, and everyone at my publishers, Boldwood Books, for the hard work they put into this and every book. Also, thanks are due to my agent Megan Carroll, and to my fellow authors in the Chelmsford RNA group for their friendship and support. I'd also like to thank the community of my home village of Galleywood, especially the staff of the village library, the heritage centre, the hospice charity shop and even the hairdressers, who all help to support me in their own ways. And lastly but definitely not least, thanks as ever to my lovely family and friends, for their encouragement and especially their tolerance when my patience and sanity were challenged by technology issues during the creation of this book! Thank you all.

# ABOUT THE AUTHOR

**Sheila Norton** lives in Chelmsford, Essex and part-time in Torquay, Devon. She is the author of over 20 novels, covering several different sub-genres of contemporary fiction, including family dramas for Boldwood Books. In 2022 she was the winner of the Romantic Novelists Association's Christmas/Winter book award with her novel *Winter at Cliff's End Cottage*.

Sign up to Sheila Norton's mailing list here for news, competitions and updates on future books.

Visit Sheila Norton's Website: www.sheilanorton.com

Follow Sheila Norton on social media:

[f] facebook.com/SheilaNortonAuthor

[O] instagram.com/sheilaann.norton

## ALSO BY SHEILA NORTON

A Good Enough Mother

Not Your Child

If I Lost You

My Daughter's Keeper

# Boldwood

Boldwood Books is an award-winning fiction publishing company seeking out the best stories from around the world.

**Find out more at www.boldwoodbooks.com**

Join our reader community for brilliant books, competitions and offers!

Follow us
@BoldwoodBooks
@TheBoldBookClub

Sign up to our weekly deals newsletter

https://bit.ly/BoldwoodBNewsletter